City of Dogs

LIVI MICHAEL

G. P. PUTNAM'S SONS

G. P. PUTNAM'S SONS

A division of Penguin Young Readers Group.

Published by The Penguin Group.

Penguin Group (USA) Inc., 375 Hudson Street, New York, NY 10014, U.S.A.

Penguin Group (Canada), 90 Eglinton Avenue East, Suite 700, Toronto, Ontario M4P 2Y3, Canada (a division of Pearson Penguin Canada Inc.). Penguin Books Ltd, 80 Strand, London WC2R 0RL, England. Penguin Ireland, 25 St. Stephen's Green, Dublin 2, Ireland (a division of Penguin Books Ltd.). Penguin Group (Australia), 250 Camberwell Road, Camberwell, Victoria 3124, Australia (a division of Pearson Australia Group Pty Ltd). Penguin Books India Pvt Ltd, 11 Community Centre, Panchsheel Park, New Delhi - 110 017, India. Penguin Group (NZ), 67 Apollo Drive, Rosedale, North Shore 0745, Auckland, New Zealand. Penguin Books (South Africa) (Pty) Ltd, 24 Sturdee Avenue, Rosebank, Johannesburg 2196, South Africa. Penguin Books Ltd, Registered Offices: 80 Strand, London WC2R 0RL, England.

Text copyright © 2007 by Livi Michael.

Printed in the United States of America. Design by Gunta Alexander. Text set in Adobe Garamond.

Library of Congress Cataloging-in-Publication Data

Michael, Livi, 1960– City of dogs / Livi Michael. p. cm. Summary: Jenny, a mysterious dog, shows up on Sam's birthday and pulls many of the other dogs in the neighborhood into her quest to prevent the destruction of the world. [1. Dogs—Fiction. 2. Fantasy.] I. Title. PZ7.M5798Cit 2007 [Fic]—dc22 2006026539

ISBN 978-0-399-24356-1

1 3 5 7 9 10 8 6 4 2

First Impression

To my good friend Jackie Robinson—
dog-walker extraordinaire!

CONTENTS

PROLOGUE

At first there was only swirling mist, then shadows, then shifting lights. Then her paws struck something solid and gritty and she was clambering upward, out from the place of no return. Still holding the precious twig in her mouth she scrabbled at the solid surface, her head and shoulders in one world and her rear end in quite another, and almost dropped back in as something thundered past.

Shaken but undeterred, she scrambled onto the road and cowered in the blaze of lights as there was another thundering roar.

Lights, more lights and noise such as she had never experienced before. Her paws shifted on the grit, and the texture of the road too was unfamiliar. She had come to a place of monsters and demons, of channeled fire and lightning and thunder and wind. She flattened herself against the blast as another demon swept past, the heat and stench. Where in the nine worlds was she?

Wherever she was, she couldn't go back. There behind her, through the mist, lay the Void, gently quivering. It made soft sounds she could barely hear. As though it was lapping at the edge of this world. But in front of her were the roaring demons with eyes that flashed along the road like lightning. Suddenly she realized they were chariots—chariots of thunder and flame. The road shook beneath them.

But she had come so far, she could not give up now. Anything was better than nothing. She would have to try somehow to reach the other side. She could just about see that there was another side, briefly but repeatedly illuminated in the flares of light. That was where she needed to go—away from the Void. She put one paw out, then hastily withdrew it as another chariot roared past and then another.

Remember, she told herself as her heart quailed, and it quailed further as she realized she had almost forgotten. But she held the flowering twig between her teeth, summoned the remaining strength in her muscles and at the next pause in the traffic shot like an arrow into the road.

Faster and faster she ran, narrowly avoiding one chariot, then another. In fury they blared their dreadful cries and she was deafened, but running still. She could feel the air whistling past her ears and through her teeth. And she could make out trees and bushes on the other side, she was almost there, when a stunning pain shot from her hip to her spine and she keeled over, hearing only the screech of the chariot as she sank once more into darkness.

CHAPTER 1

The Birthday Party

It was Sam's worst birthday party ever. He and his mum had just moved and now they lived in the middle of a strange city, where they didn't know anyone.

"You'll soon make friends at school," his mother said. She had invited her aunts, Aunty Lilith, Aunty Joan and Aunty Dot (who hadn't arrived yet), and they sat in the front room eating cake and discussing their varicose veins.

"Like bunches of grapes," said Aunty Joan. "Still, at least I've got legs," she went on briskly. "Poor Edith's having her other leg off soon."

Aunty Lilith, who was deaf, said, "Eh?"

"I SAID, EDITH'S HAVING ANOTHER LEG OFF."

"That'll be her third," said Aunty Lilith.

"No, dear, *legs*. Edith's having her other leg off."

"Why would she do that?" said Aunty Lilith, very surprised. "She's only just had them put on."

Aunty Joan turned faintly purple, then gave up. "Why don't you open your present," she said to Sam. "I don't know where Dot's got to, but I don't think she'll mind."

Reluctantly Sam picked up the bulky parcel. He'd had presents from his aunts before. As soon as he started opening it, he could tell it was a sweater they had knitted themselves. His aunts knitted all the time, so you'd think they'd have got better at it.

"Oh, that's *lovely*," his mother said. "Why don't you try it on?"

Sam just looked at her.

"Come on," she said.

With a vast sigh Sam pulled off his hoodie and tusseled his way into the knitted sweater. It was about the right size for Aunty Lilith, who was a very large lady, yet strangely, the neck was too small. It took the combined efforts of both Sam and his mother to wrestle his head through, then a mass of hairy wool fell to his knees.

"You'll grow into it," his mother said in an undertone.

"*How?*" said Sam, and indeed, the sweater was rather an odd shape. One arm seemed to be lower than the other, and it pouched out at the neck.

"Such an unusual color," his mother said brightly. Sam was just thinking that it looked as though someone had been sick down the front.

"*Scrambled egg,*" said Aunty Joan. "It was on sale at the shop. Sixteen balls of yarn for the price of one."

"I saw it first," said Aunty Lilith.

"No, you didn't."

"Yes, I did!"

"No, you didn't—you wanted to buy that *purple meringue.* Just because Edith had bought some."

"Can't hear you," said Aunty Lilith.

"Aunty Dot picked it up in the end," said Aunty Joan to Sam and his mum. "We had to ask her three times because she kept forgetting."

"It's a brilliant sweater," said Sam. "But—I think I'll take it off now. It's . . . er . . . getting a bit warm."

In fact, it was freezing since the temperature had recently dropped and the boiler wasn't working.

"Well, so long as you wear it for school," said Aunty Joan.

His mother caught the look on Sam's face. "Perhaps we should play a game," she said, and Aunty Joan suggested they could play Pass the Kidney Stone, since Aunty Lilith had brought hers with her in a jar.

But before things could get really exciting, the doorbell rang.

"I'll get it," said everyone except Aunty Lilith, who hadn't heard, but before they got to the door, they could all hear Aunty Dot.

"It's only me, dears—oh, I've had the most terrible shock—oh, just wait till you see what I've got here."

She appeared carrying a bundle wrapped in a blanket.

"What is it?" said Sam's mum, hurrying forward to help.

Just then the blanket barked. Sam's mum jumped back in alarm as a small white head with brown ears poked out of it.

"It's a dog!" cried Sam in great excitement.

"Yes, yes, my darling, don't you fret," said Aunty Dot in the voice she usually reserved for policemen and babies in strollers. "Everything's all right now. Aunty Dot didn't mean to hit you with that nasty car."

Everyone made way for Aunty Dot as she carried the small bundle through to the kitchen, explaining breathlessly what had happened.

"Just traveling here on the ring road—came out of nowhere—didn't see a thing—*felt* it, though—must have clipped her—I thought she'd be dead. . . ."

The little dog was only aware of a cacophony of light and noise. She had come from the darkness into a glaring yellow light that was quite unlike anything she was used to—torches or candlelight flickering on the walls of the great hall or the natural light of sun and moon. There was a harsh quality to this light that hurt her eyes and made her vision blur. And there was a background noise beneath the babble of voices—a whirring and ticking and clicking, and the distant roar of traffic, that made no sense to her at all. She had come to one of the realms of Chaos, she thought, and began to tremble all over.

Meanwhile, Aunty Dot began to examine her, feeling all the way along her spine.

"I think she's hurt her hip," she said.

The small white dog submitted to this examination because she could tell from her touch that Aunty Dot knew what she was doing. But when she tried to remove the twig from her mouth, the little dog braced herself and Aunty Dot succeeded only in pulling her nose forward.

"Looks like—mistletoe," she said wonderingly, and the aunts exchanged significant glances.

The little dog stared at them all. Through her blurred eyes they looked huge and impressive. There was an unusual quality to them that she couldn't place, yet something about it tugged at the threads of her memory. Everything in the room was vibrating with an energy of its own, but it was almost as though these three women had a different vibration from everything else. She didn't know whether or not to be afraid or more afraid than she already was. Then her blurred glance fell on the little boy, who was leaning over her eagerly. He had bright hair and a brightly colored tunic. A halo of light fell all around him from the lamp above. In her confused eyes he looked like the master she had left, the Shining Boy.

"Can we keep her, Mum, can we?" he asked. Then he too tried to take the twig from her mouth.

Very gently, he reached for the mistletoe, looking into her eyes the whole time. The small dog tensed all over, but she didn't growl. She could see herself reflected in each of his eyes, and she could see what he was thinking in the same way as she had always been able to read her master's thoughts. You won't bite me, he was thinking, and carefully he prized the twig away from her, and she let it go.

"Well, look at that!" said Aunty Dot as Sam turned the sprig of mistletoe over, examining it. Someone had cut and shaped it. It looked like a dart. "She knows it's your birthday. Maybe she'll grant you three wishes."

"Like a genie," said Aunty Joan.

"Jenny," said Sam, fondling the little dog's ears.

"There's no point in giving her a name," said his mother at once. "We're not keeping her."

But the little dog, who understood little of anything else, under-stood that she had been named. Naming was powerful magic. Once you were named, you were part of the world you had come to, and it was the strongest indication that you would stay. She wagged her tail feebly. *Jen-ny,* she thought. *Jen-ny.*

"Look at her," Sam said.

They all looked at the small white dog with velvety brown mark-ings who gazed back at them with soft doe eyes. She was pain-fully thin, but her eyes and her coat seemed to glow with a deep, mysterious light.

"She looks a bit like a Jack Russell," Aunty Dot said, and indeed, she did look almost, but not quite, like a Jack Russell terrier.

"I wonder where she came from?" said Sam's mum.

Sam reached out for her again. "She's my birthday present!" he said.

"Don't be silly, Sam," said his mum automatically. "I told you we can't keep her—she must belong to someone."

But Aunty Dot said she was clearly a stray. "No collar," she said.

Sam felt that he deserved one good present. And the little dog gazed up at him with dark eyes that seemed to speak of distance and mystery. He could see his face in each of them. It was almost as though she was trying to tell him something.

"Can I hold her?" said Sam, and he picked her up.

"Careful!" said Aunty Dot and Sam's mother together, but the little dog offered no resistance at all. She nestled into the crook of Sam's arm. *Safe,* she thought.

"Put her down, Sam," said his mother. "You don't know where she's been. I mean it, there's no way I want another pet."

"Well—I was hoping she could stay here, just for tonight," said Aunty Dot.

"Oh *yes!*" said Sam as his mother started to protest. Aunty Dot looked at her with eyes made huge and luminous by the extremely powerful lenses in her glasses.

"She's a nice little thing," she said. "I wish I could keep her my-self; I do miss having a dog. Life's not been the same without . . . ever since . . ."

She stopped and blew her nose. Aunty Dot had never recovered from losing her own dog. She said she didn't really want another one of her own, not since her own darling Berry had gone away. This had happened years ago, but it still brought tears to her eyes. She had become a kind of unofficial dog walker, regularly walking several dogs whose owners were too busy to walk their own pets, but she couldn't face getting so attached to another one of her own. Besides, the aunts all lived together, and Aunty Lilith had her own dog, a tiny and rather bad-tempered Chihuahua called Pico.

"We can't just throw her out," Sam said. "Look at her."

"Sam," said his mum. "We can't keep a dog. I'm at work all day, and you'll be at school. It wouldn't be fair."

"It's my birthday," Sam said.

"But Sam, we don't have a yard," his mother said.

"I'll take her out," Sam said. "Every day."

"You said you'd clean the rabbit's hutch," his mother said. "And who ended up with that job?"

Sam shuffled uncomfortably. "I'm older now," he said.

It was true that Sam's record with pets had not been great. He had forgotten all about the rabbit. His mother had cleaned out the hutch and fed it, but Sam had forgotten to take it out and play with it, and eventually it just got more and more snappy and unmanagable and one day had learned to open its hutch all by itself. The first they had known about it was when it had chased the postman up a tree. Then for three days Sam and his mother had been trapped inside the house while the savage rabbit prowled outside, snarling and making other un-rabbit-like noises so that no one could come near. Eventually, to everyone's relief, it had bounded over the garden gate and left, leav-ing a trail of mangled well-wishers in its wake.

But a dog was different. Sam had always wanted a dog. Reluctantly he put her back down on the table and placed the mistletoe twig between her paws. She picked it up immediately and stood quivering, her big eyes fixed hopefully on Sam's mum.

"Dogs cost money," she said. "Suppose she needs the vet?"

"I'll pay," said Sam, "with my pocket money," and his mother rolled her eyes.

"Please!" he said.

Sam's mother sighed. "I suppose we could hang on to her for tonight," she said, and Sam flung his arms around her. "But tomorrow we're putting signs in the shops. Someone must know something about this dog."

Sam was delighted. He took an old pillow from the bedding chest and put it in front of the kitchen door. When he got back to the table, Aunty Dot was feeding the little dog a sausage roll. She was obviously hungry, yet she hesitated, then put the mistletoe twig down between her paws and took the pieces delicately.

Sam picked her up again and put her on the kitchen floor very gently. "Come on, Jenny," he said, and she limped over to the pillow right away and sat on it. She understood that there had been some kind of discussion and that she could stay. She didn't understand fully where she was, or what she was supposed to do, or what all these people would do with her, but for now, at least, she was safe. She felt suddenly unutterably tired. She turned herself around on the pillow once and sank down, her eyes already closing.

Sam slipped the mistletoe dart back onto her pillow. The aunts all left, Aunty Dot promising to call the next day to help Sam take Jenny for a walk, and Sam was finally persuaded to go to bed after a brief, tense argument with his mother about whether or not Jenny could sleep on his bed. His mother won the argument, and Sam finally went to bed alone. He lay awake for a long time, thinking about having a dog of his own, then when he fell asleep, he dreamed strange, wonderful dreams, about a boy with a face like the sun and a white dog gleaming like a small star through the early morning mist.

CHAPTER 2

New Day, New World

When Jenny woke up the next morning, she had no idea where she was. It was still dark in the kitchen and rather cold, and the whirring and humming and clicking noises were still there. They seemed to be coming from tall, metallic slabs that stood against the wall.

She had woken from a dream in which she was playing with her master in meadows thick with flowers and the early morning sun shone down on them through the mist. But now here she was, stranded in a cold, dark, alien world. The only warm place was on the pillow where she lay, and the only reminder of her former life was the small, chewed twig between her paws. She felt lonely and afraid, and she jumped when she heard footsteps clattering down the stairs.

"Jenny!" Sam called. "Jenny?"

The little dog lifted her nose and sniffed. That was her name now, she remembered. *Jen-ny.*

Sam bounded into the kitchen. "There you are, Jenny," he said, hugging her straightaway. "Are you cold? Did you sleep well? I bet you're hungry!"

He went on talking to her in words Jenny didn't understand. But fortunately all dogs speak human to some extent. They respond to the tone of voice, the rise and fall and rhythm of the words, and Jenny knew that Sam was being kind. And she recognized the smell of him right away, though he wasn't quite as shiny as the night before. In fact, now that she could see him clearly, he didn't remind her of her master at all. He stood up and pressed a switch and immediately the room was filled with the same yellow glare as before, and Jenny couldn't see a thing. She cowered in the blinding light.

"It's only a lightbulb, Jenny," Sam said, laughing, and he opened one of the whirring metal slabs and brought out the sausage rolls from the party. He ate one himself and offered one to Jenny. She sniffed it, but she was too confused and wary to eat.

"I bet you need the toilet," Sam said, and he opened the back door, letting in a blast of cold air.

The back door opened onto a yard that was full of junk—planks of wood, buckets and ladders, an old brush and mop, a window still in its frame, and Sam's bike, draped in a plastic sheet. Jenny hung back. The yard was full of strange smells. She didn't dare go in.

"Go on then," Sam said, but Jenny didn't move. He went into the yard and called her, patting his knees, but she still wouldn't venture beyond the door.

Then Sam had an idea. He walked back into the kitchen, quickly picked up the little dart on Jenny's pillow and threw it into the yard.

Jenny leapt. She flew through the air like a bird or a very bouncy kangaroo, catching the mistletoe twig before it landed.

"Go, Jenny!" shouted Sam, and in the middle of all the confusion of the yard, Jenny squatted and made her mark. It felt strange, but she couldn't help herself. Making your mark was very powerful magic and another sign that she belonged in this world now.

Then, just as she would have done with her old master, she returned the dart to Sam.

"Good girl!" he said, patting her on the head. Then he threw it indoors and Jenny leapt after it, flying gracefully over the kitchen chair.

"Ace!" said Sam. He found a bowl in the cupboards and filled it with water, and Jenny lapped at it gratefully, then ate the sausage roll. She had eaten and drunk in this strange world, and maybe that was the third sign.

Afterward they went on playing. Sam threw the dart and Jenny caught it, no matter where he threw it, how high or how far.

"Jenny—you're amazing!" he said, and just then, the front door-bell rang, and Jenny shot backward, barking, under a chair.

It was Aunty Dot, who had pedaled all the way across the city to see them on her bike.

"I thought we'd take her out first thing, before it's too busy," she said, and she propped the bike up in the hallway and followed Sam into the front room.

"Watch this, Aunty Dot!" he said, and he threw the mistletoe dart high into the air.

"Look out!" said Aunty Dot, but before it could strike anything, Jenny leapt. She flew straight over the back of the settee, caught the dart in her jaws and descended again gracefully to the carpet.

"Goodness!" said Aunty Dot, and, "My word!" as she did it again. "Well, there can't be much wrong with her hip," she added as Jenny bounded over the high-backed chair.

"It doesn't matter where I throw it," Sam said. "She always catches it!"

"Impressive," said Aunty Dot, and she patted Jenny's head vigorously.

Jenny put up with this politely, but then Sam said, "You have a go." As soon as he handed the dart to Aunty Dot, Jenny put back her ears and growled.

It was an astonishing growl. It rattled all the knickknacks on the mantlepiece and the books and videos on the shelves. The shelves themselves started shaking, the coffee table rattled and the high-backed chair juddered toward the center of the room. Aunty Dot clutched her hat, which she could feel was about to fly off. "Oh, dear," she said. "Oh, my word," for she had a sudden, fleeting vision of volcanoes erupting and continents shifting deep within their oceanic beds.

But Sam was beaming up at her proudly. "She does that too," he said.

"Well," said Aunty Dot, "I don't think she wants me to have it."

She gave the dart back to Sam, and instantly the thunderous growling stopped and Jenny wagged her tail.

"Well," said Aunty Dot again, once she had got her breath back. "I think we'd better take her out for a walk," and from her shoulder bag she produced a collar and lead.

"Cool!" said Sam. "Can I hold the lead?"

"You'd better get dressed first," said Aunty Dot. "And tell your mum where you're going."

Sam ran upstairs to where his mother was still in bed. Aunty Dot eyed the little dog intently, and Jenny eyed her back.

"You're not quite what you seem, are you?" Aunty Dot murmured, bending forward and removing her spectacles. "I wonder what your real name is."

Jenny stared at Aunty Dot as though she had never seen her before. Without her glasses she was transformed. White light streamed from her face, which seemed suddenly not elderly and kindly, but magnificent and ageless. Her eyes radiated darkness, and pale fire streamed from her lips. It was obvious to Jenny that Aunty Dot too was not what she seemed.

Sam came thundering down the stairs again. "Can I put the lead on her?" he said.

"Yes, I think you'd better," Aunty Dot replied, replacing her glasses.

There followed a short, tense interlude in which both Sam and Aunty Dot tried to get the lead on Jenny and Jenny responded by running around in circles, twisting out of reach, rolling over and finally backing into a corner under the chair.

It was as if she didn't know what a lead was.

"Right," said Aunty Dot, out of both patience and breath. "I think I know what's going on. She's nervous of traffic since I clipped her last night. It's quite understandable, poor thing. But she'll have to get used to it. See if she'll let you pick her up."

As before, Jenny seemed quite happy to be picked up by Sam. He tucked her under his arm and followed Aunty Dot to the hallway, standing to one side of the bike as she opened the front door.

"Now you'll have to be really careful," Aunty Dot warned. "We don't want her jumping down and running into the road."

In fact, Jenny did seem to be extraordinarily nervous. She flinched at all the brightness and quivered at the noise. Sam held on to her tightly, then he saw Aunty Dot's bicycle basket.

"I know, she can have a ride in your basket!" he said, and before Aunty Dot could say, *No, don't!* he lifted the lid and lowered Jenny inside.

"WOOOFF!!" said the bicycle basket, and there followed what sounded like a small tornado. Aunty Dot hastily scooped Jenny out again.

"Pico!" she said.

It has already been mentioned that Pico was very small. He was also very loud. In fact, the one attribute had evolved out of the other since Pico lived with Aunty Lilith, who was nearsighted and very deaf. And she weighed a lot. It wasn't easy to coax her onto a set of scales or to find one that would take the full brunt of her weight, but Aunty Dot had bought an industrial-sized one specially for the purpose and had bullied Aunty Lilith onto it one day.

"Good heavens, Lilith!" she had said. "You weigh 340 pounds!"

"Too much money for a set of scales," Aunty Lilith said.

"No, dear—you'll have to go on a diet!"

"Dye it? There's nothing wrong with it!"

"Nothing wrong with what?" said Aunty Dot, getting confused.

"That's what I said!" said Aunty Lilith triumphantly.

Most conversations with Aunty Lilith went like this, and in the end, most people gave up and left her to sit in her specially designed armchair that could be maneuvered into different positions at the touch of a button, and to eat her favorite caramel toffee, which exercised her jaw at least. Other than this, Aunty Lilith was quite happy in her chair, and rarely saw the need to move out of it, but when she did, Pico had to be very careful because her size-nine feet might descend in any direction. And so this was how he had come to develop his tremendous bark.

"WOOF!"

Because Pico was too small to go for walks in the usual way, Aunty Dot carried him around in the basket of her bicycle. When anyone approached it, Pico produced a bark like a Great Dane.

"WOOF!"

"No one'll ever steal this bike," Aunty Dot said with satisfaction, and Sam, out of politeness, refrained from saying that no one would ever want to. It was a vast, unwieldy thing that clanked and groaned and looked as if it had been cobbled together from the remains of other bikes. Aunty Dot had ridden it around the city for many years. She rode on the pavements since the roads were so busy, and whenever pedestrians got in the way, she just jiggled the basket so that Pico barked again.

"WOOF!"

And they scattered to left and right, sometimes diving into the road for safety.

"Better than a car horn," Aunty Dot always said.

Now she handed Jenny back to Sam and lifted Pico out.

"Now, Jenny dear, it's all right—everything's fine," she said, holding Pico in the palm of her hand.

"Jenny, this is Pico," she said.

For a moment the two dogs tensed and bristled at each another, then Jenny moved her nose, quivering and whiffly, toward Pico, and after a moment he lifted his tiny nose to her. And this is what she said.

Little friend, I see that your body is small but your heart is great. You have within you distant horizons and marvelous deeds. You will leave the place where you are now, and travel to faraway lands. The stars shall be your compass, and your journey shall know no boundaries.

Now in the main, Pico was contented with his life. He had known nothing else, having been bought by Aunty Lilith when he was a puppy and hardly bigger than a mouse. But sometimes he did wonder if there was more to the world than Aunty Lilith's sleeve and Aunty Dot's bicycle basket. When he rode in the bicycle basket, he had a sense of immensity and noise, but Aunty Dot and Aunty Lilith were agreed that the pavements were too dangerous for him. Once when he had been taken out, he had barked at a large, mean-looking dog called Rex, and Rex had looked down in surprise to find where all the noise was coming from, then opened his great jaws and scooped him up in a single bite. Pico had to be pulled out of his mouth by the tail. Since then he had been carried about from one confined space to another, which was all he knew of the world. But he did dream, about huge mountain ranges and deserts and forests and plains so vast that run though you might, there was no end to them. He didn't know where these dreams came from, but each time he had them, he felt restless and a little more discontented with his lot. He would bark at Aunty Lilith until she put him on the window ledge, where he would peer out as well as he could at the bush that obscured his view and get terribly excited if anything happened, such as the postman coming or the window cleaner. He would trot all the way from one end of the windowsill to the other and wish that he was bigger and that he could see more.

"Where have you come from?" he would bark at them, and, "Where are you going?" and in his mind he had the sense of far horizons and horses galloping into the sun.

But all that came out of him was the same sound, WOOF! and the postman and window cleaner would laugh and say that he was a great little guard dog and leave him again, alone on the sill.

"One day, Pico," he would tell himself, "one day you will see the world!" and each time he told himself this, he had the sense that that day was coming nearer. And now for the first time he could see those dreams realized in Jenny's eyes. When he spoke finally, it was in a voice that was hushed and awed.

"You are right," he told her. "And no one has ever seen that before," and right there and then, Pico gave Jenny his heart.

Aunty Dot could sense that something had shifted between the two dogs.

"Perhaps we could try her in the basket after all," she murmured, thinking aloud. Very carefully, Sam lowered Jenny into the basket, and even more carefully, Aunty Dot lowered Pico in after her.

It worked! The two dogs nested in without protest, and as Aunty Dot wheeled her ancient bicycle along the street, Pico rode between Jenny's forepaws, and both of them looked out.

The most obvious thing about the city where Sam and his mother had come to live was that there was hardly anywhere to walk a dog. There were overpasses and bypasses and subways, and concrete buildings and apartment buildings so tall you could hardly see the sky, but hardly any grass or trees. And wherever there was grass, there were notices up saying DOGS NOT ALLOWED. More notices on lampposts read DOG OWNERS BEWARE! $1000.00 FINE IF YOUR DOG FOULS THE PAVEMENTS. They didn't say what the fine would be if the owners fouled the pavements, Aunty Dot pointed out as she showed Sam the notices. "And humans are a lot dirtier than dogs," she said.

It was true that the city was dirty. A kind of smog hung over it at all times, so that only on the brightest, hottest days could you actually see the sun, like a flat disk without rays through the smoke. Gas fumes clogged the air; road works clogged up the roads. So many different companies were drilling and digging, you could see right into the underbelly of the roads, as though they were being gutted. Dumpsters overflowed from alleys; wastepaper bins spilled their contents into the streets; people scattered their litter behind them as they went.

And there were so many people! Fat and thin, tall and short, drab or colorful and decorated with paint or metal studs. Jenny had never imagined there could be so many people. They didn't look anything like the people in her own world. For one thing, hardly any of them wore small, horned helmets. Or carried axes and shields. Some of them carried bags, and they bumped and jostled one another along the pavements, but even then they didn't look at each other but down and away, and they didn't look happy either but frustrated and sad, bad-tempered or just as though they were millions of miles away in their thoughts.

Jenny saw all this and wondered. It seemed to her, as Aunty Dot wheeled her bike slowly along the pavements, that she could hear the distant murmur of grass still struggling to grow far beneath the concrete or the soft protest of roots forced to turn inward and grow back down into the earth. But the only spare bit of land that had not been developed yet was toward the outskirts of the city, near where Aunty Dot lived, which was where she was taking Jenny now.

It was a desolate croft, with patches of black earth and stubble and tufts of grass that contained the scents of every dog in the city. Here at last Aunty Dot let Pico and Jenny out of the basket. Pico disappeared instantly behind a tuft of grass, while Jenny was assaulted by a stunning range of scents she had never encountered before. Dogs, of course, and litter—old beer cans and bags of chips or takeaway curries. There was a can of oil, an old sock and a grocery bag. But beyond this there were all the ancient scents, telling the story of that particular patch of earth since it began, nearly five billion years ago. There was the scent of marching feet drumming in her nostrils, scorched earth and fire, and before that, long before, the scent of swamp, then ocean. She took her time investigating the earth, sniffing along the length of each blade of grass she came to, parting the tufts with her nose and examining them from the roots to the tip. Even here she could smell the gas, and the residues of people, and the scent of a greater variety of dogs than she had ever known.

"This is where I bring my other dogs," Aunty Dot told Sam, clipping her lead on while Jenny was too distracted to notice. "She'll soon get used to it."

She put Pico back in the basket while Jenny practiced walking through the streets of the city, dodging and weaving what felt like millions of pairs of feet. But when they finally got back to Sam's house, his mother had copied out a notice on several index cards.

FOUND

One Jack Russell terrier, white with brown markings. Please contact—
And she had put their phone number on the bottom. She gave them to Sam along with some money for dog food. He was to go to the post office, the newsagent's, the corner shop and the supermarket, the vet's, and anywhere else he could think of that might put the signs in their window. Sam looked at Aunty Dot for support, but she only smiled at him ruefully, shook her head slightly and said she would have to be going.

Reluctantly Sam set off. He bought some cans of dog food at the corner shop and was about to put the sign into the window, tucked behind a sign for washing machine repairs and another one for secondhand bikes so that it could hardly be seen, when he stopped, left the shop and dropped all the other signs into the garbage outside. He used the rest of the money to buy another can of dog food and a lollipop for himself so that when, over the next few days, no one contacted them about the signs, Sam's mum was surprised and a little disappointed, but Sam wasn't surprised at all.

And while Sam's mum waited hopefully, Aunty Dot came every day and introduced Jenny one by one to the other dogs she walked.

CHAPTER 3

Gentleman Jim

Gentleman Jim was an enormous dog. His owner, Gordon, was fond of saying that his mother was a cross between an Irish wolfhound and a Great Dane but his father was a horse. And indeed, Gentleman Jim was almost as tall as his owner, who was not a short man. And he was very old, over sixteen years old, and was getting a bit stiff in his legs. In fact, getting up at all was becoming more and more of a problem. He would try various approaches, raising his huge head off his paws and pushing his front end to a standing position, but then if his back end refused to shift, he could only push himself backward across the floor. Or if he got his rear end up first, sometimes his front would follow, only to sag forward again unexpectedly. And then sometimes he would actually manage to get both ends up at once, but his middle would buckle.

It was sometimes said, by uncharitable people, that Gentleman Jim was not the prettiest sight.

His hair was falling out in patches and his wrinkled skin had scabbed all over. He had the ears and eyes of a bloodhound, and a long muzzle like a horse, and terribly bad teeth, which from time to time would fall out, clattering despondently to the floor. As a result of these terrible teeth, his breath was so bad that he could kill small mammals just by breathing on them.

Despite these natural disadvantages, Gentleman Jim was cheerful enough, partly because his owner was so well trained. After years of trying to train Jimbo, as he was affectionately known, to fetch the paper or his slippers, Gordon had finally learned to fetch them himself. Similarly he would run after any ball that he threw for his dog, retrieve it and lay it at Jimbo's feet. And Jim would raise his expressive eyebrows until finally Gordon would pick the ball up again, throw it again and run after it. In a similar manner he had trained Gordon to jump, roll over and beg. He had also trained him to get up when he didn't want to, simply by climbing slowly and painfully on top of him and squeezing all the breath out of him as he slept. On the occasions when this didn't work and Gordon seemed simply to be lapsing into a coma, Gentleman Jim would unroll his massive tongue, containing over half a pint of drool, and dribble it slowly into his ear until Gordon finally awoke, spluttering, sneezing and coughing all at once, and shaking his head so vigorously that droplets of drool would fly around the room.

Once his owner was thoroughly awake and had attended to all his needs—turning the heat up, cooking substantial quantities of pet mince and taking him around the corner for a constitutional—Gentleman Jim was free to go back to sleep in his favorite position in front of the fire while Gordon banged around the house in a rather bad-tempered way, wondering what on earth he would do until the sun rose and he could set off for work.

So one way or another, Gentleman Jim had his owner well trained, and he was entirely happy with this situation. His needs were few. He would sit in front of the patio doors doing his eyebrow exercises, twitching his nose if a fly landed on it, and greeting Aunty Dot, when she came by to walk him, with a slow but enthusiastic thump of his tail on the floor that sounded like applause, and generally living in peace with his world. That is, until Gordon got a girlfriend.

At first Gentleman Jim was untroubled by this development. He had got rid of no fewer than five of Gordon's previous girlfriends, mainly by sitting on them.

"Down, boy, down!" Gordon would say, struggling to extract them, and, "Bad dog!" when Gentleman Jim refused to move, and

Gentleman Jim would wag his tail in a good-humored kind of way while Gordon strained and pulled and his girlfriends squeaked out terrible language with what breath they had left.

"I'm so sorry!" he would say when they finally emerged. "He's just being affectionate. He thinks he's a lapdog." But the girlfriends, badly shaken by the experience, would usually leave in a hurry and never return.

This girlfriend, however, was different. She was small but determined and had a black belt in karate. The very first time Gentleman Jim attempted to jump on her, rather more clumsily than he used to be able to, he received a stunning blow to the nose, then found himself trapped in a kind of headlock and flipped over onto his back, where he lay for a moment, wondering what had just happened.

"Oh, he likes you!" Gordon said, reappearing with the coffee to find Gentleman Jim prostrate at his girlfriend's feet, and the girlfriend, whose name was Maureen, merely smiled as Gordon sat next to her and flexed her talons.

The worst thing about Maureen, apart from her lightning reflexes and tendency to violence, was that she seemed to want to reform Gordon. And reforming Gordon seemed to mainly involve reforming his approach to Gentleman Jim.

"What is that terrible smell?" she exclaimed one day as she entered the house after work. Gentleman Jim looked at her in surprise as she ran around the house throwing the windows and back door open. He could smell only the wonderful scents of his pet mince, a sumptuous olfactory brew of tripes and offal, the lungs, liver and mashed-up bowels of long-dead mammals, that Gentleman Jim had loved since he was a pup. It was true that Gordon wore protective clothing and a mask when he was cooking it up and that on more than one occasion the neighbors had complained and even signed a petition, but from the first moment that Gordon took it from the freezer and hammered out a chunk of it for the pan, Gentleman Jim's eyes would glaze over and he would start to drool. As the potent vapors filled the room, he would start to bark, deep, hoarse, regular barks signifying approval and anticipation, and finally when the whole house was enveloped in a succulent smog, he could contain his excitement no longer and gave vent to his feelings in a long baying howl.

"I'm not having that!" said Maureen. Her face had gone purple and her eyes were watering freely. "Give me that pan!"

"But it's the only food he likes," Gordon protested through his mask.

"I don't care!" said Maureen. "I'm not being asphyxiated by dog food. Give me the pan, now!" and Gordon, having been drilled into obedience by Gentleman Jim, meekly handed it over. Gentleman Jim's paean of praise turned into a bloodcurdling lament as Maureen dumped the whole pan into the garbage can at the end of the garden. Then she marched back in and sent Gordon to the shop for some dried dog food.

"There," she said as the tiny husks clattered into his bowl. "Nutritious, filling, and entirely smell free!"

Gentleman Jim's look said it all.

Next she threw out his dog bed, because it stank, and replaced it with a rubber mat that could be easily wiped clean. Gentleman Jim ignored this entirely and took up post on Gordon's bed, where he usually only slept at night. But Maureen's reaction to this was unfavorable in the extreme.

"You don't mean to say you let that *filthy hound* lie on your bed?" she exclaimed in horror.

Now, Gentleman Jim was very fond of that bed. It was a lovely, cushiony, rickety bed, or at least it was now, after several years of Gentleman Jim lying on it. He had marked his territory on it several times, and it was full of his own scents, and drool and hair, and the mingled scent of anxiety and sweat from Gordon.

"That bed," said Maureen, "has to go."

"Go?" said Gordon stupidly. "But where will I sleep?"

"In a new bed, of course," said Maureen. Gentleman Jim was out-raged. He had never felt the need to sleep anywhere else at all, certainly not on a new bed. He barked sharply, in a deep and commanding voice at Gordon, to tell him to assert himself immediately.

"Er, okay," Gordon said, provoking a snort of disgust from Gentleman Jim. "Do you know where from?"

Maureen not only knew where from, she got on the phone straightaway to order it, checking that the firm would take the old bed with them when they delivered the new.

"And that dog's not sleeping on it," she said, putting the phone down hard, "I can tell you that much."

Gentleman Jim felt obliged to give his owner a sharp nip in order to provoke him to speak.

"*Ow!*" said Gordon. "Well—er—where will he sleep then?"

"Downstairs in the kitchen," said Maureen promptly. "He's got his mat, hasn't he? Or even outside. There's nothing wrong with dogs sleeping outside. That's what kennels are for," she said, looking darkly at Gentleman Jim.

Gentleman Jim couldn't believe his ears. Outside? he thought. In a kennel? He waited for his owner to put his foot down, but Gordon was only gazing at Maureen with the foolish, admiring expression that dogs reserve for bones.

"You think of everything," he said, cuddling up to her.

Poor Gentleman Jim! He was so disheartened he could hardly raise a growl at the deliverymen, though he did bark furiously at the new mattress, which seemed to have a life of its own and was disinclined to go up the stairs.

Nothing in his old house smelled the same. Maureen had made Gordon clean it with disinfectant, and she installed air fresheners in every room. There were none of the old, comforting smells of pet mince and dog basket and double bed that had marked out his territory. He was too old to adjust to all this new, clean freshness, and he got terribly disoriented and confused.

One morning he awoke early as usual, in the hour before dawn. He couldn't remember why he wasn't sleeping in his usual place on Gordon's bed and lumbered upstairs to find him. Everything smelled so different he could hardly find his way, but Gordon must have left the lock off his door for once because Gentleman Jim pushed it open easily and clambered onto the bed to begin his usual ritual of waking up his owner. He lowered his considerable weight onto the sleeping form, and, when it didn't immediately show signs of struggling into life, unraveled his tongue as usual into the small pink ear.

Unfortunately, it wasn't Gordon in the bed at all, but Maureen. Once awakened by the crushing weight of what felt like a walrus descending on her and finding more than half a pint of drool dribbled into her cranial cavity, she did what any sensible woman would do. Gordon came flying in from the bathroom to find his girlfriend screaming loudly and dribbling from her ear.

"Oh, God!" he cried, and there followed the kind of perfectly ridiculous fuss that only humans in a panic can make. Maureen packed up her bag, which pleased Gentleman Jim mightily until he was ordered out of the house, and as the door slammed behind him, he just caught the words,

"Either that dog leaves or I do!" before Maureen stormed away.

Eventually, of course, Gentleman Jim was allowed back into the house. But everything had changed. The life seemed to have gone out of Gordon. He didn't wash or shave, but simply sat in front of the TV.

"What am I going to do, Jimbo?" He sighed as the great dog laid his heavy head on his master's knee. "I really loved her, you know."

Now, this was beyond Gentlman Jim's comprehension, but he did understand that his owner was very sad, sadder than he could ever remember seeing him before. He didn't even cheer up when Gentleman Jim did his impersonation of Beyoncé or wriggled across the carpet on his back. He was truly and terribly sad. For the first time the awful thought came to Gentleman Jim that if faced with a choice between his girlfriend and his dog, Gordon might actually choose Maureen. And if he did, Gentleman Jim would not know what to do about it, for at bottom, despite all his firm training of Gordon, he deeply believed, as every dog does, that his master's needs came first. But what Gentleman Jim would do, or where he would go, he did not know. So for the time being the two of them sat around the house, watching TV repeats of programs that hadn't been very good to start with and each looking doleful and lost, as only a very large hound and his brokenhearted master know how to do.

And it was in this state that Aunty Dot caught them when she called round to take Gentleman Jim for a walk with Jenny.

"Well, you two look like a pair of wet blankets," she said. "I was wondering if Gentleman Jim might want a walk."

Usually this suggestion was greeted with as much rapture as Gentleman Jim was capable of at his advanced age, but today his tail managed only a single, feeble thump.

"Dear, oh, dear," said Aunty Dot. "This won't do at all. Come on, Jimbo, there's someone I want you to meet."

She produced a doggie treat from her pocket, and Gentleman Jim struggled to rise. But it seemed as though his joints were as disheartened as the rest of him, for as soon as his front end struggled upward, his rear end collapsed and vice versa. Eventually Aunty Dot pulled his collar at the front and Gordon shoved him from behind and hurried to open doors and move furniture out of his way because once he was up and lumbering in a particular course, there wasn't much he could do about it.

He stopped abruptly, however, his back end falling over his front, when he saw Jenny. Aunty Dot had attached her lead to a hook by the back doorway, and she stood there patiently, glimmering softly in the evening light.

Both Gentleman Jim's ears flew up, and his whiskers twitched as Jenny raised her muzzle to his. And as with Pico, as soon as she sniffed his scent, she felt compelled to speak.

Dear friend, she said, *I can see you are a born hunter. The blood of your ancestors runs in you from the dawn of time, and your instincts are keen. You will hunt fiercely and swiftly again before your days are done.*

Jenny didn't know where these words came from, but as she spoke, Gentleman Jim seemed to remember it all, all the stirring of old instincts, intimate and powerful, the blood surging through his muscles and joints, which was like the surging of life itself. He remembered white woods and earth and moonlight and the thrill of battle that was like an ecstasy, a forgetfulness of self, trumpeting through him like an old war cry. And he raised his muzzle and sounded the cry from the depths of his being, frightening Aunty Dot and Gordon almost to death.

"Good heavens!" cried Aunty Dot, hanging on to her hat.

"He's never done that before!" gasped Gordon, shocked out of his melancholy stupor.

"Cool!" said Sam. "Can I hold his lead?"

But Gentleman Jim lowered his muzzle to Jenny's and gazed at himself in those liquid, fathomless eyes. And right there and then he gave her his heart.

"Well!" said Aunty Dot once she had got her breath back. "If these two are all right together, I might see if Boris and Checkers want to come out as well."

CHAPTER 4

Boris

Boris was a very slow dog. He was a Labrador and used to be a guide dog for the blind until it was discovered that he couldn't see or hear very well and had virtually no sense of smell. Sadly, this was only discovered after he had led one of his owners under a bus and deposited another in the canal. A third was only rescued by some picnickers as Boris plodded slowly toward the edge of a cliff. After this, it was decided that Boris could no longer be allowed to jeopardize the lives of the disabled, and since he was considered to be of no further use, he was taken to the dog pound, where, if no one claimed him, he was in imminent danger of being Put Down.

Fortunately for Boris, the manager of the dog pound, a kindly man called Mr. Finnegan, took a shine to Boris and took him home to his wife.

"He's a gentle soul," he told her. "I can't see him put down. He wouldn't hurt a fly."

Indeed, Boris wouldn't hurt a fly because in general flies were far too fast for him. They would crawl over his nose and into his ears and eyelids, and only sometime later, when they had gone, would Boris remember to snap.

But Mr. and Mrs. Finnegan weren't put out by Boris's slowness since they were slow, well-rounded, cheerful people themselves. The only drawback to living in their comfortable home was the food. Mrs. Finnegan didn't believe in commercial dog food and instead made her own concoctions, which were a gut-wrenching mixture of leftover dinner scraps, cereal, potato peelings, cod liver oil and any medicinal additives featured in her weekly magazine, *Canine Cuisine*, such as lavender oil and kelp.

The leftover dinner scraps were an adventure in themselves since Mrs. Finnegan was experimental with all food and attended a number of evening classes on cordon bleu cooking, which taught her to attend to matters such as height, texture and tonal variation but seemed to entirely leave out taste.

"One for the dog, I think, love," Mr. Finnegan would say. "Shall we get takeout?" And so, while Mr. and Mrs. Finnegan would eat wonderful food from a variety of unusual and exotic take-away venues, Boris, who was the only dog in the world to look depressed at mealtimes, would be given the failed results of Mrs. Finnegan's experimental cooking.

Boris bore with his mealtimes bravely, generally assuming they were a kind of punishment for something he hadn't realized he'd done. He was helped by the fact that he didn't have much of a sense of smell and only realized how bad it was when his best friend, Checkers, came to stay for the weekend.

Checkers was a lively dog with a healthy appetite. At teatime he bounded eagerly toward his dish only to keel over, stunned by the smell. When he got up, he backed away from his dish, barking madly.

"Don't be silly, Checkers," Mrs. Finnegan told him. "It won't hurt you—it's only your dinner!"

"Whatever is it?" Checkers asked Boris in a hushed voice. Boris thought hard, running through the various possibilities in his mind.

"Chicken?" he ventured at last.

"*Chicken?*" said Checkers. "It's blue!" And indeed the substance, whatever it was, was bluish and steaming.

"That'll be the ink," said Boris with a sigh.

"What ink?" said Checkers, looking more worried than ever.

"She gets it from an octopus, I think," said Boris.

Checkers advanced nervously toward the steaming mass, then backed away again. "I can't eat that," he said.

"Well, don't look at me," said Boris. "I'm still trying to digest the last one."

Checkers stepped cautiously toward it again, then ran off into a corner with his tail between his legs. "Is that an eyeball?" he said fearfully. "It winked at me!"

Checkers was a dog not easily put off his food. In fact, he rarely restricted himself to things he was supposed to eat and had gamely tried most things in his house—his owner's slippers and shirts and even, on one memorable occasion, the sofa and chairs. But now he seemed to have met his match.

"It'll all come out in the poo," said Boris encouragingly.

"That's what I'm scared of," said Checkers. And he did really look scared.

Over the course of that weekend, Mrs. Finnegan, determined to treat her guest, fed them turnip and mung bean surprise, then she prepared something tubular that slurped and sucked at the sides of their bowls.

"Blimey, mate," said Checkers. "I don't know how you stand it here, I really don't—the stuff she puts in your dish!"

Boris thought hard again. "It's not the stuff going *in* that bothers me," he said finally, "so much as when it tries to get out again."

And indeed, the tubular mess did look as if it was trying to climb out of their bowls.

All in all, Checkers was very glad when the weekend was over and his owner came to collect him. He dragged him all the way home and promptly ate a kitchen chair to relieve his feelings.

But Boris bore with all this patiently since in other respects, Mr. and Mrs. Finnegan were very good owners. That is, until they had the baby.

Mrs. Finnegan went into the hospital, and when she returned, Boris's life changed forever. She was carrying a small bundle, wrapped in blue. It had a small, wrinkled, yellowish face, rather like Checkers's bottom only less attractive. And it produced the loudest noise Boris had ever heard.

"WAAAAAAAAAA!" it said whenever Boris approached, and Mrs. Finnegan would always come running and haul Boris away. And this was the pattern of his life now. Whenever he tried to sit in any of his usual places, near the fire or on the settee, he would be hoisted up and shut into the kitchen or even outside in the yard.

Boris waited patiently for Mr. and Mrs. Finnegan to get fed up with their new toy and take it back to the shop. But this just didn't happen. They seemed entirely entranced with it, though for the life of him, Boris couldn't see why. It screamed loudly enough to send Boris, who was slightly deaf, into the nearest cupboard, and whenever Mrs. Finnegan sat down and closed her eyes briefly, it started again. But whatever it did, dribbling, puking or pulling their ears, Mr. and Mrs. Finnegan thought it was marvelous.

"Who's a clever boy, then?" they would say, and, "Ahh, isn't he lovely?"

Whereas when Boris dribbled or puked or howled along with the baby, he was smacked and put out of the room once again.

One way or another, the baby dominated the entire house. Every room was full of baby stuff. No one slept anymore or ever got to watch a full program on TV. Much as they loved the baby, Mr. and Mrs. Finnegan were exhausted, sometimes too exhausted to take Boris for a walk. Boris tried to show his owners that they didn't have to put up with it. When the garbage men came and Mrs. Finnegan had nipped inside to answer the phone, Boris pushed his paw down on the stroller brakes and nudged the stroller along the path to the trash can. But the garbage men proved even harder to train than his owners and brought the baby back. Mrs. Finnegan was very puzzled. She couldn't work out how the baby had got himself out of the gate, but fortunately she didn't suspect Boris.

Soon the baby got bigger. It changed from being an entirely helpless, useless being with a wobbly head and limbs that flailed in all directions to a creature that could crawl with determination across the kitchen floor to eat Boris's dog food and suck his ears. Mrs. Finnegan's experimental cookery had stopped for the time being, and Boris was now on canned dog food, which, as far as he could see, was the only good thing to have come out of this baby business. But one day, after the baby had eaten a full can of dog food, it was suddenly and severely sick, all over Boris. It promptly emitted a series of earsplitting shrieks, and Mrs. Finnegan came running as usual and gazed aghast at the color and consistency of the vomit.

"But you've only had milk!" she wailed.

The doctor was summoned, and he examined the baby all over but failed to find anything wrong. Eventually he shook his head gravely. "It is possible," he said, "that your baby is allergic to your dog."

Mrs. Finnegan looked stunned. "He *is* often sick when he's been near Boris," she said, and poor Boris couldn't tell her that it was because the baby was eating his food.

Fortunately, just then Aunty Dot and Sam arrived to take him out for a walk.

Boris trotted toward her happily, instantly forgetting his problems as she fastened his lead, talking to him all the time in an encouraging way. He pulled her to the front door, his enthusiasm growing as he spotted Gentleman Jim and Pico, of whom he was very fond. But he stopped in his tracks when he saw Jenny and gazed at her in astonishment, wondering whether or not to bark.

"Allow me to introduce you," said Gentleman Jim, and Pico said, "WOOF!" meaning "don't worry," but Jenny lifted her nose to Boris.

Dear friend, she said slowly as the words came to her from nowhere. *You are a natural guardian and protector. The time will come soon when you have to defend the whole world and guard life itself from danger.*

And as she spoke, Boris seemed to remember the nobility of his blood and his desire to protect the defenseless (the baby didn't count, of course, being his natural enemy). He felt himself to be towering and heroic and strong rather than stupid and slightly deaf, and he could see that image of himself reflected in Jenny's eyes.

"Amazing, isn't it?" said Gentleman Jim, and as Boris looked at him and Pico, he knew that they too had had the same experience, of seeing themselves as they really were, and right then and there, Boris gave Jenny his heart.

"Just look at how the others have taken to her straightaway," Aunty Dot said. "I've never seen anything like it," and just for a moment, she gave Jenny her penetrating look again, but this time she didn't take her glasses off, and then she added,

"Well, since you're all getting along so beautifully, we'll see how it goes with Checkers."

CHAPTER 5

Checkers

Checkers was very excited. This was nothing new since Checkers was always very excited. He got excited when it rained, which was very frequently, and particularly excited when it was windy. When the snow came, he was almost apoplectic with excitement. He barked madly when the sun shone and when it hid behind a cloud until it came out again, which might take days. Checkers seemed to think that the sun was playing some kind of game with him and that it had to be encouraged to return.

All the excitement and energy was quite entertaining when Checkers was a puppy, but much less so now that he was a full-grown dog.

"He'll grow out of it," the dog breeder told his owners, a young couple called John and Freda. "He'll calm down as he gets older." But Checkers was nearly five now, and there was no sign of this yet. If anyone walked along his street, he practically turned himself inside out with barking. And it was a busy street.

And then there was all the chewing. Checkers ate everything (apart from Mrs. Finnegan's experimental cooking, that is), from John's shoes to any papers left lying around. He chewed the ends of the curtains so that they got shorter and shorter and the table leg so that the table was crooked. He chewed his way through a set of encyclopedias on the bookshelves, which had been put there to look impressive in case John's boss ever came to tea, and when the new settee arrived, he ate that too.

Chewing was just one of the ways Checkers relieved his excitement. And there were always so many things to be excited about. John and Freda were often out working and didn't really spend enough time with Checkers, so that all his energy remained pent up inside him, and he had to relieve his feelings any way he could.

Right now, he was excited because he was having a bath.

Bathing Checkers was a strenuous occupation and not to be lightly undertaken. Checkers *hated* being bathed, partly because he couldn't see where he was going afterward.

No one knew what kind of a dog Checkers actually was. He had a mass of black hair, and when he was bathed, it was impossible to tell one end of him from another until one end bit you.

It took the combined strength of both John and Freda to haul Checkers toward the frothy water in the dog bath. Freda pushed, and John pulled, and finally they all tumbled in, upsetting the water all over the floor. Fortunately they had bathed him before and had covered the entire house in plastic, so that no real damage was done. They simply filled the bath again, and there was a short, tense interlude when it was not quite certain which one of them was having the bath. Then once they were all in together, with John and Freda sitting firmly down on Checkers, he promptly ate the soap, and when they tried to scrub him with a special mitten for his long coat, he ate that as well. When finally it was all over and John and Freda had collapsed in an exhausted heap, Checkers gave vent to his feelings by widdling all over the floor.

Freda wailed aloud. John buried his head in his hands.

"I never thought I'd say this," he said when he could trust himself to speak. "But that dog is getting worse."

"Cooee," sang Aunty Dot, letting herself in. "It's only me! I thought Checkers might want a walk."

John and Freda tried to explain that Checkers had just had one and they had just finished giving him a bath, but since Checkers was tearing around the house barking madly in excitement at seeing Aunty Dot, no one could hear themselves think, let alone speak.

"We won't be long," shouted Aunty Dot above the noise. "I've got someone I want him to meet."

That was all she managed to say before plunging toward the door on the other end of Checkers's lead. Checkers had just succeeded in dragging her through the outsize dog flap John and Freda had installed in their back door when he caught sight of Jenny and skidded abruptly to a halt.

"What?" he said, staring at Boris.

"Who?" then, "Why?" and he was so surprised, he completely forgot to bark. Boris was still grappling with the first of these questions, and Aunty Dot was still picking herself up, but Sam said, "This is Jenny, Checkers." Checkers pushed his nose forward and sniffed a scent that while doglike was like no other dog scent he had ever sniffed. He could smell stars in it, a whole universe of stars, and a vision came into his mind, of a vast tree, its branches spreading into the sky.

Then he found himself standing next to Boris and gazing deep into Jenny's dark and fathomless eyes, and a great calmness entered him. He felt as tall as a mountain and twice as still.

Dear friend, said Jenny. *You are a natural warrior, with the great gift of courage.* Then she looked at both Boris and Checkers. *You belong together,* she said, *and together you will accomplish great things.*

Checkers didn't fully understand this, and Boris didn't even try, but both of them felt that Jenny was speaking to the depths of their being and saying only what they had always already known. Boris felt himself grow strong and patient as a tree, whereas Checkers felt as though he came from a long line of the bravest dogs that had ever lived. He didn't move, he didn't bark, but stood still as a statue, as one who has waited for his destiny to call, and now that it had, waited only to know what to do with it. He could see that in other circumstances, all his tremendous qualities, his keen sense of smell, his boundless energy, his reckless courage and determination would win him praise rather than getting him constantly into trouble. He saw those other circumstances and a whole other world in Jenny's eyes, and right then and there he gave her his heart.

John and Freda had never seen him calm before.

"Look at that!" said John, astonished. "Is he ill?" For Checkers normally dealt with strange dogs by trying to eat them.

"No," said Aunty Dot, smiling and petting Checkers. "He isn't ill. He's just met Jenny, that's all. And Jenny's no ordinary dog."

"Can I walk Checkers, *please*," said Sam, and while John and Freda started to protest that if they couldn't hold Checkers on a lead, then a child certainly couldn't, Aunty Dot thought about it, then smiled and said he could give it a try. And Sam walked, holding both Checkers and Jenny, while Aunty Dot took Gentleman Jim and Boris and Pico, of course, who was in her pocket, and as long as he was walking with Jenny, Checkers behaved perfectly, just like a dog in a show. John and Freda watched openmouthed as they disappeared out of the drive and onto the busy street.

"Now," said Aunty Dot. "There's only Flo."

CHAPTER 6

Flo

Normally, Aunty Dot wouldn't attempt to walk six dogs together, but Flo's house backed onto the croft where they could all be set free, and since they were all behaving so well and Jenny was having such a miraculous effect on them, she thought she might as well get the last of the dogs she regularly walked.

"Who's Flo?" Sam asked, and Aunty Dot told him she was a poodle, though one of the bigger ones, standard-sized.

"I haven't introduced you to her yet," she said, "because she's a very nervous dog. Very nervous indeed. But you never know," she added mysteriously. "And there's no time like the present. We'll give it a try, shall we? We'll go and pick up Flo."

Flo peered nervously around the living room doorway.

"Easy does it," she told herself. She stepped very cautiously into the hallway.

"One step at a time," she murmured, then retreated in terror as she stood on a creaking board.

"Forward and onward," she quavered, sidestepping the board this time.

"Walk, don't run."

"So far, so good," she encouraged herself as she reached the dining room door and nothing untoward sprang out at her, and she remembered another of her owner's many proverbs.

"Fortune favors the brave."

Flo was one of the very few standard poodles who had mastered the art of tiptoeing. She tiptoed now past the utility room and into the kitchen, where the smell of breakfast temporarily overcame her fear. She glanced nervously to left and right, then trotted swiftly toward her dish.

Unfortunately, like most standard poodles, she had not mastered the art of glancing upward for danger. If asked about this, she would probably say that she had enough to cope with at eye level and with all the hazards of the ground. But in this case, not looking upward was a serious mistake. Just as she reached her dish, her jaws opening in anticipation, the Thing from the Topmost Cupboards sprang.

It sounded like this:

YEEEOAWWWWOOEEEEEIOW!!!!

And it sank all its claws into Flo's back.

Flo tore up the stairs yelping and belted back down them again howling, but the Thing on her back only released its hold when she collapsed on the carpet and rolled over in an attitude of abject submission. Then it stalked into the kitchen with its tail twitching and calmly ate her breakfast.

Poor Flo! It was a while before she could even summon the courage to sit up. And when she did, she realized that she had widdled in terror all over the carpet. It was enough to make a dog weep, especially a dog as naturally fastidious as Flo.

The Thing had turned away from her dish and was glaring around suspiciously with its luminous eyes. Flo barely had the presence of mind to cower behind the dining room door as it stalked past, radiating pure evil, its yellow eyes scouring the hallway as though still hungry for another chance of attack.

"It's just a cat, Flo," Gentleman Jim had told her one morning when Aunty Dot was walking them both and Flo had been particularly distressed.

"It's not a cat!" Flo insisted. "It's a horrible stripy—*thing*—and it's got fangs, and . . . and . . ."

"It's a *cat*," repeated Gentleman Jim.

"Oh no, it can't be," Flo quavered. "You haven't seen its eyes.

Its eyes are—horrible—monstrous—they—they glow in the dark—like—like—"

"Like cat's eyes?" queried Gentleman Jim, but there was no convincing Flo that the ferocious being that had taken over her household was, in reality, no more than a cat.

Gentleman Jim tried a different approach. "Look," he said. "You are actually bigger than it, you know."

But Flo's terror had apparently affected her eyesight.

"Oh no. I don't think I am," she said. "You haven't seen it. It's *huge*! *Much* bigger than me."

In vain, Gentleman Jim pointed out that for a cat to be much bigger than a standard poodle, it would have to be a tiger, and though Flo's owner, Myrtle Sowerbutts, was a renowned eccentric who dyed her pet poodle pink to match her own clothes and had her clipped into unusual geometric shapes like a kind of abstract topiary, even she might draw the line at taking a tiger in.

"Besides," he said, "if a tiger had jumped on you from the top of the kitchen cupboard, you'd hardly be here to tell the tale."

Eventually Flo was forced to concede the point. "Well, it might not be *quite* as big as me," she admitted. "But it's much, *much* meaner."

Life had been fine, a little scary, but manageable before her owner, for no good reason that Flo could think of, had taken in this foul predator and assassin.

"She calls it *Henry*," she said, as though this was like calling the Prince of Darkness Fred. "She says her sister *left* it to her. In her will!"

It was true that the Sowerbuttses were notoriously eccentric. Myrtle's sister Holly had left her house to the cats' home and her cat to Myrtle, and though everyone, including Myrtle, thought that this should probably have been the other way around, there were no real grounds for contesting the will. And since it was the only thing she had been left, Myrtle seemed determined to keep it.

"But it's ruining my life!" Flo said, almost in tears as they approached her home again. "I don't know how much longer I can go on like this!"

And it was true that under the fantastically clipped pink-and-purple mane, Flo was actually getting quite thin. Whereas the cat was getting fatter and fatter because it always ate Flo's food.

While Jenny was being taken for her walk, Flo was clinging to the wall, feeling the reassuring texture of wallpaper on her back. If she could just make it to her bed and lie down for a little while, she might feel better. She was quite exhausted after the morning's trauma. She nosed the door to the front room open carefully and sniffed.

"Feel the fear and do it anyway," she reminded herself, which was another of Myrtle's favorite sayings. The coast seemed to be clear.

"Lightning doesn't strike twice," she remembered as she tiptoed behind the back of the settee toward her bed.

Nothing. The clock ticked; the shadows did not move. Vastly reassured, Flo reached her bed and was about to sink down gratefully when the bed itself rose before her into a huge and monstrous cloud of ginger fur with staring eyes, making a noise like the snakes around a Gorgon's head would make if they all hissed at once.

Flo just had time to wonder whether she was having a heart attack when she realized that it wasn't her heart, but the Beast that was attacking. It flung itself at her face and she careered around the house backward, totally unable to see, hear or think. The smell of it was enough to render her unconscious. And in fact she *did* seem to pass out for a moment, and when she came to, she was somehow locked in the cellar, alone.

Poor Flo stayed in the cellar a long time because Myrtle was out with a friend, and when she came back, she was rather tipsy and had completely forgotten that she had a dog. She opened a can of dog food for the cat and fell asleep with him on her lap. Eventually she woke out of a dream in which the cat was barking at her and looked at him in surprise.

"Henry?" she said. At the same time there was a knock on the front door.

"It's only me," called Aunty Dot. "I've come to take Flo for a walk."

"Flo!" said Myrtle, remembering all at once that she had a dog.

"Just thought I'd take her out for an evening constitutional," said Aunty Dot, letting herself in.

It was part of Myrtle's eccentricity that though she had a dog, she wouldn't walk. She didn't like the outdoors at all; there was too much of it, she always said. She had an elderly chauffeur called Ryan who drove her everywhere, even next door, and she had hired Aunty Dot to walk Flo twice a day.

"Well, where is she, then?" said Aunty Dot, and finally Flo was extracted from the cellar.

"How did she get down there?" said Myrtle.

"How did she lock the door?" said Aunty Dot, and she looked toward Henry, who squatted with eyes like yellow slits, twitching his evil tail.

"Well, never mind," said Aunty Dot, when Henry failed to speak. "Come along now, Flo, dear, there's someone I want you to meet."

Poor Flo hung back, cringing and trembling. "Will it hurt?" she asked, but Aunty Dot coaxed her to the door with dog biscuits and then to the end of the yard, where she could make out her friends, Gentleman Jim and Pico, and a boy with reddish hair, who might have been alarming, but he was standing on the other side of the gate.

"I've had the most terrible time," she started to say. "I've—oh!"

The boy had opened the gate, and there was Jenny.

Instantly Flo cringed, her whole body clinging to the earth as though it might rock dangerously and fling her off. There are not many dogs who close their eyes when meeting a potential threat, but Flo had an optical condition that made frightening objects appear five times larger than their actual size and so had discovered that it was best. She shut her eyes tightly and clung to the lawn.

"Don't be silly, dear," said Aunty Dot, and Sam and all the dogs tried to tell her that it was all right. But Jenny trotted right up to Flo and touched her nose. Instantly Flo's nostrils were filled with the scent of meadows and summer streams and, well, kindliness. It is not often that one female dog takes instantly to another, but the scent in Flo's nostrils said "friend." Very cautiously she opened her eyes and realized that Jenny was not, in fact, the size of a pony.

Dear friend, said Jenny, in the voice that was at once strange and instantly recognizable, as though Flo had been listening to it for years. *You will be an invaluable companion through the peril that is to come.*

"P-peril?" stuttered Flo, getting ready to close her eyes again. "I'm not very good at peril. I—I'm a bit of a coward, actually."

Cowardice is just one of the forms of wisdom, said Jenny. *And it is your wisdom and perception that we need.*

"Oh," said Flo. It was not often that she received a compliment, and she was so taken by surprise that she forgot to ask, *For what?* Instead she was remembering that poodles are in fact among the most intelligent of dogs, and that her great-grandfather had been a leading performer in a circus, and that Flo herself learned new tricks very rapidly. She felt suddenly aware of the vast possibilities of her brain, and she raised herself up properly, feeling brave enough to look all around.

"There you are," said Aunty Dot triumphantly. "Jenny's even made friends with Flo!"

"I told you she was special," said Sam, and Aunty Dot said she didn't need telling that. Between them they led all the dogs onto the croft, and watched as they sniffed and explored and Checkers ran around and around in circles, but sooner or later they all returned to Jenny.

"It's like they're making a pack," said Sam, and in fact, this was exactly what they were doing.

My friends, Jenny said. *I can see that all of you are sad, for one reason or another. That is because you are not leading the lives you were born to lead. None of you can live out your full potential. But all that is about to change. You are all members of my pack.*

"Hooray!" cried Checkers, belting all the way around the croft again. "I've always wanted to be in a pack. Can I be the leader?"

No, said Jenny.

"But every pack should have a leader," said Flo, who had watched a documentary. "And an underdog."

"That'll be Pico," said Checkers, tearing around again.

"WOOF!" said Pico from underneath a twig.

Jenny paused for a moment, wrapped in thought. There was a reason she was here, in this new world, and a reason they had all come together. Only she didn't know what it was. A ripple of sadness passed through her, and she had a sense of something else dark and flickering in the corners of her mind.

This pack has neither leader nor underdog, she said eventually. *Each of you is needed for the danger that lies ahead.*

Boris looked at Checkers, and Flo looked at Gentleman Jim. Pico stood underneath Jenny and looked up but couldn't see at all. But they were all thinking the same thing, though only Gentleman Jim put it into words.

"Danger?" he said. "What danger?"

CHAPTER 7

The Doggie Post

I do not know yet, Jenny said. Flo closed her eyes. Checkers, how-ever, ran around the croft again, barking madly. "Danger!" he shouted. "Hurrah!"

Now the colors of the sky were deepening and the first pale stars appeared. Jenny looked up at them and sighed and wondered briefly if she would ever see her own, very different stars again.

"When will you know?" asked Gentleman Jim, but Jenny only said that she would know when the time came.

"Come along, you lot," called Aunty Dot. "Checkers, Boris, Flo—time to go home."

And slowly, reluctantly, the dogs returned. Their mood had changed, and they were all serious and quiet, wondering what their new friend might possibly mean.

Over the next few days, Jenny adjusted to life in her new home. There was a lot to adjust to. Electric lights, which went on and off unpredictably, so that the rooms did not go dark when night came, and music, blaring out from a small box. There was a bigger box, full of moving pictures, that Sam and Jenny watched entranced every evening until Sam's mum told him off for not doing his homework or sent him upstairs to bed, and then she sat in front of it, entranced. Then there was the washing machine. Jenny got in trouble for at-tempting to rescue the clothes as Sam's mum loaded them in, then she guarded them fiercely, her head going around and around, until the machine reached the spin cycle, when she ran off backward, with her tail between her legs.

"It's almost as if she's not used to electricity," Sam's mum said as Jenny stared out of the window, entranced by the street lamps. "I wonder where she lived before?"

Then, at the end of that week, Sam's mum got the vacuum cleaner out. Jenny cowered to the ground, appalled, as it was plugged in and switched on. She watched in horror as Sam's mum kept pushing it away from her and it came back, roaring horribly. Jenny was terrified, but her duty was clear. She flattened herself to the floor, emitting a volley of barks, then advanced on it in a growling rush, gripping the base of it with her teeth and hanging on for grim death while it pulled her back and forth across the carpet. But Sam's mum did not appear to be grateful for Jenny's heroic struggle.

"Sam!" she thundered. "Take the dog away!"

And Sam had to haul Jenny into the kitchen on her lead. Even there she wouldn't give up on the battle. She kept on barking and sounding the alarm until Sam's mum had finally won the fight and tied the beast up with its own tail.

There was so much that was strange and new that Jenny was often exhausted at the end of the day. She had come to a very noisy world. The garbage men arrived with their huge truck that made a grinding noise as they lifted the cars. Police sirens sounded regularly, and once a fire engine thundered past, almost deafening Jenny with its alarm. Many enemies attacked the house in that first week. There was a strange man in uniform who came every morning and a boy with a big bag of papers. Both of them seemed to be trying to get in through the letter box, but each time they tried, Jenny barked furiously until she had seen them off. When the window cleaner came, Jenny nearly had a fit. He attacked all the windows with a soapy solution so that he thought he was hidden, but Jenny wasn't fooled, and she barked so loudly and for so long that everyone on the street came out to see what was going on.

Gradually Jenny adjusted to the clamor of her new world, though she was still very nervous and still didn't much like being taken out on a lead. No one turned up to claim her, much to the bemusement of Sam's mum and Aunty Dot. But Sam kept his word about taking her out every day, before and after school. She wagged her tail furiously at him when he got up in the morning and looked very sad when he left for school, then overjoyed to see him again in the afternoon. He was the first person she had trusted in this strange new world, and she followed him whenever she could.

If Aunty Dot came to take Sam and Jenny out, Jenny would meet all her new friends. When Sam took her out on her own, she learned to communicate with them by using the doggie post.

When dogs leave their mark on lampposts or fences or tufts of grass, it usually contains a message for other dogs. In this way Jenny learned when Gentleman Jim's rheumatism was bad or Boris's food had disagreed with him again, when Flo was feeling especially nervous or Pico especially cross. Checkers was always very excited about something, often too excited to leave a proper message.

"Come *on*, Jenny," Sam would say because he was impatient to play with his new friends. "What's so good about that one blade of grass?"

But Jenny would move the blade around carefully, sniffing over and under it and nudging it at the root before moving on to the next blade. There were the scents she was familiar with, of earthworm and mole and hedgehog, the silvery trails of snails. Then there were the little piles of poo scattered all over the croft. Boris's poo was especially interesting, and she couldn't understand what made it glow with a mysterious purple light until she worked out his message, that Mrs. Finnegan had bought a new cookbook and he was suffering from the results. The chemicals in Flo's poo suggested that she had become sensitive to the new hair dye her human was using on her. She could tell that Checkers had been eating the wallpaper and that Pico was having trouble with his teeth.

"Get a move on, Jenny!" Sam complained. "It's getting dark!"

But Jenny had her own messages to leave, of comfort and hope to her friends who were leading such unnaturally stressful lives and about her daily battles with the postman, the washing machine and the vacuum cleaner.

Apart from these misadventures, however, Jenny felt that her humans were shaping up nicely and that she was getting to grips with the new world and settling in. Aunty Dot thought so too.

"She's a little miracle, that dog," she said, spoiling Jenny with one of the special treats she always brought. "I wonder how she came to be a stray?"

Jenny could have told her, of course, but she preferred to lie in her basket in front of the fire, keeping one eye on them all even when she fell asleep. Then as the weeks passed, she found that she was forgetting that she had a former life, and she preferred not to think about it. Her life now was full. She had her food, such as it was, she had her family and she had her friends. She was learning to speak to them in a voice that was more like theirs. And of course, she still had the mistletoe dart. She kept it under her cushion and took it out with her when she went for a walk. Sam was still the only person she allowed to touch it, and it was getting rather mangled now from the games they played. Still she refused to give it up since it was her last reminder of her other life. Sometimes when she tucked it into her mouth, she had an old, sweet feeling of former times, the image of a golden boy to whom she was absolutely devoted, and then she would get the pressing sensation that there was something she should be doing, but try as she might, she could no longer remember what it was. She worried about this at first, but as time went on and she became more and more content, she allowed the fragments of her former life to settle like dust into the hollows of her mind.

CHAPTER 8

In Which Something Very Unusual Happens

Aunty Dot and Aunty Joan and Aunty Lilith sat in their front room, knitting. At least Aunty Dot was actually knitting. Aunty Lilith was holding the ball of wool and sucking her tea through her false teeth, while from time to time Aunty Joan leaned forward with an enormous pair of scissors and cut the wool. This didn't seem to bother Aunty Dot much—she just carried on knitting with another ball of wool that Aunty Lilith passed to her, in a different color. Pico was asleep in his tea cozy in another room.

This room was very quiet, except for the ticking of the clock, which was very loud. It was an old-fashioned clock that had a sun and moon traveling around the face on separate dials, and if you looked at it closely enough, you would see that instead of numbers, it had the words PAST, PRESENT and FUTURE inscribed on it where the numbers 9, 6 and 3 would normally be. And at the top, instead of the number 12, there was the word ETERNITY in bold letters. It was quite hard to tell the time from this particular clock, especially since there seemed to be an almost infinite number of hands of different sizes, from the microscopically small to the huge. The biggest hand, however, seemed to be pointing at one minute to eternity.

Aunty Joan cut yet another strand of wool, and Aunty Dot put her knitting down. Both she and Aunty Lilith looked expectantly at Aunty Joan, who sat up suddenly.

"Sisters," she said. "It is time."

"It is time," echoed Aunty Lilith and Aunty Dot, and then all three of them did something very surprising. They unfolded their wings.

CHAPTER 9

An Unwelcome Guest

Jenny lay asleep on the rug in front of the fire. She was breathing heavily, and her paws were twitching.

"I wonder what she's dreaming about," Sam said.

"Bones," his mother replied. "Chasing a ball in a field. Come on, you'll be late for school."

But in fact Jenny wasn't dreaming about bones or balls. She was dreaming that a great tree had spread over the world. Its branches covered the sky and its roots lay in a chasm of darkness. The universe lay suspended beneath the roots of the tree, quivering with life like a great egg that was about to crack, and a serpent coiled from the branches to the roots.

IT IS TIME, a great voice said, and there, filling the kitchen, was the biggest wolf she had ever seen.

Jenny tore herself out of her dream. Nothing had changed. She was in the living room, not the kitchen, and the room was quiet and empty, though very cold because Sam's mum had turned the fire off. She shook her ears to warm them and to help her wake up properly. She had had these dreams before, and she always found them unsettling. She trotted into the kitchen to finish what was left of her food, then paused, looking in astonishment through the glass door.

Snow was falling—a few gentle flakes at first, then thicker and thicker until the whole yard was covered in a whirling whiteness. But only yesterday the sun had shone, and it had been quite warm.

IT HAS BEGUN, said a deep voice behind her. Jenny spun around. There was a huge wolf in the kitchen.

It is a characteristic of the Jack Russell breed that they don't know they are small. No enemy, however large, goes unattacked. Jenny crouched, barking for all she was worth, then sprang at the intruder. She didn't know what he was doing there or how he'd got in, but she was determined to see him off. She wasn't even put off by the fact that if he had opened his great mouth, he would simply have swallowed her. But no matter how often she sprang, the enormous wolf didn't seem to be quite where she thought he was. Yet he didn't seem to move.

HAVE YOU FINISHED? he said as she leapt at him for the fifth time.

"Ow!" said Jenny as she crashed into a cupboard. "Stay still, can't you?"

I THINK YOU'LL FIND I'M NOT MOVING, said the wolf. YOU ARE MOVING, AND SO IS THE WORLD. I AM QUITE STILL.

None of this made sense to Jenny. All she knew was that there was a strange wolf in her territory. She rushed at him again, barking, but the great wolf simply raised a paw and flattened her.

It was a force like an electric shock. Jenny lay stunned and gasping.

THAT'S BETTER, said the wolf.

Jenny closed her eyes briefly. Something was tugging at her memory. Her mind ran over the facts. There was a strange wolf in her kitchen. He was huge and glowing. His eyes were like two blow-torches and there was a kind of electric drool from his massive jaws that disappeared before it hit the floor.

I HAVE TRAVELED THE NINE WORLDS TO FIND YOU, said the wolf, and Jenny had a strange sinking sensation. She knew that she ought to know who he was. She tried to bark again, but all that came out was a kind of rattle.

"Why are you here?" she managed to ask.

I THINK YOU KNOW WHY, said the wolf, and added, IT HAS BEGUN.

Slowly, warily, Jenny got up. She couldn't bear to look at him, so she looked at the floor instead, which was gently smoking. Sam's mum would be furious, she thought.

"You already said that," she said quietly.

THE FIMBULWINTER IS HERE, said the wolf.

Jenny shook her ears. *Fimbulwinter,* she thought. The word echoed strangely in her mind.

"Wh-who are you?" she asked.

The strange wolf lowered his massive head. His eyes seemed to burn right through Jenny.

I THINK YOU KNOW, he said.

"No," said Jenny, though again she had the awful feeling that in fact she did.

I THINK YOU DO.

Jenny felt a spasm of annoyance. There was a strange wolf talking riddles in her kitchen.

"No, I don't," she said waspishly. "Or I wouldn't ask."

MY NAME IS FENRIR, HOUND OF RAGNAROK, said the wolf, and the kitchen rattled as he said these words. Slowly, horribly, Jenny's memories came tumbling back. She licked her lips.

"What are you doing here?" she whispered.

I THINK YOU KNOW, said the wolf.

"Don't start that again," said Jenny.

The wolf put back his head and howled, and it was as though suns were bursting inside Jenny's skull and stars were pouring over the edge of the sky.

MY NAME IS FENRIR, SON OF LOKI, HOUND OF RAG-NAROK, said the wolf, and Jenny stood, shocked into silence.

YOU HAVE TAKEN SOMETHING THAT DOES NOT BE-LONG TO YOU, said the wolf, and Jenny waited, bracing herself.

YOU MUST RETURN TO YOUR WORLD, he said.

"No," said Jenny. The great wolf lowered his terrible gaze toward her once more.

DO YOU REMEMBER GINNUNGAGAP? he asked.

"What?"

GINNUNGAGAP.

"Er . . . ," said Jenny.

THE GREAT ABYSS? IN WHICH EVEN LIGHT AND TIME ARE RENDERED VOID?

"Oh, that?" said Jenny. "No."

The great wolf gave the mildest sigh.

DO YOU REMEMBER EMERGING FROM THE ABYSS ONTO THE PLAIN OF VIGRID?

"I don't *think* so," Jenny said.

WHAT DO YOU REMEMBER, FROM THE TIME BEFORE?

Jenny looked at him blankly. "Nothing," she said.

THAT'S IT.

"No, I mean, I don't remember anything. Nothing at all."

YES, said Fenrir. THAT IS GINNUNGAGAP.

Jenny began to feel that this conversation wasn't getting anywhere.

"I don't remember anything," she said, a little peevishly. "And I'd like you to leave. Now."

NOT WITHOUT THE MISTLETOE DART, said the wolf, and Jenny's heart lurched. She knew where the dart was, of course. It was under her pillow, a bit chewed and scraggy because Sam and Jenny played with it every day. All Jenny knew was that it was precious to her—her favorite thing. She would never give it up. But she couldn't remember why.

YOU MUST GIVE ME THE MISTLETOE DART, said the wolf.

"Suppose I don't?" said Jenny, and the wolf put back his head and howled again, a deafening, blasting howl that had the cries of many beasts in it, a bellowing, roaring howl that flattened Jenny back against the cupboards. Lightning and thunder flashed around the kitchen units.

"I wish you wouldn't do that," said Jenny as a thunderbolt left a huge scorch mark on the kitchen floor. Fenrir ignored her.

YOU HAVE ALTERED THE COURSE OF DESTINY THAT WAS SUPPOSED TO BEGIN WITH BALDUR'S DEATH, he said. YOU KNOW THIS. BALDUR'S DEATH WAS TO BE THE FIRST IN THE GREAT CYCLE OF EVENTS THAT BRINGS ABOUT RAGNAROK. NOW RAGNAROK IS COMING ANY-WAY, AND ALL THE EVIL OF THE WORLD WILL BURST ITS BONDS. THREE COCKS WILL SOUND THE ALARM FROM VALHALLA, MIDGARD AND NIFLHEIM; HEL AND HER MINIONS WILL SPILL FROM THE GREAT ABYSS. VAL-KYRIES WILL HOVER OVER THE BATTLEFIELD OF VI-GRID, DRINKING THE BLOOD OF THE WOUNDED AND EATING THEIR FLESH, THEN THE HELLHOUNDS SHALL DEVOUR THE SUN AND MOON, THE SEAS WILL BOIL, ENGULFING THE LAND, THE HEAVENS WILL BE RENT ASUNDER AND THE STARS WILL FALL INTO THE GREAT ABYSS THAT IS GINNUNGAGAP.

Jenny's mouth felt entirely dry. "Is that all?" she managed to say.

YES, said the wolf.

Jenny began to feel that she might have a headache coming on. The great wolf said nothing, gazing at her with scorching eyes.

"Look," said Jenny, "are you trying to say that my world—the world I came from—will come to an end?"

YES.

"And its sun and moon—and stars—and seas?"

YES.

"Are you sure?"

YES.

"Well, then," said Jenny helplessly. "I mean—when?"

IT IS HAPPENING NOW, Fenrir said patiently. THE FIM-BULWINTER HAS BEGUN. I TOLD YOU THAT ALREADY. WERE YOU NOT LISTENING?

"Yes—yes," said Jenny hurriedly, for the great wolf looked as though it might bite. "But, I mean, what can I do?"

YOU CAN GIVE ME THE MISTLETOE DART.

"But why?" said Jenny. "Will that stop the end of my world?"

NO.

"No?" said Jenny. "Then why bother?"

The great wolf Fenrir bared his mighty teeth, and for a moment Jenny thought he would swallow her in a single bite, then he lowered his massive head and spoke.

IF YOU STAY HERE, IN THIS WORLD, he said, speaking slowly and clearly, THEN RAGNAROK WILL COME HERE AS WELL. SEE—THE FIMBULWINTER IS HERE NOW, NOT ONLY IN YOUR OWN WORLD. THIS WORLD WILL BE DESTROYED WITH YOUR OWN. IS THAT WHAT YOU WANT?

Jenny's heart sank like a stone. She knew he was speaking the truth. She had known all along that she might not be able to stay here. But she did not know what else to do.

The great wolf pawed impatiently at the kitchen floor. YOU MUST RETURN TO YOUR WORLD, he said. YOU CANNOT STOP RAGNAROK, BUT YOU CAN STOP IT FROM COMING HERE. YOU HAVE A CHANCE TO SAVE ONE WORLD AT LEAST.

Jenny said nothing. She was remembering, finally, with a fierce pain, why she had run away with the dart in the first place and what she had started.

WHERE IS THE DART? the wolf said.

"Why do you care?" said Jenny, suddenly curious. "I thought you wanted Ragnarok. In Ragnarok you are free. Why should you want to save this world?"

And she started to back away from him, though in fact there was nowhere to run to, nowhere to hide.

The great wolf bellowed again.

FOOL! he roared. DO YOU STAND HERE ARGUING WITH

ME WHEN THE FATE OF TWO WORLDS IS AT STAKE?
GIVE ME THE DART—NOWWW!

And this last word ended in a terrible howl. Jenny was horribly
frightened. But she thought she could see something on the other
side of the wolf. She tried to look around him, but he was too big.
She could sense the Void, lapping and quivering behind him, and
something else. Something that had stopped him from coming farther into the kitchen and simply attacking her or carrying her away.
All of a sudden, she knew what it was.

"Fenrir," she said. "This is not your world. You are bound to the
Void. The gods bound you, with a rope as light as silk but stronger than anything in the known universe. It was made by the Dark
Dwarves, from the footfall of a cat, the roots of a mountain, the
sinews of a bear, the breath of a fish, a woman's beard and the spittle
of a bird. This is not your world, and you cannot come in."

The great wolf roared and bellowed, rolling back his terrible
eyes.

YOU DO NOT BELONG HERE, he roared.

"No, *you* do not belong here," Jenny said. "And you can't have
my dart."

The great wolf strained and frothed, then was suddenly still.
There was a cunning look in his eye.

SHOW IT TO ME, he said. Jenny stepped sideways, toward the
cushion. If she was right, she could run right past him, to the dog
flap in the door. If she was wrong, she would die.

"Here it is," she said, holding it in her mouth. And as Fenrir's
great jaws snapped toward it, Jenny ran.

CHAPTER 10

In Which More
Unusual Things Happen

Pico woke up alone. He stared around for a moment, bemused. One minute he'd been on the coffee table, watching Aunty Lilith polish her bunions, the next he'd fallen asleep in the tea cozy. And now he didn't know where everyone was.

Pico struggled out of the opening for a spout. Aunty Lilith had knitted the tea cozy, which meant that it was a very peculiar shape and seemed to have holes for three spouts. He stood up on the coffee table and shook himself, then looked all around.

Since Pico was so very small, it was difficult to see over the various things around him, but he felt absolutely sure that the room was empty. This was very odd. He was never alone since one or other of the aunts would carry him wherever they went, in their sleeves or even under their hats. Worse, the silence around him seemed bigger than the room, as though the whole house was empty. Surely the aunts wouldn't have gone dog walking without Pico?

"Woof!" he said, experimentally, then louder, "WOOF!"

But there was no reply.

One thing was certain. He couldn't stay perched on the coffee table all alone. Somehow he would have to get down.

It wasn't a very big table, but to Pico it seemed very high. It wasn't as bad as the time that Aunty Lilith had absentmindedly put him on the top shelf of the dresser and he had to knock all the knickknacks off before anyone realized he was there, but still the coffee table stood two feet off the floor, which was almost five times Pico's height, and he had to run all the way around it before finding the best place to jump from so that he would land on the thick hearth rug.

Once safely down, Pico trotted through the door onto the landing and was further taken aback to realize that the front door was open.

What was going on?

A cold wind was howling, and it flung the front door back with a crash. Pico summoned his courage, stepped forward into the gap where the door had been and warily looked out. He sniffed the scent of snow. The aunts must have gone out without him, but they couldn't have gone very far in this weather, leaving all the doors open.

As Pico peered out along the garden path, which was flanked to either side by a dense undergrowth that looked like a jungle to him, he was suddenly struck by a new thought. For the first time in his life that he could remember, he was alone, unsupervised. This was his big chance! If he was ever going to realize his dreams of travel and adventure, now was the time.

But it was very cold, and the first snowflakes were gathering. The leaves and roots and twigs all around him looked enormous.

"Come on, Pico," he said to himself sternly. "How many times have you waited for an opportunity like this?" He tried to summon the images of stars and rivers and mountains that beckoned him in his dreams, but he was finding, as many people do, that the moment of realizing his wildest dreams was a rather scary one. He was suddenly very aware of himself as a two-pound Chihuahua, alone in an enormous world, and his heart quailed. Why, there were spiders out there in the garden that were nearly as big as him.

Then just at that moment, the wind blew again. It brought with it the scent of rain, and traffic and trees and something else, delicate and sweet to Pico's nostrils. It was the scent of Jenny, the new friend to whom he had given his heart. Jenny had passed that way recently, as far as he could tell, and he instantly remembered the way she had looked at him and the things she had said. *Your body is small but your heart is great,* she had told him, *you have within you distant horizons and marvelous deeds,* and just the memory of this made him swell with pride, so that he was nearly six inches tall rather than five. If

Jenny was out there, he wanted to be with her, and the one place he could think they would be likely to meet was the croft.

Without further delay, Pico made the enormous leap from the front door step to the path and landed unhurt. Glancing around quickly for obvious hazards such as a falling leaf, he stuck his nose in the air so that he could follow Jenny's scent and trotted quickly to the end of the path. The gate was closed, but he just trotted under it, and he was out on the pavement, tracking a scent, alone and free for the first time in his life.

Gentleman Jim lay asleep on his rug by the fire. He had started to dream, a wonderful, exciting dream about being led into battle and running alongside a chariot with soldiers, their swords and shields flashing in the sun, when he was woken by the sound of voices at the front door.

"No, Gordon," one of the voices was saying. "I won't come in—not while you've still got that disgusting hound."

Gentleman Jim twitched all over convulsively. It was the one voice he had hoped never to hear again—Maureen's.

"It's for the best, Gordon," she said. "He's getting too old to enjoy life now."

Gentleman Jim didn't know what she was talking about, but he was suddenly, absolutely sure that he needed to know. He struggled to his feet, which wasn't easy since his back end seemed to want to go a different way from his front, and just as he'd got his hips locked into position, his knees gave way. But once he was up, he crept as quietly as he could into the hallway, only knocking over a coffee table and two lamps on the way.

He could see his owner and Maureen through the glass in the vestibule door, talking earnestly.

"It's a kindness, really," Maureen was saying. "It can't be any fun being that old. How are you going to look after him when he needs full-time care?"

Gordon hung his head. As usual, when Maureen was talking, he seemed to have no capacity to assert himself. She fiddled with a button on his shirt.

"We could be so happy together, just the two of us," she murmured. "I'm sure if you ask the vet, he'll agree with me."

Vet? thought Gentleman Jim. That was one of his least favorite words. He could even spell it since Gordon had taken to saying V-E-T in Gentleman Jim's presence.

"It's only one little injection," she said. "He won't feel a thing."

Slowly the full horror of what Maureen was saying sank in.

No! thought Gentleman Jim. Don't let her get to you! Send her packing!

But Gordon seemed to be mesmerized by Maureen's eyes.

"Promise me you'll take him," she said.

"Well—I—I—" Gordon said, and Gentleman Jim nearly bit through the coat stand in frustration. Tell her you'll take her to the vet's, he thought furiously as Maureen rested her cheek on Gordon's shoulder.

"It's for his own good," Maureen said, and Gordon murmured, "I suppose so."

Gentleman Jim stared at them both in disbelief. He felt a long shudder, from his tail bone to the top of his skull. He had heard enough. He didn't know when he'd felt more desolate, or betrayed. He turned away, blundering blindly back into the living room.

He would have to leave, he thought. But how?

When Gordon finally came in, he couldn't look at Gentleman Jim, but Gentleman Jim stared accusingly at Gordon, his outraged gaze following him around the room.

"What?" said Gordon finally, and, "Stop looking at me like that!"

The clock ticked loudly in the quiet room, and Gentleman Jim was horribly aware that each tick was bringing him closer to the end of his life. Then suddenly Gordon put away his paper and stretched and remained for a moment staring at the ceiling.

"Shall we go for a walk?" he said, looking at last toward Gentleman Jim. The big dog stared at him. Gordon was a creature of habit and never went out for a walk at this time. He might almost have said *one last time,* thought Gentleman Jim, but at the same time, he was aware that this was an opportunity, and he thumped his tail slowly on the floor.

Then once again, while Gordon got his coat and boots, Gentleman Jim struggled to his feet. He was a warrior, he told himself, remembering his dreams of battle. He could not be so easily defeated. He didn't know where he was going or what he would do when he got there, but as Gordon opened the front door to a blast of freezing air and reached for Gentleman Jim's lead, he was suddenly flattened against the vestibule wall. Gentleman Jim blundered past him before he had chance to recover his breath and shout *"Hoy!"* and lumbered along the garden path toward the gate. The gate was shut, but Gentleman Jim didn't let that stop him. He gained speed, crashing straight through it, and he was out, in the freezing air.

Boris was in trouble again, and this time it was serious. His mum, Mrs. Finnegan, had finally caught him in the act of leaving the baby out for the garbage men.

He had been tugging the baby, whose name was Sean, along the garden path by the seat of his disposable diaper, when suddenly he was deafened by a powerful shriek.

"Boris!" screamed Mrs. Finnegan. "What are you *doing?*"

In fright, Boris dropped the baby, who rolled onto one side and started to roar. Mrs. Finnegan picked him up instantly but carried on screaming and shouting at Boris, so that Boris's brain and ears quietly shut down. If people shouted at him for long enough, he simply went to sleep. But Mrs. Finnegan took in the arrival of the garbage men, and the direction in which Boris had been hauling the hapless Sean, and the truth hit her in all its enormity. She even stopped screaming for a moment as she took it all in. Then, when she recovered her breath, she towered over Boris, looking tall and terrible, though in fact she was short and round.

"Right!" she said, clipping his lead onto his collar. "You're coming with me!"

And she hauled Boris into the garden shed, attached his lead to a hook and slammed the door shut.

"You can stay there for the rest of the day!" she shouted through it. "You wicked, *wicked* dog!"

She said one or two more things, about waiting until his father got home, but Boris wasn't listening. He sat on the damp stone floor, sniffing all the strange, moldy, musty smells, then nudged at a slug with his nose. It clung to the end of his nose and he got very distracted for several moments, trying to shake it off, while Mrs. Finnegan harangued him outside. Then eventually she turned away, and he could hear her heels clicking on the path. He let his head sink onto his paws, feeling very sad. It was cold in the shed. Outside he had sniffed a hint of snow.

There had to be some mistake. He had only been trying to help— the baby was getting everyone down, and Boris thought he had come up with the perfect solution. Surely Mrs. Finnegan would come back for him soon?

But no one did, and Boris spent a miserable, freezing day in the shed. The cobwebs and dust made him sneeze, small beetles crawled over him and he was forced to relieve himself on the floor. When Mr. Finnegan finally opened the door, Boris was overjoyed. But Mr. Finnegan was clearly not happy at all.

"Boris, Boris," he said when Boris had finally stopped barking, and he squatted down and took Boris's head in his hands. "Whatever am I going to do with you?" and he shook his own head.

"It's no good, Boris," he said, and, "If only it wasn't the baby," and, "You do understand, don't you, old fella?"

But of course, Boris didn't. He understood that Mr. Finnegan wasn't happy, and, when he gave him a great lick on the nose, was astonished to find a tear on the end of it and was immediately terribly miserable too. But Mr. Finnegan stood up, brushing his tears away, and took hold of Boris's lead.

This was more like it, Boris thought—a walk. Though he would rather have got warm first. Still, maybe a walk would warm him up, and he trotted along happily at Mr. Finnegan's side.

But Mr. Finnegan went straight to his car. Boris was stumped by this development until he remembered that in the good old days before the baby arrived, Mr. and Mrs. Finnegan would sometimes drive out to the seaside and then take Boris for a walk. Of course it was rather cold for the seaside, actually snowing now, but still Boris wagged his tail hopefully when Mr. Finnegan opened the door.

And once he was in the car, Boris began to warm up. Mr. Finnegan put some nice music on and began to talk to Boris, though he was still saying things that Boris didn't understand, like, "I wish I didn't have to do this to you, old son," and, "Still, maybe it's all for the best."

Then a feeling began to grow in Boris that he actually did know where he was going. But it was only when they rounded the final corner and he saw the sign for the dog pound that he fully understood what was going on.

Mr. Finnegan stopped the car and opened the door.

"Come on, Boris, old son," he said. Boris stared at him in anxiety and dismay. Mr. Finnegan *couldn't* be taking him back to the dog pound! It was horrible there! Boris would have to live in a cage again and would only be taken out once a day to walk past all the other abandoned dogs. Worst of all, he, Boris, would not belong to anyone anymore. He would be no one's dog.

Boris backed away along the seat as Mr. Finnegan took hold of the lead.

"Out you come, Boris," he said.

Boris wasn't coming out. He braced himself against the lead as Mr. Finnegan tugged. Boris was quite a weighty dog in spite of all the terrible food, and though Mr. Finnegan tugged hard, he wouldn't budge. Mr. Finnegan tried reasoning and pleading and finally swore, but it wasn't any use. Then Mr. Finnegan let go of the lead.

"Suit yourself," he said, and he walked away.

Boris was so busy trying to work out what was going on now that he didn't notice Mr. Finnegan sneaking around the other side of the car. He had backed himself up against the other door and was taken completely by surprise when Mr. Finnegan flung that door open and seized him by the collar crying, "Gotcha!"

For the first time in his life, Boris acted fast. He lunged forward, hauling Mr. Finnegan with him through the open door in front of him so that Mr. Finnegan was dragged the length of the car's back-seat and pulled out on the other side.

"OW!" he roared as he hit the pavement. But he let go of Boris's collar, and Boris lumbered off, straight into the traffic of the main road.

Checkers was very excited. There hadn't been a real storm for ages—ever since, well, ever since the last one. He barked when the wind got up and when it dropped again. He barked when some leaves flew past the window, and when the TV flickered, he barked at that. When hailstones clattered against the window, he went barking mad.

"For goodness' sakes, Checkers," Freda said. "Give it a rest, can't you? My nerves are shot!"

But Checkers charged from one window to another all around the house, raising the alarm and sounding his special war cry, which was part growl and part howl. When the wind howled threateningly at him, he howled back, and when a door slammed shut, he went completely insane, convinced that the enemy was finally inside and after them.

"Checkers—*Checkers!*" Freda roared, but Checkers was barking too loudly to hear. At last she caught hold of his collar and hauled him upstairs, into the little room they called the study.

Checkers hated the study. It was a tiny room, queerly shaped, that the real estate agent had optimistically referred to as having "third-bedroom potential." He hung back, growling, as Freda tugged and pushed him into it. It was the one room in the house where he couldn't charge madly at the window since there wasn't one. Freda finally managed to thrust him in and lock the door.

"I'm sorry, Checkers," she called to him through it. "But you're driving me mad. I'll let you out when the storm dies down."

But Checkers didn't want to be let out when the storm died down. He wanted to be out, fighting the storm while it attacked the house. Freda obviously didn't understand. He barked at the door for a long time, trying to explain, then, when she didn't come back, he vented his feelings by eating all the papers on the desk, then chewing the wires that led into the computer.

Eventually he calmed down. He couldn't hear the storm so well, locked into the tiny room, and anyway, his voice was getting hoarse. This didn't mean that he could let himself off duty, however, and he sat erect as a sentinel by the door, guarding it until either John or Freda let him out.

Sometime later, he heard John's footsteps coming up the stairs and started barking all over again, overjoyed that he might be let out at last. When John opened the door, he leapt at him in a single bound.

"All right, Checkers, all right," John said, laughing and tugging his ears. "Calm down now, settle down. I've just come up here to collect my—"

Then he stopped, looking at the mass of chewed-up papers on his desk, and the computer wires.

"Oh—my—God," he said, and his eyes bulged, and his face turned a funny color.

"Checkers," he said weakly. "You didn't—you haven't—?" and

he fumbled frantically through the scraps of paper while Checkers watched him, astonished, his head cocked to one side.

John's face changed color again, from pale green to puce. He stopped fumbling through the papers and picked up the chewed computer wires. He closed his eyes. He appeared to be holding his breath. He held it for so long that Checkers got quite worried and was about to bound onto his back to make him breathe again when John emitted an earsplitting, anguished sound.

"NYYAAAARRRGGGHH!"

An almighty row ensued. Checkers tried to help by tearing around the house, chewing the furniture and barking. Doors were slammed; pots and books flew around.

"IT'S THAT BLOODY DOG!" John yelled at last. "HE'LL HAVE TO GO!" and he advanced on Checkers, holding the special lead that was a kind of chain.

Checkers knew he was in trouble. He had never before been thrashed, but as John advanced toward him, with a berserk expression on his face, Checkers ran. He bounded down the stairs, knocking pictures from the wall as he went, burst through the kitchen door, scattering all the chairs, dived through the dog flap in the back door and charged straight through the hedge. Traffic roared and blared as he shot across the main road, leaving John waving his arms helplessly on the other side. He had no clear idea where he was going, just that he had to put as much distance as possible between himself and his enraged master. A freezing wind blew, and on it he thought he caught the scent of his friend Boris.

The croft, he thought. That's where he would go. To the croft, to meet his friends.

For once, Flo was having a peaceful afternoon. She was safe and warm in her house, not lost in a horrid cold storm. She lay on her side on her soft bed and closed her eyes, twitching slightly as she began to dream.

She dreamed that she was running away from Henry. She couldn't see him, but she could hear his unearthly howl behind her to the left, then the right. Flo swerved away from the howling, up the stairs, through all the bedrooms, in and out of the bathroom, back down the stairs and down another flight of stairs.

Gradually it began to dawn on Flo that she didn't know where she was running to. The dimensions of the house seemed to be changing; there were corridors and stairs she had never previously encountered and doors leading into rooms she didn't know. What's more, she seemed to be traveling through them all quite silently, and the yowling of the cat became distant.

What's happening? thought Flo, and, Where am I going?

There was no sign of Henry and no sensation of weight on her back. There was only Flo, traveling weightlessly and soundlessly through corridors and past stairways and doors. Till at last she came to a halt in front of a door at the very end of the corridor.

It was an old, oak door. It looked as though it hadn't been opened for years. Flo stood in front of it panting and gradually brought her trembling breath under control. She hadn't the faintest idea where she was or how she had got there, but she was too afraid to look behind her to see where she had come from in case the fiend called Henry should suddenly pounce. So she trotted toward the door and opened it, quite easily, with her nose.

It was an exact replica of the room she had curled up in so peacefully such a short time ago. A fire burned brightly in the hearth, and a huge curved mirror hung over the fireplace. In the rocking chair there was a basket, full of the odds and ends of ribbon with which her owner had been tying Flo's hair.

Flo was mystified but too exhausted to think. She trotted gratefully toward her spot near the fire, wanting only to sink into sleep, but just as she reached the patterned rug, the mirror leaned forward.

Now dogs, as you may know, don't take much notice of mirrors. The surface of a mirror seems like brightly patterned glass to them, and usually they show no interest in their reflection or anything else reflected in it. Yet this time, as the mirror leaned toward her, Flo saw everything with startling clarity.

There were three ancient women in the depths of the mirror. They were dressed in white and their hair hung over their faces like trailing fronds.

Flo yelped in fear and spun around, expecting to see the three hags behind her, but there was nothing. The little clock ticked on, the fire spat and the chintz cushions glowed brightly.

Flo didn't know much about mirrors, but she did know they were supposed to reflect the room they were in. She turned around again, slowly, fearfully, and there were the three white figures, leaning forward. They appeared to be spinning something, and as Flo stared, with a dreadful fascination, the central one lifted her head and gazed at Flo with milky eyes. And at the same time the surface of the mirror rippled and changed to a kind of smoke.

Oh, dear, thought Flo as the smoke wreathed its silky way toward her. "Oh, dear. Oh, dear, oh, dear."

And she wrenched herself awake, trembling and sweating.

Nothing had changed. The room was empty and quiet apart from the ticking of the clock and the crackling of the fire. Outside, the wind mourned.

Flo couldn't bring herself to look at the mirror. There was no sign of Henry or Myrtle. Flo felt disturbed by her terrible dream. She wanted company, and though she was afraid to leave the room, she padded quietly to the door and poked her nose into the hallway.

A blast of cold air came in through the front door, which was open. Flo felt more confused than ever. Myrtle never left the front door open—it let the outdoors in, she always said. Fearfully, in case Henry was waiting for her on the stairs, she trotted toward it and peeped out.

The light had changed to a greenish yellow and there were snowflakes whirling around in it, dancing lightly in the air rather than falling to earth. Flo shivered, then, more disoriented than ever, she ventured onto the path, looking for her mistress. She didn't dare to bark in case Henry heard, but as she advanced toward the gate, she saw that it too hung open.

Something was terribly wrong, Flo thought. No one was more security conscious than Myrtle, who kept most of the doors and windows locked even when she was in. Finally she remembered that Myrtle was visiting her next-door neighbor, Mrs. Drum.

Next door couldn't be that far, Flo told herself. She could go there, all by herself, and bark at the window until someone appeared. Still she hesitated. Terrible things happened to dogs who stepped outside their own gates. Beyond her gate was the croft, and she didn't feel safe without a lead. She wished very much that Aunty Dot would come along and attach her to one. She didn't even know if she could walk properly without one. Gingerly, as though the earth might open up beneath her and swallow her into its gaping mouth, Flo took one step forward, then another, and soon the gate was behind her, and she stood, gasping a little in fright, on the scrubby grass of the croft.

Lightning crashed and thunder rolled as Jenny reached the croft. The wind whipped leaves, twigs and small stones up into the air in a flurry before pelting them down again toward all the small creatures who lived there. Shrews, mice and beetles ran for cover. Jenny paused, squatting to begin the message she had to leave for her friends. It was the most complicated message she had ever sent by the doggie post. It began with the creation of the world and ended with Ragnarok. She was out of breath already, and didn't know if she had enough widdle in her to fully explain.

Dear friends, she began, sniffing the electric air. *I am running away from Fenrir, Hound of Ragnarok.*

She moved on to the next clump of grass. *I have to return the mistletoe dart, which was the reason I ran away. . . .*

As she left her messages, Jenny felt terribly alone. She could smell the scents left by her friends on previous, happier days. She could smell the disturbance in the air and something else, which was more like the complete absence of smell. Ginnungagap, the Void, lapping at the edges of the storm, surrounding the croft. It was waiting for her; she knew that now. She had been summoned, and she would have to return. All her memories had come flooding back, and she knew it was useless to attempt to escape. Who was she, a small Jack Russell, to defy Fenrir, Hound of Destruction?

The last thing Jenny wanted to do was to jump into the Void again. Just contemplating it made her feel even more lonely and afraid.

"I wish I wasn't alone," she said aloud.

"WOOF!" said Pico, and Jenny jumped violently. She looked all around before realizing that he was underneath her and she had been about to widdle on him.

"Pico!" she exclaimed. "What are you doing here?"

But before he could answer, a quavering voice said, "Hello? Is anyone there? Oh, please, don't jump out at me if you are."

"Flo!" cried Jenny and Pico together, so that Flo bolted backward in fright, closing her eyes.

"Who—who is it?" she said, too nervous to recognize their voices.

"Well, if you opened your eyes," said Gentleman Jim, rounding the corner and nudging Flo from behind so that she yelped in fright, "you'd stand a much better chance of finding out."

"Gentleman Jim!" said Jenny, and Flo opened her eyes and instantly felt much better. "Oh, it's you!" she said, wagging her little pink pom-pom of a tail.

"So it is," said Gentleman Jim. "It looks like it's all of us. Apart from Boris and Checkers," he added, and was immediately bowled over by Checkers.

"Watch it, G. J.," he said, bounding all the way around the croft and back again. "Anyone seen Boris? He was here a moment ago."

"Here I am," said Boris, plodding slowly out from behind a bush. He had met Checkers several moments ago and since that time had been leapt upon, sucked, nuzzled, pummeled and chewed and so was feeling a little dazed, but very glad to see all his friends.

"Well, here we all are," said Gentleman Jim, picking himself up again and looking sternly at Checkers, who was too busy belting around to notice. "And none of us with our owners. Or Aunty Dot. I must say, this is very unusual. What brings you all here?"

And immediately everyone began talking at once and trying to explain, so that Jenny, who at first had been overwhelmed with delight to see them all, could hardly hear herself think. And she was very afraid that all the noise would attract some unwelcome attention.

"Stop talking, all of you," she said, and when no one heard, she lifted her voice and cried, *"Silence!"* and everyone stopped talking at once.

"There is no time," she said earnestly. "We are all in terrible danger."

"WOOF!" said Pico, and Flo said, "D-danger?" and Checkers bounded all around everyone three times in excitement. Jenny raised a paw and stamped it on the ground in impatience. "You must listen, all of you," she said. "I have to tell you my tale."

"Tail?" said Boris, but Gentleman Jim said, "Quiet, everyone. Let Jenny speak."

And Jenny looked at him gratefully, for she had such a lot to tell them that she hardly knew where to begin.

"First of all," she said, as they all looked at her expectantly, "my name is not Jenny."

CHAPTER 11

Jenny's Tale

I come from a different world," Jenny said, gazing into the far distance. "And there my name is Leysa, meaning 'to set free.'"

All the dogs followed the direction of Jenny's gaze, as if they expected to see a different world appearing suddenly on the croft. Then they looked at one another in bewilderment. However, dogs very rarely tell lies, and in general, they are trusting animals who believe, implicitly, everything they are told. They looked back at Jenny, waiting for her to go on, and Jenny sighed.

"A long time ago, when my world was young," she said, "Odin the All-Father and his beloved wife, Frigg, gave birth to a baby son, named Baldur. He was not like their other children, who were harsh and violent. He was known as the wisest of the Aesir, the fairest and most merciful. He was gentle and kind and everyone loved him. He was my master, my Golden Boy, who saved me from the jaws of a wolf when I was out hunting. We went everywhere together."

Jenny looked at the others with an indescribably sad expression on her face, so that they all too felt very sad. "I owed him my life, you see," she said, and the dogs bowed their heads. Loyalty was a concept they all understood. Jenny went on.

"When he was born, his mother, Frigg the Gentle, Lady of Flowers, extracted a promise from all the plants in the world that they would not harm him. But she overlooked one plant, the mistletoe," and Jenny nudged the mistletoe dart at her feet. "One day, all the gods, in sport, decided to put this to the test. They shot arrows at him and threw spears, but everything missed or bounced off him harmlessly. Then Loki, the most evil of the gods, found this sprig of mistletoe and shaped it into a dart."

All the dogs looked at the mistletoe. It was chewed and misshapen, but they could see that it might once have been a dart.

"He put it into the hands of Baldur's brother, Hod, who was hanging back because of his blindness, and said to him, 'Do as the others, enjoy yourself, and I will guide your hand.' So the mistletoe dart flew through the air. But I was watching, and I knew Loki could be up to no good. Before it could strike Baldur, I leapt into the air and caught it."

"WOOF!" said Pico, and Checkers leapt into the air too, exactly as if he was catching the dart. They all understood. Every single one of them would have done the same, for a dog's first loyalty is always to his master.

"And then what?" asked Gentleman Jim.

"Then I ran," said Jenny. "With Loki howling behind me, for if a dog disturbs the games of the gods, the penalty is death."

"That . . . seems a little . . . harsh," said Flo.

"No," said Jenny, "for the gods do not play their games for amusement only. The outcome decides the fate of men, and the world, and even the gods themselves."

Now the dogs looked baffled, and Boris started to say, "I don't understand," but Jenny went on.

"Baldur was supposed to die that day, and his death was the first in a long chain of events that would bring about Ragnarok."

Jenny lowered her voice as she said this, yet still the earth around them rumbled and shook.

"Ragnarok?" said Gentleman Jim, and it rumbled and shook again.

"Do not speak that name unless you have to," said Jenny earnestly. "It is the last battle at the end of the world."

"Battle?" said Checkers.

"The end of the world?" said Flo nervously, and Boris, who was catching up, said, "Mistletoe dart?"

"I'm sorry," said Gentleman Jim. "Could you run that by me again?"

"Ragnarok," said Jenny patiently, and the dogs all huddled together as earthquake-like tremors reverberated through the ground. "It's the last battle, between the gods and the forces of destruction. When the evil of the world will burst its bonds and Hel and her minions will rise from the abyss. The seas will boil, engulfing the land, the heavens will be rent asunder and the stars shall fall into endless night."

"Oh, dear," said Flo, feeling faint, and Checkers said, "Battle!" and ran around everyone again.

Gentleman Jim said, "But luckily you've stopped all that."

"No," said Jenny. "You don't understand," and Boris was glad she'd noticed. Jenny sighed. It was hard for her to put everything she had to say into words.

"The gods are angry," she said finally. "I was not supposed to alter the course of destiny. Baldur was supposed to be slain. I don't know why. But if Ragnarok comes and Baldur is not slain—then—something terrible will happen."

She looked at them all earnestly.

"Something terrible—*apart* from Ragnarok?" said Gentleman Jim, and Flo said, "Can you *please* stop saying that?"

But Jenny just said, "Baldur—has to die. That's the way it's supposed to be. It is written."

"Where?" asked Gentleman Jim.

"I don't know where," said Jenny, a little peevishly. "It just is."

There was a short silence, then Gentleman Jim said, "If you came from another world, then how did you end up here?"

"I fell into the Void," said Jenny.

"Okay," said Gentleman Jim cautiously, "and what void would that be?"

"The great Void that is Ginnungagap," Jenny said.

"Ah," said Gentleman Jim, and Jenny could see that he didn't fully believe her. She gave him a hard stare.

"I set off running, without knowing where, knowing only that the gods were giving chase," she said. "I ran over a field and through a river, and suddenly I was on a vast, deserted plain. And around the edges of this plain a mist was swirling, and I could see nothing beyond this mist. The war cries of the gods grew faint behind me and still I ran, until the mist closed around me and I could see and hear no more. And then suddenly—whoosh!"

Flo jumped in nervous alarm. "Wh-what?" she said.

"The earth itself disappeared beneath my feet," Jenny said solemnly, shaking her ears as she remembered the horror of that moment. "I was falling, falling," she said. "I do not know how long I fell. Time itself disappeared. I remember nothing until my paws struck something hard, gravel, and I was climbing out of the Void onto the ring road. There I was struck by one of the iron chariots you call cars, and Aunty Dot picked me up and took me to Sam's house. The rest you know."

Gentleman Jim looked at Boris, Boris looked at Checkers and Checkers looked at Flo. Flo looked down at the ground. Gentleman Jim cleared his throat. "So—this Void," he began.

"Ginnungagap."

"Ginnun—"

"Ginnungagap. It is all around us now, lapping at the edges of your world."

"I can't see anything," said Boris.

"Yes, that's it."

"No, I mean I can't see anything," said Boris, while Checkers ran off to find it.

"Yes," said Jenny. "That is Ginnungagap. It surrounds the known world and leads into other worlds unknown. It is always with us, though it cannot be seen."

"Well," said Gentleman Jim, after he too had looked around. "It's an amazing story. Quite the best I've heard."

Jenny almost stamped her paw in impatience. "It's not a story," she said. "It's the truth. I have to return."

"What?" said Flo in alarm. "To certain death?"

Jenny bowed her head. "The great wolf Fenrir appeared in my kitchen," she said. "He couldn't do anything because he was bound to his world by the cord Gleipnir, which is the strongest cord in the world. It was made by the Dark Dwarves from the footfall of a cat, the roots of a mountain, the spittle of a bird, the breath of a fish, the sinews of a bear and a woman's beard."

"Oh, *that* cord," said Gentleman Jim, and Jenny couldn't be sure, but she thought he was smiling. She ignored him and carried on.

"He said that if I did not return, then—" She whispered, so that only the trees shook. "Ragnarok would come to this world as well."

All the dogs, even Checkers, looked shocked.

"I see," said Gentleman Jim after a short pause. "So you have to return."

"Yes."

"And take the mistletoe back to—what was his name again?"

"Baldur."

"How?" asked Flo.

Jenny looked away for a moment, then said, "I think I must jump once again into the Void."

"And then what?" asked Gentleman Jim, after a short pause.

"I don't know," said Jenny. She tried to speak for a moment but failed, then tried again. "Baldur must die." She looked so sad as she said this that Pico nuzzled her in sympathy.

"And Ragnarok—"

"Stop *saying* that," said Flo as the earth lurched.

Gentleman Jim shook his head and gave a great snort, like a

horse. "How do we know any of this is coming? It might not happen at all."

"We do know," said Jenny. "Because the Fimbulwinter is already here."

The dogs all looked blank. Boris opened his mouth, then shut it again, convinced he would only say something stupid, but Checkers said, "Fimbulwinter?"

"The snow and ice are the first signs," said Jenny. "Then three cocks will sound the alarm, from Valhalla, Midgard and Niflheim, and two wolves, Skoll and Hati, shall devour the sun and moon. Then the great Giallarhorn will sound to summon the forces of the universe to do battle on the plain of Vigrid."

"Sounds like quite a party," said Gentleman Jim, and when Jenny just looked at him, he said, "I suppose there's no chance at all that someone's pulling your leg?"

Jenny stared at him. "It's not a *joke!*" she said. "It's happening now, all around you! Look—the Fimbulwinter has begun!"

And indeed the snow was falling more thickly now, and the light in the sky had disappeared.

All this time Pico had stood beside Jenny without saying anything. He wasn't sure he understood fully what was going on, but he understood that he was being buried slowly in snow and that his bones were rattling with cold. He shook the snow off him and stamped his paws. "Now, look," he said. "I'm not sure what's going on here, but I know that Jenny is our friend, and if she says she's come from another world, then I for one believe her. We all knew she was special."

Jenny touched her nose to his in gratitude.

"And if she's in trouble, then I for one will stand by her. She's not jumping into this Void thingy alone. I think I'm not alone in saying that. We will all go with you, Jenny," he said, shaking the snow off his pelt again.

"Er, well—" said Flo.

"We cannot all plunge into the Void," said Jenny, and Flo said, "No, indeed!" and when they all looked at her, she added feebly, "It's getting late."

"We will *all* go with you," Pico said fiercely. "Even to certain death."

"Hurrah!" said Checkers, for no obvious reason, but Flo said, "Excuse me," and Gentleman Jim said, "Now just wait a minute, all of you. It's all very well, all this talk of wolves and battles and Voids, whatever they are, but we don't live in a world of Gods and demons—we live in the real world. Look around you. There's the croft, and there are all the houses. It sounds to me," he said kindly, "as if you've had a very bad dream."

"That's what I thought!" said Boris, amazed and delighted that someone else had had the same idea. "I used to have terrible dreams when Mrs. Finnegan started that course on experimental cookery!"

"That's what I mean," said Gentleman Jim. "It's probably something you ate."

Jenny trembled all over in protest. She opened her mouth to give Gentleman Jim a piece of her mind, but before she could say anything, there was the unmistakable sound of a cock crowing. Checkers charged off barking while the others looked all around, but there was no sign of a cock or any other domestic bird. Jenny shivered.

"The first cockerel has crowed," she said, and just as she said this, the sky started flickering. "Look!" cried Flo.

Everyone looked upward. As if in appreciation of this, the sky flickered some more. Black clouds broiled, then rolled apart like theatrical curtains to reveal a bloodred sun. In the eastern corner, where the sky was clear, there was a pale, full moon. But what attracted the dogs' attention was the shape of the surrounding clouds. They looked, unmistakably, like wolves, two great wolves in fact, one galloping toward the sun with open jaws and the other toward the moon.

"Good grief," murmured Gentleman Jim, and his great ears flopped forward over his eyes while Flo stared in horror and Checkers ran backward and forward, barking madly at the sun and moon as though to warn them.

"Skoll and Hati," murmured Jenny, her heart sinking in dread.

"Oh, dear, oh, my word!" gasped Flo. "Oh, I think one of my funny turns is coming on. OW!" she said, because Jenny had nipped her slightly.

"Come on, all of you!" Jenny said. "We need to find shelter!" and she trotted toward a cluster of low-lying bushes.

"What's happening?" said Boris desperately, following Checkers, and Flo shrieked, "We're all going to die!"

"No," said Jenny firmly. "None of you is going to die. I can prevent Ragnarok from coming here. I will return."

Then Pico stood in the middle of the circle of dogs and raised himself to his full, unimpressive height. "I have already said that you will not go alone," he said. "But what I want to know is, if you have changed the course of destiny once, can it not be done again? Is there no other way?"

Jenny closed her eyes for such a long time that Boris thought she might have fallen asleep. "Yes," she said eventually. "There might be another way."

Then she lowered the mistletoe dart toward Pico. "You must prick me with this," she said, "until the blood flows."

"Ooh, er," said Flo, and Pico said, "I can't do that," looking very shocked.

"You must!" said Jenny impatiently. "For there will be a message in the blood that falls."

Pico could hardly bear to watch as he held out the mistletoe dart and Jenny drove her paw down onto it and held it there until nine drops of blood fell onto the snow. Then shakily she held the wounded paw up and sniffed at the blood on the ground.

"Yes," she said finally. "There is a message."

CHAPTER 12

Sam

By the time Sam got home from school, the snow was falling fast. He couldn't wait to take Jenny out into it. He let himself in at the back door and shouted, "Jenny!" then stopped. Jenny was always there, waiting for him. Sometimes she started barking before he had even reached the backyard gate, and when he got to the door, she would jump up and down, wagging her tail so hard that it looked as if she was doing a funny kind of dance. When he let himself in, they would both leap around the kitchen in excitement, and then Sam would take her for a walk. But the kitchen was empty. She wasn't there.

Mystified, Sam dropped his school bag onto the floor and ran into the living room. "Jenny!" he called. "Jenny?"

He ran into each room of his house, but there was no sign of her. Panic rising, he hurried back into the kitchen. There he noticed for the first time that the dog flap fitted by their neighbor looked as though it had been disturbed, and he remembered that the backyard gate had been open when he had run through it. His heart gave a hollow thump. Surely she couldn't—she wouldn't—have run away? Why would she?

Sam stared at the back door without seeing it. He was so distracted, he didn't even notice the scorch marks on the cupboards and floor. His mind was filled with a single, awful thought. Suppose Jenny had run back to where she had come from?

No, she wouldn't do that, Sam thought fiercely, brushing a

tear from his eye. She would never leave without saying good-bye.

Suddenly he knew he had to do something. He lifted Jenny's lead from the hook by the door, and though his mother had told him to wait inside after school until she got home and do his homework, he opened the door and ran out into the whirling storm.

CHAPTER 13

The Task Revealed

Jenny lowered her nose to the first drop of blood.

"The great hound seeks the mistletoe twig," she said, and the other dogs looked at one another, mystified. "He must on no account be allowed to have it, for with it, he can unleash Ragnarok on the nine worlds and reign supreme."

She paused, and the other dogs looked at her dumbly as this sank in.

"Only one other hound can defeat Fenrir," she said, sniffing the second drop. "The greatest of all hounds. The Guardian of the Darkest Way."

"Er, who?" asked Boris, but Jenny ignored him as she moved on to the third drop of blood.

"The greatest hunter must sound his horn," she said, "to end the final battle."

"And who might that be?" asked Gentleman Jim, but Jenny only moved on to the next drop.

"He shines above three worlds, but his soul is in a place far below," she said, and paused for a moment, perplexed.

"What's she talking about?" Boris wanted to know, but Checkers hushed him.

"His soul must be released," said Jenny, sniffing the next drop.

"Er—how?" whispered Flo, but Gentleman Jim nudged her warningly.

"The Guardian of the Darkest Way will not come willingly," she added after examining the sixth drop of blood. "He must be fought, if necessary, and brought from his lair. So that the soul of the hunter can be released."

"A fight—hooray!" said Checkers, but no one else spoke.

"The great wolves must be kept at bay until the hunter returns," Jenny said, after sniffing the seventh drop. "So that they do not swallow the sun and moon.

"Only the thread of destiny can restrain the great wolves," she said, touching the next drop with her nose, then she paused for a moment, deep in thought.

"Well, go on then," said Checkers, bounding around them all. "What's next?"

"The mistletoe dart must be returned," said Jenny, and she looked up. There was a short silence.

"Er, it doesn't say *how* we're supposed to do all this, does it?" asked Gentleman Jim. Jenny sniffed back along the nine drops of blood.

She sniffed for a long time, so that Checkers nearly burst with impatience.

"Each of you will have to enter the Void," she said finally. "Follow the Dog Star. It will take you on your separate journeys."

And she looked up at the blank expressions of her five friends. "That's all," she said.

"Oh, right," said Gentleman Jim. "Er—you do know that none of that made sense, don't you?"

Checkers looked ready to bound off straightaway, then he paused and said, "Void?"

"Fimbulwinter?" said Boris, who was still trying hard to keep up.

And Gentleman Jim said, "It doesn't make sense. What does it all mean? What are the nine worlds?"

But Jenny shook her head. "I do not know them," she said. "I only know my world and yours. Each of the worlds has its own gods. Mine has the ancient gods of the Norse world—Odin and Freya and Thor. This hunter, whoever he is, must belong to a different world, with different gods, but I do not know which one."

"Oh, well, then," said Flo, who was suffering from the cold now and anxious to get back home. "We can't go there unless we know where it is, can we? And we don't because, as Gentleman Jim says, the message doesn't make sense—"

"It does make sense," said Jenny. "I have to return the mistletoe dart."

"Yes, but how?" said Flo. "I vote we all go home and think about it after tea."

"Some of us don't have homes to go to," said Gentleman Jim, looking very sad, and briefly he told them about monstrous Maureen. Then Checkers said he wouldn't be in a hurry to get back either and told them about John, who had turned into a raving lunatic just because Checkers had eaten a bit of paper. And Boris said he didn't care where he went, so long as it wasn't back to the pound.

"Well, but some of us *do* have homes to go to," Flo said, a little desperately. "Pico? Your mum must be missing you by now."

Pico seemed sunk in a reverie. "I don't know," he said in a distant tone. "I always wondered when my time would come to travel to far horizons. And I think this may be it."

Flo shook herself to get rid of the snow. "You're mad, all of you," she said. "All this talk about wolves and gods and strange messages in the snow. I know what that message means. It means we should all go home and have a good night's sleep."

Just then, a terrible howling filled the air, above the howling of the storm. It was a howl of desolation, destruction and ravening hunger. If the end of the world could be put into a howl, it would sound like this one. All who heard it felt that they had gone temporarily insane. Flo shrieked and tried to hide, rather unsuccessfully, behind Pico, and all Checkers's hair stood on end, so that he looked like an enormous toilet brush.

"*What—was—that?*" gasped Gentleman Jim.

Jenny stood her ground, though her bones were rattling with fear. "Fenrir," she said. Fearfully, the dogs followed the direction of her gaze. They could all see that the great wolf clouds were nearer to the sun and moon now. They seemed to be traveling slowly, which was a good thing, but not if you considered that they were actually covering immeasurable distances of time and space. Exactly between them, on the far horizon, they could see a dark speck, growing bigger.

"He has burst his bonds," Jenny said in despair. "Nothing can stop him now. He is coming here."

Checkers ran forward immediately, barking for all he was worth.

"Here?" squeaked Flo. "Whatever for?"

"For the mistletoe dart," Jenny said. "Were you not listening?"

"Oh," said Flo. "Oh. Well. That's all right, then—you could just give it to him, you know, it's got to be returned anyway. Hasn't it?"

Her voice rose in panic, but Jenny shook her head impatiently. "I cannot return it to Fenrir," she said, "for with it he will bring chaos and destruction to all the nine worlds and reign supreme."

"Oh, well, now you're being picky," Flo said, gabbling a little. "Just get *rid* of the thing and we can all go home."

"No," said Gentleman Jim, looking considerably shaken. "No, I don't think that's how it works, is it?"

Jenny's eyes were dark with despair. "Ragnarok is already coming to this world," she said. "Unless we do as the mistletoe tells us, all the worlds will be destroyed. We have to find the greatest hunter of all and release his soul so that he can blow his horn and prevent it."

"Because unless we do—the hound that just made that terrible noise—" said Gentleman Jim.

"Will reign supreme, yes," said Jenny, and all the dogs fell into an appalled silence as they began to realize what this might mean.

"Well, I for one will not stand for it," said Pico. "I shall keep the great wolves at bay until the hunter returns."

"Pico," said Gentleman Jim, "you are a two-pound Chihuahua."

Pico bristled all over until he looked at least half a pound bigger. "You heard the prophecy," he said earnestly to Gentleman Jim. "We cannot just stand by and let some demented canine unleash the forces of destruction on the earth!"

"But how are we going to stop him?" said Gentleman Jim.

"Discretion is the better part of valor," said Flo.

"I'm with Pico," said Checkers unexpectedly. "This is our earth, and we love it. Who has not smelled the scent of rabbits at dawn or followed the trail of a hare? Who has not experienced all the rich tangled scents of a wood in rain? We're not just going to let some howling beast come along and take all that from us! What are we—dogs or cats? If there's a battle to be fought—I'm your dog! I'm with Pico—and Boris is with me—aren't you, Boris?"

"I . . . expect so," said Boris dubiously. "But I still don't understand what we have to do."

Jenny looked upward, but could only see the frightful sight of the wolf clouds and the black speck that was Fenrir growing steadily larger. She closed her eyes briefly.

"We must each claim the quest that is our own," she said, opening them again, "and follow the Dog Star in our hearts, and it will take us where we need to go."

"Will do," said Checkers, bounding off. Then he bounded back again. "Er—what *is* the Dog Star exactly?"

"The Dog Star is Sirius," said Jenny. "But I do not think it can be seen in this storm."

"No," said Flo, more cheerfully. "And we can't do anything without that, can we? So I vote we all go home and—"

"YEEEEAAAAAWWWOOOOOHHH!" howled Fenrir again, and Flo fell to the ground, gibbering in fear. Checkers bolted backward into a thornbush, then barked like a lunatic at all the prickles. Gentleman Jim's knees gave way and he crashed heavily into Boris, who simply stood, stunned. Only Pico barked back at the great wolf.

"WOOF!" he said.

"My dear girl," said Gentleman Jim, when he could finally speak. "I am so sorry for doubting you."

Jenny trembled and shook until the blast of the howl subsided. Already the black speck in the distance seemed wolflike in shape.

When she could trust herself to speak, she said, "This task may be too great for us. It is too dangerous."

"Nonsense," said Checkers, whose blood was up. "There's six of us and only one of him!"

"What about those other wolves?" said Flo, and they all glanced upward toward the galloping wolf clouds.

"Look," said Gentleman Jim. "Let's just go through it again. What is it exactly that we're meant to do?"

Jenny sighed. "We all carry our paths within us," she said. "I saw them in you the first moment that we met. Gentleman Jim, you are a hunting dog. I imagine that it is your destiny to find the great hunter. And Pico must travel with you to fulfill his own destiny."

"WOOF!" said Pico, happy to be given something to do.

"Checkers, you are a natural warrior. Only you can fight the Guardian of the Darkest Way. The path is full of dangers. Will you try?"

"Just watch me!" said Checkers, emerging finally from the thorn-bush with at least half of it still in his pelt. "Let me get at him!"

"Boris shall go with you, for it is too dangerous to travel alone, and he will be your guardian. Boris, do you accept this task?"

"Er . . . " said Boris, but Checkers said, "Of course he will!"

"It is very important that you all accept your tasks," said Jenny, and everyone looked at Flo.

"That leaves someone to hold off the great wolves, Skoll and Hati," Gentleman Jim observed, while Flo wondered frantically what excuse she could possibly make.

"Does it?" she said, since he seemed to expect her to say something.

"And restrain them with the threads of destiny."

"Whatever they are," said Flo.

"Flo," said Jenny. "Do you accept this task?"

"Me?" said Flo, stepping backward. "Good heavens, no. You said I was wise, not brave," she added accusingly.

"It is your wisdom you will need. There is no point trying to fight the great wolves—"

"Good," said Flo. "Because I wasn't planning to."

"You must outwit them."

"I don't want to outwit them," said Flo. "I don't want to do anything with them. I just want to go home!"

The last bit came out in a kind of yelp. Jenny just looked at her, her head on one side.

"Definitely not," said Flo. "I don't even know what the threads of destiny *are*!"

"Flo," said Jenny, "only you can do this."

All the dogs looked at Flo. Flo stared back at them. It was a solemn moment—the kind of moment in which Flo should have said, "Very well, then, I will," in an impressive kind of way. Flo could feel that it was that kind of moment. She licked her lips.

"I can't," she said. She could see the disappointment in their eyes and began to babble. "I'll have to get back," she said. "My owner will be wondering where I've got to. Or else she'll forget and lock the door. And I can't be locked out—not in this weather. Really, you should all get back too."

"I can't do it," she went on as they all continued to look at her. "It's not fair. It's really not my kind of thing at all. I never said I was brave," she finished lamely.

All the time she was talking, she was backing away, and the others watched her solemnly. Then Gentleman Jim turned to Jenny.

"What happens if one of us does not accept the task?" he asked.

"Then the quest will surely fail," said Jenny. "We will go to certain death. And the world will end."

"I thought so," said Gentleman Jim. There was a short, depressed silence, then Pico raised his head.

"But we have to try," he said to Jenny. "Don't we?"

And Jenny smiled, looking down at him.

"Yes, Pico," she said. "We have to try."

"There are still five of us," Pico said. "Together we will fight the Hound of Destruction and save the world!"

Flo felt horrible. She turned her back on them all and slunk away, gradually gaining speed.

"I didn't ask to be given a quest," she muttered to herself. "It's all right for them—they've not got homes to go to anymore. Except for Pico, and he's always wanted to travel. I don't want to travel, and I've got a perfectly good home, with a nice fire and food and a good bed."

She had forgotten for the moment about Henry, but even if she had remembered, he would have faded into insignificance in her mind compared to the appalling task Jenny had tried to give her.

"Wolves devouring the sun and moon indeed," she muttered to herself, gaining more speed. "Why would anyone in their right minds take on a dangerous quest? At this time of night? And in this weather?"

For now indeed the storm was building up.

CHAPTER 14

The Chapter of
Being Lost in a Storm

What's a Fimbulwinter again?" said Boris, who was still trying to understand.

Checkers pelted back toward him through the swirling snow. "I think you'll find this is it, boss!" he said.

"There is not much time," said Jenny, raising her voice above the storm. "Dear friends, we must separate. I must go north. I do not know where you must go . . ." She looked at them anxiously for a moment. Checkers looked alert and ready for anything, Pico determined, and Gentleman Jim very serious. Boris wagged his tail hopefully. Any minute now, he thought, he would start to understand. Jenny sighed. She did not know what dangers lay ahead for them; she could only hope that they would all make it back.

"Hold the image of the Dog Star in your hearts," she said. "It will take you where you need to go. When you come to the end of the storm, the Void will be there." She paused again. Already the snow was so thick that she could hardly see them. "I must go," she said. "I will keep you all in my heart. I hope and trust that we will meet again. Farewell," and without another word, she turned and walked into the storm.

The others watched her go, a small white dog in the swirling whiteness of snow, then a dark shadow, then nothing.

"Good luck," called Checkers.

"Take care," said Gentleman Jim.

"Where's she going?" asked Boris.

Only Pico trotted after Jenny for a few paces, sniffing anxiously, then he turned. "She should not go alone," he said.

"She must," said Gentleman Jim. "And we must go too."

"Off we go!" cried Checkers, then pelted back. "Come on, Boris!"

"I don't think—" said Boris.

"No, don't think," said Checkers. "Whatever you do, don't think. Follow me!"

Boris looked around, baffled, for a moment at Gentleman Jim and Pico, then gave up and trotted after Checkers.

Gentleman Jim looked down at Pico, who was once again practically covered in snow. They were the only two left on the croft. "Well, little fellow," he said. "It looks as though it's just you and me."

Pico shook the snow off. He had no idea where they were going or what they were about to do, but this was his first taste of freedom, and he was in no hurry to give it up, despite the bitter cold that was rattling his bones.

"Why don't you climb up on my shoulders?" said Gentleman Jim.

Pico was about to protest when the wind blew a flurry of snow right over him. He was completely submerged, and Gentleman Jim had to nudge him out.

"Come on, climb up," the great hound said.

Pico was so cold he could hardly speak. His teeth were chattering. He clambered onto Gentleman Jim's back and clutched his collar, trying unsuccessfully to see between the big dog's ears. Soon he was raised rather unsteadily to a dizzying height as Gentleman Jim began to plod through the storm.

"I—I don't know where we're going, do you?" he managed to say.

"Nope," said Gentleman Jim.

It wasn't the most encouraging reply, but Pico kept his mouth shut because every time he opened it, snow whirled inside. And some of the snow was hard, like little pellets of ice. It whipped about his ears and into his eyes, so he shut them as well. Instantly he could see the glimmering of a star. It winked and disappeared, then reappeared again. Pico opened his eyes, and all he could see was the swirling snow, then he shut them again. There the star was, clearer and brighter this time, over to the east. He clutched at the folds of Gentleman Jim's neck in excitement.

"There—over there," he said. He had to repeat this two or three times before Gentleman Jim heard.

"What's that?" he asked.

"Close your eyes," said Pico. Obediently Gentleman Jim closed them.

"Can you see it?" asked Pico.

"My eyes are closed," said Gentleman Jim, opening them again. "So, no."

"Keep your eyes closed," said Pico, hopping a little in excitement. "What can you see?"

"Well, nothing," said Gentleman Jim, a little confused by this instruction. In fact, even with his eyes closed, he could still see the swirling storm.

"Can't you see the star?"

"Er, no," said Gentleman Jim.

"I can see it!" said Pico, hardly able to contain himself. "When my eyes are closed, I can see the star!"

"Really?" said Gentleman Jim. "Where is it then?"

"Over to the left," said Pico. "I can see it clearly now."

Slowly Gentleman Jim turned himself around. It was easier to walk in this other direction since the wind seemed now to be behind them.

"Are you sure?" he asked.

"Yes, yes," said Pico, scrambling up his neck, then falling down again. "It's there—behind that tree!"

"Little friend," said Gentleman Jim. "It looks as though there was a good reason for you and I to travel together."

And so they set off, Pico's hind legs braced against Gentleman

Jim's collar so that he could tug at first one ear, then the other in order to steer his enormous friend.

Checkers had bounded into the swirling storm at his usual speed, and Boris was finding it hard to keep up.

"Wait for me!" he called plaintively, and was rewarded by being suddenly bumped to the ground.

"I've never seen so much snow!" Checkers said, shaking himself vigorously so that it fell all over Boris, then he ran off again.

"Where've you gone *now*?" said Boris, but Checkers couldn't hear him. He was too busy barking at each of the thousands of snowflakes whirling around him. He was being pelted hard by little grains of ice, so that it felt as though he was under attack, and he responded accordingly by snapping furiously at every grain and flake, barking and running around in circles.

Boris felt tired. He often felt tired when he was with Checkers, but now the cold and the storm were getting to him as well. When Checkers bounded past him for the fifth time, he simply sat down.

"I don't know where I'm going," he said to himself, "so I might as well not move," and he sat back on his haunches and waited.

"Come on, Boris!" yelled Checkers, flying past. "We're nearly there!"

"Nearly where?" asked Boris, but Checkers had disappeared again.

"Forward and onward!" he cried, reappearing, then disappearing again.

"Forward and onward where?" asked Boris, but Checkers didn't answer. Boris was hardly surprised. No one ever answered his questions.

"We've got to follow it—" called Checkers, rushing past, but Boris didn't hear the rest of what he was saying because he had already gone again.

"Because—" explained Checkers, dashing past again.

"Oh, well," thought Boris, settling down. Experience had told

him that sooner or later he would either understand what was happening or it would stop happening and then there was no need
to bother.

"—save the world!" concluded Checkers, skidding to a halt in
front of Boris.

Boris looked at Checkers, and Checkers looked at Boris.

"You don't know where we're going, do you?" said Boris.

"Er, no," said Checkers. "But I do know," he added, bounding
around Boris in a circle, "that we've got to find it. And when we've
found it, we've got to fight it, and then . . . and then . . . well . . ."

"What?" asked Boris.

"Then we can go home," said Checkers firmly. "But not before
we've found it, or we'll never find the way. That's the problem, Boris,
old chum," he said, finally standing still. "Finding it in the first
place. She never said how we could do that," and he chewed Boris's
ear in a distracted way.

"Do you mean that star?" said Boris.

"What star?" said Checkers, leaping up again.

"That star—there," said Boris. Checkers ran around and around
barking, but all he could see was the storm.

"I can't see any star," he said, returning.

"Well, I can," said Boris.

Checkers ran off again, determined to find it. If Boris could see it,
then Checkers must be able to. It was unheard of for Boris to have
spotted anything before Checkers. But the snow was falling thicker
and faster than ever, swirling into his eyes and blinding him.

"What star? Where?" he said eventually, frustrated.

"Just there," said Boris, lifting his nose, and Checkers looked and
looked, but he couldn't see anything other than the swirling whiteness of snow.

"It is a star we're supposed to be following, isn't it?" said Boris.

"Well, yes," said Checkers, completely stumped.

"Then you'd better follow me," said Boris, getting up.

He tried not to, but he couldn't help looking just a little bit smug. This was the first time ever in their long friendship that he had led the way and Checkers followed, and he could tell that his friend wasn't happy from the way he was snapping at Boris's tail.

"Get a move on," he said. "We haven't got all day," and, "You're sure it's a star you can see, Boris, and not more of your mum's food playing tricks on you again?"

But Boris wouldn't be goaded. He kept on trotting to the right, keeping the star clear and luminous and steady in his mind, and Checkers, vastly disgruntled, was forced to follow slowly behind.

CHAPTER 15

In Which Flo Looks
Before She Leaps

As soon as Flo could see her own house again, she felt better. Her guilt faded rapidly in her relief at being home. She was so unnerved by what had happened to her that she didn't even notice that all the doors and windows were still open.

Thank goodness for that, she thought, stepping over the threshold. All that nasty "quest" business has given me a headache!

All Flo wanted was her nice warm bed. She hurried toward the front room, not even bothering to glance over her shoulder in case Henry was there. Henry, she had decided, was the least of her problems.

She pushed the door open and was surprised to find that it led to another corridor.

That's funny, she thought. I'm sure the living room was there when I left it.

However, there was another door at the end of this corridor, and Flo, still dazed and freezing from the storm, trotted toward it.

This time, as she pushed the door open, she could have sworn that the house gave itself a little shake and *rejigged* itself somehow. There, in front of her, was another passageway, bending around to the left.

Definitely perplexed (had she come to the wrong house? Had she come into the right house by the wrong door?), Flo stepped warily into the passageway. She felt weary, almost too tired to be nervous. All she wanted was to lie down. And there ahead of her was the door to the living room. She was sure she'd got it right this time—she recognized the peculiar handle, which was shaped like a snake.

Thankfully she pushed it open, and indeed this time there was the living room, looking much as she remembered it, with the fire flickering brightly in the hearth.

At last, thought Flo, crossing the room gratefully. There was her bed, there was the coffee table and the chintz covers on the little settee, and there was the mirror, in its usual place. Henry was nowhere to be seen, and for this Flo was profoundly grateful. She didn't know where Myrtle was, and she was almost too tired to care. She flopped exhausted onto her bed, where, despite the rattling of windows and the creaking of doors, she began, very slowly, to relax. After all, she was safe and warm now, not lost in a horrid cold storm. She didn't know where her friends were, but she hoped they were safe and had been sensible enough to make their own way home. She told herself that she could hardly be responsible if they hadn't and were foolish enough to go risking their lives on some terrible quest that involved leaping into Voids and battling wolves. Whatever happened now, there was nothing that Flo could do about it except try to get some sleep and wait for the storm to be over. And thank her lucky stars that nothing dangerous could happen to her here.

Unfortunately for Flo, she hadn't quite closed her eyes when the mirror started to lean toward her.

A cold shudder ran along her spine. A bark rose to her throat and stuck there. She couldn't remember her dream, but she knew with absolute certainty that this had happened before. She wanted very badly to close her eyes but couldn't. There, in the mirror, were the three ancient hags. One was knitting, one holding a ball of wool and one held an enormous pair of scissors.

Run, Flo told herself, but she couldn't move. She remembered suddenly what Jenny had said. Was this the thread of destiny? And if so, was she supposed to take it and use it to restrain the great wolves, who were even now galloping toward the sun and moon?

No way, she thought. Then one of the hags spoke, in an ancient, creaking voice.

"Sisters," she said, "is it time?"

"It is time," the other two said, like a chorus.

"Then why doesn't she get on with it?"

"Don't worry," said the second sister, in the same creaking, rusty voice that sounded oddly familiar. "She knows what she has to do," and she held the ball of wool out toward Flo.

At the same time, the surface of the mirror changed. It rippled, then wreathed like smoke. Flo stared at it in anguish. They were talking about her. Could they see her?

As if in answer, the one holding the ball of wool raised milky, sightless eyes in her direction.

"What are you waiting for?" she asked.

Flo gave a yelp that turned into a strangled whine. Trembling all over, she rose to her feet. The mirror wreathed before her. She could run, but there was nowhere to hide. She glanced all the way around the room, but the door seemed to have disappeared. There was no way out. So, in fact, she couldn't even run.

Trapped, she thought. I'm trapped. Through the cloudy surface of the mirror she could still see the clawlike hand holding out the ball of thread. There was nothing else to do. Summoning whatever she had instead of courage, Flo leapt at the surface of the mirror.

CHAPTER 16

Beyond the Void

Jenny plowed on, walking northward into the swirling whiteness of a storm that would take her directly to Ginnungagap, the Void.

The cold got colder. The whiteness got whiter and swirled even more. It was hard to see or even think. Jenny's ears were blasted backward by the wind. She felt as though the tips of them were freezing off, then soon, she couldn't feel them at all. She didn't even miss them because it was as though the storm had got inside her somehow and was howling and raging inside her skull. When the ground ended beneath her feet, she didn't stop to think but plunged headlong into the Void.

Silence.

It was a silence so dense she could almost feel it. It wrapped itself around her like a thick blanket that was, strangely, neither reassuring nor warm. If anything, it was even colder than before, and as the sounds of the storm died away inside her, Jenny began to wonder if she had, in fact, left her ears behind. She couldn't see or feel anything either, not even the sensation of falling, and the silence itself was so complete it was as though sound itself had never existed.

After a while of seeing, hearing and feeling nothing, it was hard to believe in her own existence. Perhaps she had died and this was death, she thought, and then reminded herself that she was at least still thinking.

Then, all around her, the nothingness began to swirl. It swirled around her like a freezing fog. In fact, it was a freezing fog, and Jenny was traveling into the heart of it. With a pang of fear, she realized where she was.

Niflheim.

The far northern region of darkness and cold, where the bitter winter of despair breathed icy fogs of desolation. Niflheim, containing Helheim, realm of death, and Nastrond, the shore of corpses.

And even as she realized this, the stony ground rushed up to meet her. Her paws struck frozen rock, and she fell along it somehow, bumping and scraping herself, until the angle of it corrected itself with a lurch, and she realized that she was standing up. A little way ahead of her, through the mist, was a single root of an enormous tree.

And propped up against the root of the tree was her master, Baldur.

Despite her frozen paws, Jenny broke into a stumbling run. She tried to bark, but it came out as a strangled yelp that was quickly muffled by the fog. And as she ran, she had the nightmarish feeling that she wasn't, in fact, getting anywhere. And that something was wrong, terribly wrong, with Baldur.

He seemed to be entwined in the root itself. His limbs were twisted into positions that should have been agonizing; his hair, frost-stiffened, seemed part of the twisted pattern of the bark. Jenny ran with all her might, straining every muscle and nerve, but either Baldur was much farther away than she had thought or the tree itself was moving because the distance between them did not close. And at last she stopped, in terrible despair, and lifted her voice and cried, *"Master!"*

And the next moment she was stumbling over his frozen, lichen-encrusted feet.

CHAPTER 17

Black Shuck

Where are we now, then?" asked Checkers. This was at least the fifth time he had asked this question, along with, "Are we nearly there yet?" (seven times) and, "Can you still see that star?" (four). Boris had given up answering. He could still see the star, but he had no idea about the other two questions. He rather suspected that Checkers was trying to annoy him because he wasn't the leader and was forced to go along at Boris's slow pace.

As far as the first question was concerned, they seemed to be in a wood. Boris couldn't remember when the first trees had started to appear, but now there were more and more of them, springing up dense and fast. More like a forest than a wood, even, Boris thought, and he tried to remember where in the city there might be room for a forest.

At least the snow was disappearing, and that was one good thing. It had been replaced by the dank dripping of water from trailing branches, which was less good and had a rather depressing effect. Twigs crackled underfoot, and the light had drained away like water from a sink. The holes in tree trunks looked like open mouths, and the fungus covering the bark of tree stumps made extraordinary patterns, like distorted faces. Everything was very still.

"Gives me the creeps, this place," muttered Checkers, and Boris had to agree with him. It was so silent, and there was no sign of life. Even though Boris wasn't used to forests, he thought that some kind of life might be living there—rabbits or birds or even beetles. But no life stirred, and there was nothing to be seen or heard.

Until they saw the shadow.

It flickered in front of them briefly and disappeared along a bend in the path.

Checkers charged after it, barking for all he was worth. He had skidded to a halt, still barking, when he realized he couldn't see anything, then plunged into some undergrowth. He emerged from a tangle of thistles, then dived off in the other direction. By the time Boris caught up with him, he had almost barked himself hoarse. Each bark fell into the air with a slightly muffled sound.

"Did you find anything?" Boris asked when Checkers had finally finished.

"Er, no," said Checkers. Boris lowered his nose to the ground and sniffed. It was a curious, distinctive smell, like ashes and mold. And like dog, though not like any dog Boris had ever scented before. Unless it was a huge, ancient dog that had been lying around for a few hundred years in ashes and mold.

"Are you looking for me?" said a huge, black and rather moldy-looking dog.

Checkers leapt into the air in surprise, then barked so hard he almost turned himself inside out. Boris said nothing. He felt a great awe. An awe that turned his bones to water, bowed his head and rooted his feet to the ground. The big dog was bigger, even, than Gentleman Jim. He had great eyes like calves' eyes, and in the center of each was a scarlet flame. His coat was like a black fungus, and he seemed to have emerged from the earth itself.

Checkers fell over himself, barking, then ran around the great dog in decreasing circles until the huge hound raised one of its shaggy paws and pressed him to the ground. "Gnnumpphh," he said.

"Who are you?" Boris asked slowly.

"My name is Black Shuck," said the great dog, in a voice that seemed to come directly from the bowels of the earth.

From the position he was in, pressed to the earth, Checkers couldn't help noticing the scorch marks around the black dog's feet. Where he stood, the earth was smoldering.

"Hey," he said, stuggling out from beneath the enormous paw. "How do you do that?"

The great dog was silent.

Checkers licked his lips. "Are—are you the Guardian of the Darkest Way?" he asked, rather hoping that he wasn't because if he was, then Checkers would have to fight him.

"No," said the black dog, and gave a short, barking sound that might have been a laugh. *"Next to him I am but a lap dog."*

"Oh, right," said Checkers weakly. He had a funny feeling in the pit of his stomach, a feeling he didn't recognize because he'd never had it before. Dimly he realized that this must be how Flo felt all the time. He glanced at Boris for help, but Boris looked sunk in thought.

"Why do you seek the Guardian?" asked Black Shuck, and Checkers said simply, "Because we've got to fight him."

Now Black Shuck did laugh, a long, baying laugh that made the trees shake and the stones tremble. All around him the earth scorched and withered.

"Fight the Guardian?" he roared. *"But the Guardian is a monster that feeds on living flesh and crunches the bones of the dead. He is rabid with a hunger that can never be assuaged, and his jaws drip with gore. He is the brazen-voiced hound of Hades, and all who hear him die."*

There was a brief, tense pause.

"Right," said Checkers. "Well, we have to fight him anyway."

Black Shuck raised his voice in a howl that blasted the last leaves from the shrubs. *"Tell me another one,"* he said.

Checkers wondered where all the knocking noises were coming from, then he realized it was his knees. The dreadful pounding noise must be his heart, and the funny rattling and clattering would be his teeth. If he could just untangle the muscles of his throat, he might be able to say something sensible.

"Can you take us to him?" Boris asked.

Black Shuck laughed again—a terrible, howling laugh. It sounded as though several screech owls were practicing their wolf impersonations while being passed slowly through a vacuum cleaner. Checkers flattened himself to the ground. At least, he hoped it was the ground for he had lost all sense of where anything was.

"Take you to him?" Black Shuck bellowed/roared/howled/screeched. *"The way to his dread abode may not even be described! It is a vast quagmire of boiling whirlpools surrounded by desolate wastes, through which lost souls pass like numberless insects, moaning and whooping and gibbering and trailing their blood-soaked limbs. The boiling whirlpools belch corrosive slime into the river of death. And the stench,"* Black Shuck said, *"passeth all understanding."*

Boris turned to Checkers. "Sounds like summer camp," he said. "I've heard all about it."

"It is not like summer camp," said Black Shuck. *"It is a vast, desolate plain where the mountains of corruption loom over the chasms of despair and the deplorable gloom is relieved only by diabolical shade. None who go there may return."*

"Right," said Boris. "So, how do we get there?"

Checkers looked at him with admiration. He couldn't even speak, but Boris was managing to ask all the right questions.

The great hound flicked his monstrous tail. It might almost have been a wag, but it was much more sinister. He looked at Boris with an appreciative light in his eyes.

"No living creatures may cross the waters of the underworld," he said. *"But if you like, I will take you as far as the birdless lake."*

Checkers couldn't help wondering why Boris did not appear to be frightened. Checkers was the brave one who knew no fear, but now look at him. He was clinging desperately to the ground as though he might be about to fall off. He felt winded and shown up at the same time.

Boris didn't have the sense to be frightened, he realized suddenly. It was Checkers's duty to protect him from himself. Besides, he couldn't stay cowering on the ground forever; it wasn't dignified. Shakily, he stood. "Right, then," he said. "Which way do we go?"

Black Shuck bayed, a long, drooling call that sounded like the cries of lost souls. Checkers flattened himself against Boris and managed not to fall over this time. "Don't you worry, Boris old son," he gasped. "I'm here."

"Round here, all roads lead to that dread entrance," Black Shuck said. *"I will take you to the birdless lake, where you may enter the caverns of darkness, that lead to the river of death."*

"Thank you very much, Mr.—er—Shuck," Boris said.

Checkers was speechless. River of death? he was thinking. But he fell in behind Boris as the great dog set off in front of them, scorching the earth with his feet as he passed. He had the feeling that things were about to go terribly wrong, if in fact they hadn't already. But Boris seemed to be in a conversational mood.

"So, if you're not the Guardian," he said, "what is it that you do, exactly?"

"I am one of the hounds of hell," said Black Shuck, turning his head a little. *"I hunt for human souls. For thousands of years I have traversed lonely roads, stalking the souls of the damned so that I may take them to the Guardian. Most do not see me, but those that do invariably die."*

"Sounds a bit grim," said Boris, trying to keep up. The great dog expelled a sound that might have been a sigh.

"Yes," he said. *"It is unutterably boring. Apart from when people beg. That livens things up a little."*

"So, why do you do it, then?" Boris asked, and the great dog paused.

"Why?" he said. *"What else is there to do?"*

"Well, I don't know," said Boris. "Lots. You could hunt rabbits, run after cats—or chase balls."

Black Shuck turned around, baring his enormous teeth. *"Chase balls?"* he said. *"Do I look like a pet?"*

"No," said Boris, very definitely.

"Chase balls," said Black Shuck with withering contempt. Obviously no one had ever suggested that to him before. *"That is man's*

game. Along with every other foolish game ever invented for the race of dog. In fact, you could say that man invented the race of dog just so that he had some way of playing his foolish games. For man is afflicted with imagination, and man's imagination is the dog's curse."

"Hang on a minute," said Checkers, appearing finally from behind Boris. "Men didn't *invent* dogs!"

"Indeed they did," said Black Shuck. *"For in the ancient times, dogs were wild, like wolves and jackals. Man used both their hunger and their intelligence to tame them. Dogs were the first domestic creatures,"* Black Shuck said, imbuing the term with a world of scorn. *"We were soon indispensable as hunters and guides, as warriors and herders and trackers and guardians. We fought their battles, herded their flocks, protected them, hunted for them, tracked them down when they were lost. It might almost be said, in fact, that dogs invented the race of man, for without dogs, man as we know him would not exist. He would never have farmed his animals, built his cities, vanquished his enemies without us. And what is our reward?"*

Black Shuck looked at them with enormous, glowing eyes.

"Kennels!" he said with a scorching contempt. *"Leads. Canned dog food! He has built his cities with the help of dogs and now there is no room in them for us. He prevents us breeding and curtails our right to sniff, our freedom to even move. He calls us his best friend, but when he has no further use for us, it is a quick trip to the butchers they call vets. Barbaric."*

Boris and Checkers looked at each other. They had never thought about it that way before.

"I don't think it's that bad," Boris ventured.

"No?" said Black Shuck, turning on them his thousand-watt gaze. *"What about your own homes? Happy are you? Well-treated? And if so, why are you here, instead of stretched out on your own comfortable hearths?"*

Boris opened his mouth to protest but said nothing. He was remembering the dog pound. Checkers too was remembering, with unease and a growing resentment, how his mistress had locked him into the tiny room, without light or food, and then, when he had chewed up a bit of paper, as any dog would, his master had threatened to beat him.

"*See?*" said Black Shuck, just as if they had spoken aloud. "*And you probably haven't seen the worst of it. I've seen sights that would make a grown dog howl. Stray dogs kicked and abused, pelted with stones, forced to fight one another, starving around restaurants where humans glutted themselves with food or flung out of cars onto roads by men who think no one is watching. But I am watching. Because that is what I do.*"

He turned again and trotted on briskly through the dripping wood.

"Well, but some of them are nice," Boris said, almost pleadingly.

"*Nice?*" said Black Shuck, stopping so suddenly that they almost fell over him. "*Nice? Because they pet you and take you for walks? Because they feed you that indigestible muck they call dog food? Or because they decide when you live or die, when and if you will mate, when, if ever, you get to go out?*"

"Sometimes they play," said Boris, trying to remember the time before the baby came, but Black Shuck gave an indescribable snort.

"*When it suits them,*" he said. "*But mainly they play at building roads and railways and huge apartment buildings and creating a world where no dog belongs. They use dogs for sport and throw them away. They have forgotten, conveniently, that they ever needed us. How many times have you waited patiently, all day, for your human to return and take you out, then, when he comes in, he collapses in a chair and doesn't want to go? They are so obsessed with themselves and the world they have created that they don't even know they are doing wrong. Until they meet me on some lonely road,*" Black Shuck said ominously. "*Then they do.*"

Checkers and Boris didn't know what to make of all this. Black Shuck seemed very sure of himself and very knowledgeable and wise. Everything he said seemed to make awful sense. They could each remember the times when they had been neglected or ignored, then punished for behaving badly. Checkers had been smacked for widdling on the carpet when no one had taken him out. Boris had tried to help his owners get rid of the baby and look where that had got him. They each thought there must be a flaw in the argument somewhere, but neither of them could think what it was, and secretly, their grievances and resentments began to burn.

Around them the trees started to thin out, but a swirling mist filled the spaces between, so that they still couldn't see where they were. They could smell water that was not like the water that dripped from the trees, but only when Black Shuck paused again did they realize that they were near the edge of a vast, dark lake.

"This is the birdless lake," Black Shuck said, and indeed there was an oppressive silence, as if no bird nor any other living creature had ever flapped, crawled or croaked in that vicinity. *"On the other side of this lake there is a cavern, with a hundred broad shafts like mouths. Only one will take you into the underworld. Its rocky throat will lead steeply down to the bowels of the world, where flows the River Styx. No living creature may set foot in those waters, but the ferryman may be induced to take you across—if he is in a good mood."* He looked at them. *"He is not usually in a good mood. In fact, he has been in a bad mood as long as I have known him."*

"H-how long is that?" asked Checkers.

"Since the dawn of time," Black Shuck said. *"But who knows. You may be lucky. And whether you are lucky or not, you will have to cross the water, to reach the Guardian's lair. That is,"* he added, with an amused glint, *"if you are still determined to fight him."*

Neither Checkers nor Boris felt very determined at that moment.

"Er, isn't there another way?" asked Boris.

"No," said Black Shuck, who seemed to be enjoying himself.

"Well, how do we get across the lake?"

"You must swim it, of course. Unless you can fly."

Checkers and Boris looked at the lake. It was black and stagnant and looked very deep. A sulfurous vapor rose from its murky depths.

"Try not to swallow any," Black Shuck said unnecessarily. *"For to taste the waters of the birdless lake means certain death."*

"Now you're just trying to cheer us up," muttered Checkers, but Boris said, "How will we know which cave to go into?"

"When the wind blows, the mouths of the cave will speak," Black Shuck said. *"One of them will call your names. Try not to go in that one—it will be the Harpies, I'm afraid. They sound just like Sirens, but if you follow them, they will feast on your flesh and drink your blood. Follow the one that sounds like the tolling of a bell. It will lead you steeply downward to the bowels of the earth, wherein lies the river of death."*

Boris and Checkers looked at each other in growing dismay. The air was oppressive and very still, as if no wind had blown for a thousand years.

"Sometimes the wind doesn't blow for a thousand years," Black Shuck said. *"You'll just have to wait. Seems like a waste of time to me. Might I ask why you are so intent on fighting the Guardian?"*

Checkers looked at Boris, and Boris looked at Checkers. "Well, it might not come to that," Boris said. "He might just . . . come with us."

Black Shuck shook his head a little, as if he couldn't have heard correctly. *"Why would he do that?"* he said.

Hesitantly, interrupting each other, Boris and Checkers told him their tale. It seemed much less convincing as they told it, and certainly it no longer seemed like a good idea except that it had something to do with preventing the end of the world.

"So you see, we don't want to *fight* him as *such*," Boris finished lamely. "We just want him to come with us—and defeat Fenrir."

Black Shuck looked as amused as a smoldering hellhound could. *"Well, that's all right, then,"* he said. *"Maybe you could throw a ball for him. Oh, I forgot, you haven't got one."*

Checkers and Boris were feeling definitely discouraged by now. Squashed, even.

"Ragnarok," Black Shuck said thoughtfully, as though to himself, and the ground around them quivered. *"So you are trying to save mankind. Just like a dog,"* he added in tones that suggested they deserved everything coming to them.

"Not just mankind," Checkers said.

"We have to save the whole world," said Boris.

"Because a mistletoe twig told you to," Black Shuck said, and both the dogs were silent.

"Of course, it's always possible," he went on, *"that if this world were to end, another, better world would take its place. One in which mankind did not dominate the rest of creation, and in which each animal had its rightful place."*

Boris and Checkers looked at him.

"Just a thought," he said. *"Well, I'd love to hang around a bit longer, discussing the best way to save mankind, but there're people to stalk, lonely travelers to frighten out of their wits, that kind of thing. I'll have to be going."*

And he twitched his mighty tail and turned around.

"Wait a minute," Checkers called. "You can't just leave us here!"

"I'm afraid I can," Black Shuck said, then he reached up toward a single, flowering twig and snapped it off with his great jaws. *"You might need this,"* he said to Boris, and he lowered his head and tucked it into Boris's collar. *"For the ferryman,"* then he turned and walked into the mist, leaving a trail of smoking stubble in his wake.

"Come back!" Checkers barked, his voice falling on muffled air. He stared regretfully at the space where the great hound had been. "I quite liked him," he said to Boris. "He was all right, really. Better than . . ."

He meant better than being all alone on the shores of the birdless lake that led to the caverns of the underworld and the river of death. Not to mention the unspeakable Guardian. Boris understood this, but neither dog wanted to finish the sentence. And at that moment, the mist swirled back, and they could see the farthest shore.

On a bright, sunny, cloudless day, the scene in front of them would have been merely depressing. However, in the dank gray mist it was a sight grim enough to make both dogs burst into tears, if only they'd known how. The water looked as though it was coated with slime. It was more like a swamp than a lake. From time to time stinking bubbles broke the surface, discharging noxious vapors into the reeking air. No life stirred; only a few straggling reeds hung over the edges of the lake as though broken in spirit. And then, on the other side of the lake, was a vast rock face, full of caves that looked exactly, as Black Shuck had said, like open mouths.

"Right," said Checkers on an out breath. "Er, what did he say about crossing it?"

"You mean about the certain death?"

"No," said Checkers. "Not that bit."

"He said we had to swim," said Boris.

Checkers was not a dog who usually held back from swimming. He had swum in the sea, in the canal, in a swimming pool and even in a silage tank. Wherever there was water, Checkers dived in. But this black, stinking swamp was something new in his experience, something he had no desire at all to go near. He hung back. "You can go first if you like," he said generously to Boris. After a moment Boris trotted to the edge of it and gingerly stuck one paw in, withdrawing it instantly.

"Boris," said Checkers, "this is your big chance. You always wanted to be a hero."

"No, I didn't," said Boris. "That was you." He looked at the water. The paw he had dipped in felt curiously deadened. "There's something funny about this place," he said.

And at that moment the caves began to moan.

CHAPTER 18

In Which Gentleman Jim and Pico Come to the End of the World

Meanwhile, Gentleman Jim and Pico had also emerged from the storm, into a snow-covered world. The snow was crisp and dry and crunched under Gentleman Jim's paws. Frost-stiffened grass crackled as they passed, and an occasional shower of snow fell from the branches of a shrub as they went by.

The snow glittered all around them, in all directions as far as they could see, and the frost formed itself into patterns on rocks and stones so that they looked as though they were wreathed in flowers. Everything was perfectly still, as though they were the only living creatures on the earth. It was rather beautiful, but Gentleman Jim felt a growing unease.

Apart from the imminent ending of the world and other concerns such as where were they and how were they supposed to find this mighty hunter, there were three things troubling Gentleman Jim.

First, the silence was rather eerie. Where were all the birds and wild animals? Had everything gone suddenly into hibernation? Where was all the noise of the city? In all of Gentleman Jim's considerable life, he had never been anywhere where there was no noise at all.

Second, there was no sign of the sun or moon. They seemed to have entered a vast twilight, where only the first pale stars pricked the dull sky. The stars were in themselves beautiful, but Gentleman Jim hoped very much that the sun and moon hadn't already been devoured by ravening wolves, in which case, they were already too late.

And third, though his eyesight was no longer what it was, he thought he could see a point ahead where everything simply ended, as though the whole world had fallen off a cliff.

He hadn't mentioned any of these concerns to Pico yet because he didn't want to worry the little dog and also because any noise he made seemed unnaturally loud in the silence. Besides, he suspected that Pico's eyes were sharper than his own and that from his look-out point between Gentleman Jim's ears, he had probably already worked out what there was to know.

Pico, however, was facing the other way. Worried that they wouldn't be able to find their way back, he had scrambled around so that he was looking behind, at the way they had come. This had enabled him to come up with a troubling fact of his own.

There were no tracks. Gentleman Jim had been crunching his way through the snow for hours now, and his tracks should have been clearly visible. The snow had virtually stopped falling, apart from an occasional flake drifting lazily downward as though trying to make up its mind whether to land or not, and there was no wind. Gentleman Jim's great paws should have left a clear trail all the way back to the croft, but the snow seemed to be covering them up. Pico found himself watching the tracks very hard, but the snow didn't seem to be moving at all, yet three or four paw prints behind them, Gentleman Jim's tracks simply disappeared. And there were no tracks of any other kind either, bird or fox or rabbit.

Pico was paying such close attention to the disappearing tracks that he almost fell off Gentleman Jim's collar when the great dog cleared his throat.

"AHEM!" said Gentleman Jim, and a nearby shrub quivered, sending cascades of snow from its branches. "Er, I don't suppose you know where we are, do you?"

Pico scrambled around hastily so that he was facing the back of Gentleman Jim's neck.

"Can you still see that star?" Gentleman Jim inquired.

"Oh yes," Pico said, gazing around quickly, though in fact, now that there were a few stars out, he was no longer sure which was the right one. "I'm sure we're still going in the right direction."

Gentleman Jim nodded. "Take a look ahead, will you?" he said.

Pico pulled himself up Gentleman Jim's neck until he was looking out between his ears. "I can't see anything," he said.

"That's right," said Gentleman Jim.

"Oh," Pico said, suddenly understanding. "I see."

For ahead of them was a ridge of snow, slightly too high to see over and very long. It extended to the left and right as far as the small dog could see. Beyond this ridge, there appeared to be—nothing. Only the stars twinkling in the deepening sky. It was as if the whole world had suddenly ended there.

Gentleman Jim sighed. "I didn't like to mention it before," he said, "but the earth seems to be coming to an end."

Pico slid a little way down Gentleman Jim's neck, then scrambled up again. "My word," he said.

Neither of them could see over the ridge of snow, but both of them had the horrible impression of nothingness on the other side. It was almost as though someone had rolled the world up like a carpet. Behind them stretched the vast, glittering plain they had just crossed; before them, it seemed, was the end of the world.

Pico licked his lips. "It is clear what we must do," he said.

"Is it?" said Gentleman Jim, surprised.

"Yes," said Pico, very definitely. "We must clamber up that icy ridge and leap into the Void."

Gentleman Jim seemed less convinced. "Well, that's *one* idea," he said.

"Do you have another?" asked Pico.

"No, but—"

"Then I suggest we do not delay."

Gentleman Jim stayed where he was, oppressed by the sense of vast immeasurable emptiness on the other side. He looked up at the ridge. Even the sky seemed blacker beyond it, as though emptied of stars.

"Gentleman Jim," said Pico. "Remember the nobility of your blood."

What Gentleman Jim was remembering was that he had almost no desire at all to discover a Void, whatever it was. He coughed, playing for time.

"Hrrrummppph!" he said. "Did Jenny say what we were supposed to do once we were *in* the Void?" he asked.

Pico thought hard for a moment.

"No," he said.

"Ah," said Gentleman Jim.

"But surely that is for us to find out."

"Hmmm," said Gentleman Jim, whose instincts were telling him that he should definitely not, on any account, go over that ridge. "Are you sure you can still see that star?" he asked suddenly.

"Gentleman Jim," said Pico sternly. "You cannot be thinking of backing out now?"

"Well," said Gentleman Jim, "not backing out as *such,* but—"

"Put me down!"

"Pardon?"

"Put me down at once! If you will not take me to the Void, I will go there myself!"

There followed a short, tense discussion in which Gentleman Jim pointed out that there was no need to get huffy, and Pico pointed out that Gentleman Jim should be ashamed of himself, and Gentleman Jim said that Pico was far too bossy for a midget, then yelped as Pico nipped his ears, and finally Gentleman Jim said that if Pico was determined to go flinging himself into any old Void that came along, who was he, Gentleman Jim, to prevent him, and he lowered himself to the ground so that Pico could slide down his nose.

For the next few minutes, Gentleman Jim watched in a resigned kind of way as Pico tried and failed to clamber up the ridge. He tried approaching it scientifically, by looking for footholds, but the walls were glassy and sheer. Then he tried running at it, from increasing distances, but he got hardly any farther than his own height before tumbling back down again and burying himself in snow. Finally, he spent several moments jumping up and down at it, like a miniature kangaroo, but it was hopeless. He was far too small to project himself over the ridge.

Frustrated, he turned around and mustered what was left of his dignity. "Gentleman Jim?" he said.

"Ye-es?" yawned the big dog.

"Would you be so kind as to assist me? Please?"

Gentleman Jim thought of saying that even with his assistance, Pico was unlikely to get very far since the ridge was much bigger than both of them, but he knew that Pico would just take this as a further sign of giving up. Pico was the kind of dog who never, ever gave up. Gentleman Jim would get no peace unless he went along with him. Besides, he reflected, they were perfectly safe. There was no way that either of them could climb that ridge.

So, rolling his eyes and muttering to himself, Gentleman Jim stood up. And as he did so, he saw something he had never seen before.

A constellation was rising over the edge of the ridge. This was nothing unusual in itself, of course, and Gentleman Jim even knew the name of it since Gordon was a keen amateur astronomer. Orion was rising as usual, but then, much less usually, Gentleman Jim thought, it began walking toward them.

Several expressions of surprise and disbelief battled for possession of Gentleman Jim's face. His jaw flopped about for a while, then he barked loudly. "Look!"

"What is it? What is it?" barked Pico, jumping up and down again, and Gentleman Jim just had the presence of mind to lower his nose so that Pico could scramble up again; then when he did, he almost fell off Gentleman Jim's neck in shock. Both dogs stared in astonishment as the great constellation approached, its stars burning brighter and brighter. Gentleman Jim thought of running, but where was there to run to? All the short hair on his back bristled as the outline of the constellation resolved itself into an enormous burning man. His eyes, hair and sword gleamed with a cold, white fire. He rose over the edge of the ridge and remained poised in mid-air, gazing down at them.

"ARE YOU LOOKING FOR ME?" he said.

CHAPTER 19

The Chapter of Not Being
Devoured by Wolves

In the ordinary course of things, Flo would have expected to land sometime shortly after leaping. Her whole experience of the world had taught her that if you leapt, you landed, or indeed fell. She had been a particularly bouncy puppy and had learned this lesson many times.

"What goes up must come down," her owner, Myrtle, had told her.

"Pride goes before a fall."

"He who climbs farthest falls hardest," and so on.

Flo, the most intelligent of poodles, had learned all these lessons by heart. But they weren't helping her now. Because, in fact, she had leapt, but had not landed.

She had jumped at the mirror, closing both eyes as a sensible precaution against further fright. She was now waiting a reasonable length of time before opening them again, sure that at any moment she would collide with something hard and probably dangerous, like, say, the ground.

This didn't happen.

Flo was familiar with the unpleasant lurching feeling of descent, when the earth rushed up to meet you and smacked you hard for attempting to leave. She was even familiar with the laws of gravity since Myrtle had once taken a diploma in advanced physics at the university. But in fact the unpleasant sinking feeling wasn't happening either. It had been replaced by an even more unpleasant *soaring* feeling.

Flo, not alone among her kind, had never wanted to fly. If she had somehow learned by accident, she knew she should open her eyes since, as every bird learns in its first flying lesson, it is very unwise to fly with them closed. But Flo really didn't want to open her eyes. Surely, any minute now, her feet would touch something solid and secure.

But they didn't.

In a further attempt to delay the dreadful moment of opening her eyes and seeing what was happening to her, Flo ran through the facts in her mind.

First, in an uncharacteristically reckless moment, she had jumped at the mirror.

The mirror should have been hard but wasn't, and Flo appeared to have passed right through it. This was abnormal fact one.

Seconds later, something large and hairy had attempted to stuff itself down her throat. This had to be abnormal fact two since even in Flo's limited experience of hunting, small furry creatures did not just stuff themselves down your throat. Flo had gagged and almost thrown up midair, eventually coughing up what seemed like a giant hair ball. So this, actually, could be abnormal fact three since poodles don't have the kind of hair that comes off and forms itself into balls. Now the thing, whatever it was, was stuck between her teeth; Flo had tried to shake it out of her mouth but couldn't. Was this abnormal fact four? Or three? Flo was getting confused now as the general abnormality of the situation swept over her. There was the mirror, which perversely reflected a bizarre scene unrelated to the room it was in; there was the house, which refused to resemble itself and had kept sprouting further corridors and doors; *and* there were the three horrible hags.

So numerous were the abnormal occurrences that Flo had experienced in the course of just one afternoon that she had lost count. It might almost be said that she had lost all sense of normal. Apparently she had leapt through a smoking mirror over the heads of three grotesque old women and simultaneously learned to fly.

It was this last factor, of course, that was troubling her most of all. Not landing just wasn't normal, not by anyone's definition of the term. Her paws craved solid ground, her eyes itched to open so that her brain could relay them some kind of message that would hopefully make sense. After all, how much worse could things get?

Flo opened her eyes.

And immediately everything got much worse.

Now look what you've done, said her brain, and quietly but firmly shut down most of its circuits in protest.

Flo was in the sky. She wasn't just hovering above the ground at the sort of distance she might comfortably have leapt to—she was thousands of feet above the earth. Waves of horror rushed over her as she realized that the tiny specks and lines far below were buildings and rivers and roads. Wreaths of mist passed over the scene, and Flo realized, with mind-numbing shock, that she was looking at clouds, *from the other side.* Worse, she was still ascending.

In terrible dismay Flo tried to shut her eyes again, but without her permission they went on looking. The sun seemed huge without its helpful screen of clouds and atmosphere, pulsating with light. And in her direct line of vision, there was an enormous wolf galloping toward it.

Even without Flo's optical condition that made frightening objects appear five times larger than they actually were, the wolf was enormous. Its ravening jaws were open wide; its eyes glared fire. Behind it was a pack of lesser wolves, though they didn't look lesser to Flo. They all seemed hideous and terrifying. And she was hurtling toward them at an incomprehensible speed.

With what was left of her brain, Flo tried to jam the brakes on in midair. She thrust all her paws out before her in an attempt to skid to a halt and wriggled frantically but succeeded only in turning a sickening somersault, then continuing to fly upside down.

This is it, she thought sadly. *This is the end.* And she just had time to reflect that of all the many ways in which she had anticipated her final moments, crashing airborne into a pack of flying wolves seemed the least likely before the rest of her brain closed down.

Meanwhile, the pack of flying wolves had noticed something unusual.

"What's that, boss?" said one of them, who was near the front. But their leader, Skoll, was too intent on opening his jaws wide enough to swallow the sun to hear.

"Looks like a flying pink poodle," the wolf went on, and this time Skoll did hear.

"A flying pink poodle?" he said, with vast contempt. "Give me a break, Garm."

"No, boss, look," Garm protested. "It *is* a flying pink poodle."

"And I'm a cuddly toy," Skoll said, still intent on the sun. "I told you what would happen if you didn't take your altitude tablets."

But by now the other wolves were joining in.

"He's right, boss, look!"

"It *is* a flying pink poodle!"

"Why's it upside down?"

"What's a poodle?" and so on.

Skoll heaved a sigh of absolute exasperation. He'd told his mistress, Hel, the Queen of Darkness, that he'd be better off on his own, but she'd insisted that the other wolves needed the exercise. More skillfully than Flo, he managed to turn around midair to glare at them all.

"First of all," he said, "poodles can't fly. And they ain't pink. I—oh."

For now that he had turned he could see Flo, careering erratically toward them upside down with her eyes firmly shut.

Skoll had seen many things in his time. The flight of the Valkyries, the march of the frost giants of Ymir, the birth of the world tree, Yggdrasil, from the cosmic egg. He had become, over the millennia, almost jaded to novelty. But now he was genuinely astonished.

"Wow," he said.

It was all he had time to say before Flo crashed into the heart of the pack, scattering them left and right.

In the resulting cacophony, Flo's brain, much to her distress, started working again. Her eyes, despite every instruction she gave them, opened.

"Oh, dear," she gasped, and ordered herself to faint. But against her will, she remained conscious.

She was in the middle of a howling, snarling pack of wolves, each many times larger than Flo. Drool dripped from their ravening jaws; their eyes were bloodred. Several of them lunged toward her, snarling. Flo tried hard to remember how to pray.

But then a strange thing happened.

As she scrambled away from first one, then another, the cord she was carrying in her mouth wound itself around them—a paw here, a throat there, a muzzle somewhere else. Their bloodcurdling howls changed to baffled roars and barks of frustration.

"'Ere, you!" bellowed their leader. "What do you think you're doing?"

"I wish I knew," moaned poor Flo as the cord looped itself around another wolf's tail.

"Stop it this minute!" Skoll howled, lunging toward her. "Cut it out!"

"Believe me, I'm trying," cried Flo, ducking under another wolf and tangling his feet in the cord. "I'm terribly sorry," she added as another one practically choked. "Do excuse me," she said to a third as she looped his ears together. "I hope it's not too tight."

Soon all the wolves apart from Skoll were roped together in the cord that kept unraveling itself from Flo's mouth. They struggled and kicked and writhed, but they were joined together in a howling mass, and no matter how they tried to bite the cord, it merely cut into their mouths. There was only Skoll left, facing Flo.

Skoll's ears flattened, his fur lifted and his teeth were bared in a terrible grin. He had faced many enemies before, and while this one, a very polite pink poodle who had somehow learned to fly, was not in his handbook of supernatural foes and demons, he was not about to be tied up by a poodle who looked as though she was suffering from a very bad perm.

"Right," he snarled. "I don't know who or what you are, but I do know this. I am Skoll the Terrible. No living creature has ever defeated me in single combat, and I have never been chained. Not even by the Queen of Darkness herself. You might've tied up those jokers there"—he jerked his head at the struggling pack—"they probably deserve it. But if you think for one moment that you're going to rope me up with the rest of them, you've got another thing coming. However," he said, grinning evilly, "you're welcome to try. All you have to do," he said, drawing an imaginary line in the air in front of him, "is to step over that line there."

Flo looked at the enormous, ravening wolf. Single combat really wasn't her thing, and if she was going to try it, she would pick someone more her size. Like Pico. She wondered briefly whether the great wolf would follow her if she set off now, dragging all the other wolves behind her, but somehow she doubted it. He would carry on relentlessly until he had fulfilled his mission of swallowing the sun.

Flo's heart quailed as she looked at the monster before her. She wondered how far she would get if she simply ran away. She hadn't asked for this task, she reminded herself. It wasn't fair. She, the least brave of poodles, was being forced to fight a supernaturally evil wolf, who was also supernaturally big and strong. The others had chosen their tasks, or at least picked ones that suited their personalities. Pico had always wanted to travel; Checkers loved a good fight. All Flo wanted was to go home and lie down.

Then, as if from far away, she remembered Jenny's voice. *It is your wisdom and perception that we need,* she had said.

"I'm waiting," said the wolf.

Flo swallowed. "Skoll the Terrible," she said, as if thinking aloud.

"Yes?"

"That's a funny name, isn't it?"

The wolf looked distracted by this different tactic, as she had hoped he would be. "What's wrong with it?" he said.

"Oh, nothing," said Flo carelessly. "It's a lovely name. I just wonder what your mother was thinking of when she called you 'the Terrible,' that's all."

The great wolf's bloodred eyes kindled. "You leave my mother out of it," he growled.

"I mean, she *could* have called you Skoll the Handsome," Flo went on as if she hadn't heard, "or Skoll the Wise. But no," she added smoothly, "I can see why she wouldn't call you that."

The great wolf's growl changed to a rumbling roar, and behind Flo one of the captive wolves tittered. "She's got you there, Skoll," he said.

"At least she didn't dress me up as a cake decoration," he snarled, and more of the wolves yelped with laughter.

"Nice one, nice one," they said.

"Hmmm," said Flo. "Looks like she didn't dress you up at all, in fact. Never thought, 'Poor Skoll, a dog with a face like that could do with a bit of grooming,' no. Just left you till you looked like a badly trampled goat."

Now the wolves behind Flo howled with laughter while Skoll prowled up and down in midair, growling, but still keeping to one side of the imaginary line.

"I mean, Skoll the Terrible what?" Flo went on, now actually enjoying herself. "The terrible hairdo? The terrible body odor? Or just the terrible excuse for a dog?"

Flo had gone too far. Skoll's growl rose several notches in pitch and he crouched back on his haunches in classic spring pose. The next moment he was leaping through the air and Flo just had time to step neatly to one side so that he landed in the thick of the howling wolves. Flo acted swiftly, tossing the cord toward him. Impelled by its own magic, it looped itself around him several times.

"*#@*!" said Skoll.

"Language," said Flo.

Skoll's rage was terrible to see. He writhed and howled and bit several of the wolves nearest to him so that they howled too. Flo watched with interest as he struggled and kicked, only tying himself up tighter. Once she was sure that he couldn't free himself, she felt much calmer, and almost brave, and even a tiny bit proud of herself.

Eventually the great wolf stopped struggling. He looked at Flo with an evil glare. Under normal circumstances this glare would have been enough to reduce Flo to a quivering mass, but now she couldn't help feeling that she had the upper hand.

"You won't get away with this," he said.

"Looks like I just did," said Flo pertly.

The great wolf's breathing was heavy and hoarse. "All right, then, Miss Hair Crime," he said. "You've got us all here. Now what are you going to do?"

He'd got Flo there. She hadn't a clue. Skoll saw the fleeting expression of doubt on her face and his glare changed to an evil grin.

"You needn't think you can stop Ragnarok, you know," he said. "You might've stopped me from swallowing the sun—for now, but you've still got Hati to deal with."

Flo glanced nervously over her shoulder. "Hati?" she said, and all the wolves began making appreciative noises.

"Hati!"

"She's the most evillest wolf of all!"

"No one's ever defeated Hati!"

"Hati'll have her for breakfast!"

"All right," Flo said, with a bravado she did not feel. "Who is this Hati, then?"

"Why, the third great wolf of Ragnarok, of course," said Skoll, affecting surprise. "She's on her way to devour the moon. She'll be getting there around about now, I should think."

Flo turned. There on the far horizon the sky was darkening, the moon round and full and clear. The shadow of a great wolf was rapidly approaching it. Flo couldn't help it; her heart sank. She was in midair, with a pack of bound wolves, and her task wasn't over yet. She didn't know what to do with the pack, and the moon seemed a long way off. But while she was waiting, another great wolf was drawing ever closer to it.

"Hat-i, Hat-i, Hat-i," chanted the wolves.

"I'd go home now if I was you," said Skoll.

But Flo had come this far, and she wasn't going to give up now. Besides, she had no idea how to descend. "Right," she said. "I'd better stop her, then," and behind her all the wolves howled with laughter.

"Stop Hati!"

"That's a good one!"

"This should be worth watching!"

Flo ignored them. The cord tugged in her mouth and she followed it, moving more gracefully now and gaining speed. The pack of heckling wolves streamed behind her like an evil balloon as she flew.

CHAPTER 20

In Which Boris and Checkers Plunge into a Hole

Boris," moaned the caves. "Checkers!"

Checkers flattened himself to the ground, snarling and ready to spring. Boris looked worried.

"Don't go running off, Checkers," he said. "Remember what Black Shuck said about the Harpies."

"Boris and Checkers," the caves moaned. "Come to us!"

Checkers barked furiously and looked as if he would dive straight into the swamp. Boris sighed and sat on him. All the air shot out of Checkers as Boris's considerable weight descended.

"What did you do that for?" he gasped when he could speak.

"Shut up," said Boris, uncharacteristically. "I'm thinking."

"I—don't—suppose—you—could—do—it—somewhere—else—could—you?" puffed Checkers.

"No," said Boris.

"Come to us," moaned the caves.

"What's—there to think—about anyway?" grunted Checkers, squirming.

"Well, for one thing," said Boris, "I'm trying to work out how we cross the lake."

"Come, Boris, come, Checkers," sang the caves. Black Shuck had said that only one of them would call their names, but at this distance it was impossible to tell which one.

"Look," said Checkers, with a desperate wriggle. "If you'd—just—get—up—I promise—I won't go—running off—or do—anything—stupid. Okay?"

With a grunt, Boris heaved himself off Checkers. Immediately Checkers ran off, plunging straight into the lake.

"Checkers, Checkers," moaned the caves.

"Look, Boris," Checkers called. "It's like I thought. It's quite solid around the edges. We can walk across, easy—"

Then he sank like a stone.

"Your turn, Boris," sang the caves, evidently enjoying themselves.

Boris heaved a sigh of absolute exasperation. Sometimes he lost patience with Checkers, he really did. He got up slowly and plodded toward the edge of the lake. Checkers's head surfaced briefly, struggling for breath, then sank again.

Boris thought. He thought about crossing the lake and about how the voices on the other side seemed to be able to see them. But they couldn't leave the caves, presumably, or the Harpies, whatever they were, would have attacked them by now. For some reason, they wanted to lure them into the lake.

Checkers's head broke the surface of the water again.

"Bo—" he said, and sank once more.

Boris thought he should probably speed up his thought processes, but speeding up was not something Boris did. The lake would be difficult to swim through since it was more like a swamp and there was the flowering branch to carry. It was a long time since Boris had swum.

"Come on, Boris," chanted the caves, and Checkers, rising again, said, "B—"

Boris sighed, then turned around slowly and lowered his tail into the water toward Checkers, still thinking. Almost immediately he felt the curious deadening effect he had felt in his paw. There was definitely something very wrong with the lake. Yet Black Shuck had told them to swim it, and the Harpies (whatever they were) evidently wanted them to as well. Of course, that wasn't the best reason for doing it. . . .

Boris felt Checkers's jaws closing on his tail. He stood and heaved, moving slowly, slowly away from the water's edge. And very slowly, a muddy and bedraggled Checkers emerged like some great sea creature from primordial slime.

"Thanks, Boris," he said, and keeled over like a stone.

Boris waited. The caves had stopped chanting now, temporarily thwarted. Slowly the feeling returned to his tail, and Checkers started to cough. It occurred to Boris that the reason the Harpies wanted them to swim the lake was because they knew they wouldn't survive the experience. And maybe that was what Black Shuck had intended all along. What was it he had said? *No living creatures may cross the waters of the underworld.*

Checkers made an attempt to rise, then slumped again.

And Black Shuck had also said something else. *Around here, all roads lead to that dread entrance.*

"Hmmm," Boris said. Checkers struggled to a sitting position.

"Oh, Boris," he said. "I thought I was a goner there."

His speech was slow and slurred. Boris stared away from the lake, back toward the wood. Then he glanced at Checkers. "Can you walk?" he asked.

"I—think—so," Checkers said. He struggled to get up and made it on the fourth attempt.

"Good," said Boris. "Follow me." And he set off, plodding back along the path they had so recently walked with Black Shuck.

Although he was going slowly, Checkers had some difficulty keeping up, and it occurred to Boris that the lake, which would have stunned or killed a less energetic dog, had simply slowed Checkers down. Really, he was almost normal now.

"Where are we going, boss?" he said.

"Back into the wood," said Boris.

"Oh, right," said Checkers. "Er, why?"

Boris didn't answer. The path was curving now, as he'd thought it might, though it hadn't curved before.

"Eh, that's funny," said Checkers. Boris plodded on. The path left the wood again and curved steeply uphill.

"We didn't come this way before," said Checkers, his voice sounding stronger and more normal with every step. "What's it doing *now*?"

For the path was twisting now, leading sharply up through rocks.

Checkers caught up to Boris and began nudging him from behind. "Where're we going?" he said.

"What's happening?"

"Are we nearly there yet?"

"Hang on a minute," he said. "What about that lake? And the caves, remember?"

Boris didn't answer. He was too busy clambering over rocks. Mist swirled around him so that he could hardly see, but at last he seemed to have reached the highest point of the climb. They were on a plateau of rock. He paused for a moment, recovering his breath, then trotted over to the edge of the plateau and looked down.

"What?" said Checkers behind him. "Where are we?"

"Come and look," said Boris.

Checkers looked. He let out a long breath of admiration that was almost a wolf whistle. "Boris, old son," he said. "You're a flipping genius."

For there below them was the lake, steaming gently. They could see that they had gone all around it and were now on the other side. They could see, as they peered over the edge, that they were looking down a cliff that was pitted with openings, as though it had a hundred mouths.

"Boris," Checkers said. "You're a star! Mind you," he added, "I don't fancy climbing down there."

"We might not need to," Boris said. "Look."

Just behind them and a little to the left, there was an opening in the plateau of rock. Beyond it was another opening that neither of them had noticed. Checkers was astonished. "Wow," he said. "They weren't here before."

But even as he spoke, the rocky ridge rumbled and quaked and several small stones scattered past them over the edge. A third fissure appeared to the right.

"Checkers," Boris said warningly. "Don't go bounding off."

"As if I would," Checkers had began when the rumbling and quaking started again and the rock parted, almost beneath their feet. Checkers poked his nose into it right away.

"Rabbits!" he said, quivering all over, and he would have dived straight in if Boris hadn't caught hold of his collar.

"Checkers!" he said. "There's only one opening for us, remember?"

"Mmm rabbits," Checkers said. His eyes had glazed over already. Somewhat reluctantly he allowed himself to be hauled over to the next hole.

"Now look, Checkers," Boris said. "When we come to the right opening, it'll sound like the tolling of a bell. My hearing isn't what it used to be. You'll have to find it. But it won't work if you go diving down every hole you come to. Whatever you smell down there, whatever you hear, promise me you won't dive in."

Checkers promised. He sniffed cautiously at the next hole, then cocked his ear at it. Then he looked at Boris with a strange light in his eye.

"It's an ice-cream truck!" he said, wagging his tail furiously. Checkers had once chased an ice-cream truck clear across the city.

Boris sighed. He caught hold of Checkers's tail just in time to stop him disappearing into the hole.

"It's the Harpies again," he explained when he had dragged Checkers clear. "They're still trying to lure us in. We'll have to be very careful."

"That's me, boss," Checkers said promptly. "You know me."

He stuck his head right into the next hole and began barking in a muffled way. Boris caught his tail again.

"But boss, there's *cats* down there," he said. "Hundreds of them! Just let me get at them—"

"*No*, Checkers," Boris said firmly. "What did I tell you—?"

But he was interrupted by the terrible rumbling and quaking of the ridge once more as yet another hole appeared. If this went on, Boris realized, they wouldn't have any decision to make. They would simply fall through.

The next hole smelled like barbecued sausages, and Checkers had trouble restraining himself again. The baying of hounds got him all excited, and Boris had to bite his tail hard. But finally, on the seventh or eighth try, they could hear a noise like the tolling of a bell, faint but distinct, from the depths of the earth. Boris looked at Checkers, and Checkers looked at Boris. It was the one hole neither of them had any desire to go down.

"Er, after you, boss," said Checkers. Boris sighed. He retraced his steps a little and picked up the flowering branch that he'd had to drop in order to hold Checkers back. Then they both peered over the edge of the hole.

It seemed a long way down. Checkers's paw dislodged a small stone, and it was ages before they heard a muffled *plop* as though it had fallen into dank water at the bottom of the deepest, darkest well. Both dogs' ears went down at once.

"Well," said Boris. "I think we—" but he never got to finish his sentence because at that moment, the whole of the rocky ridge shook itself violently, with a terrific, rumbling roar, and the hole in front of them widened so that they lost their footing and plunged downward into it, tumbling over and over into the deep, dark pit.

CHAPTER 21

In Which Gentleman Jim and Pico Leap into the Void

Gentleman Jim and Pico gazed in astonishment at the giant man suspended before them in midair. He was so tall that his head seemed to merge with the surrounding stars in the sky, while his feet hung well below the cliff edge and could not be seen. They could see the three dazzling stars of his belt, and from them hung the hilt of a sword and a short, curving horn.

At last, Pico found his voice. "WOOF!" he said, meaning, Who are you, and how can you stand in midair like that, and how did you get to be that big?

Orion sighed, and his sigh was like the rustling of stars. "My name is Orion," he said, in a voice as distant as starlight. "I am doomed to travel the skies for all eternity."

"Doomed?" said Gentleman Jim slowly, and Pico said, "Travel the skies!" in an impressed kind of way.

"Yes," said Orion. "I am doomed."

"It doesn't sound like much of a doom to me," Pico said.

"What would you know?" said Orion, with a trace of bitterness. "Do you know how far you have to travel up here before you see anything? How long you have to wait before anything happens? Thousands of light-years—that's how far *and* how long. Thousands of light-years of nothing. Vast oceans of emptiness, the rolling wastes of time, followed by, just for variation, nothing at all."

Gentleman Jim cleared his throat. *"Hrrruummph!"* he said, meaning that they should get on.

But Pico wasn't listening. "I thought the universe was a very exciting place," he said.

"No," said Orion.

"I don't understand," said Pico. "You must have seen amazing things—stars and galaxies and—and things that we mortals can only dream about!"

"Don't get me started on that one," said Orion. "It is true that I have seen remarkable things. Meteor showers, the birth of suns . . . but so few and so far between. Do you know how far it is from one constellation to another? Or what lies between? I can tell you. Nothing. Nothing at all. Do you know what nothing looks like?"

Gentleman Jim thought that this line of conversation had gone on long enough. "What is it that you did, exactly, to have deserved such punishment?" he asked.

Orion bent his mighty head toward them. Beams of starlight showered from his eyes. "Once when the earth was young," said Orion, "and all the stars more brilliant than they are today, and the morning breeze fragrant with the all the scents of nature, and the dew on the grass sweet and piercing, I made a boast that I, Orion, mightiest of hunters, could kill any living thing the earth produced. It was no idle boast. The earth ran wild with game, and whatever I saw, I killed. No beast escaped the flight of my arrow or the shaft of my spear, neither bird, nor fish, nor four-footed creature. And I killed for pleasure, not need."

Pico clutched Gentleman Jim's ears. "Senseless slaughter," he muttered. "Carnage!"

"Indeed," murmured Orion. "And the great goddess, Gaia, Mother Earth, thought so too. It was she who sent the scorpion to kill me. Only Artemis, Goddess of the Hunt, took pity on me. She transmuted my flesh into stars, though my soul was lost. No living creature mourned for me apart from my dogs, who were ever my companions in the chase. And two of these, my best beloved, she placed with me in the sky for company. Without them I should indeed have been alone."

He glanced over to where two stars shone in the space where

Orion should have been. "They were once my beloved hounds." He sighed. "Sirius and Procyon. But now they too are doomed to wander, soulless, through the trackless wastes of eternity. They are known simply as Canis Major and Canis Minor, and without their souls they are but pale imitations of the living, loving beings they once were. I miss them."

He looked down at Gentleman Jim and Pico. "You remind me of them a bit," he said.

Gentleman Jim ignored this. "Do you mean to say," he said, "that you deliberately set out to kill every kind of animal on earth just because of a *boast*?"

"I had my reputation to think of," said Orion, and as Gentleman Jim gasped in outrage, he added, "but I have never killed a dog."

"Well, that's something, at any rate," muttered Gentleman Jim. Then, remembering the prophecy made by the mistletoe dart, he said, "So, would you say that you are the greatest hunter that ever lived?"

"I was," said Orion, with more than a touch of pride.

"Okay," said Gentleman Jim. "Now we're getting somewhere."

"I am getting nowhere," said Orion, and he sighed his rustling sigh.

"Can't you find your soul?" asked Pico, and Orion sighed again.

"This is my doom. Each night I travel westward to the farthest point of darkness before the sun can rise, flooding the sky with light. There, at the worlds' farthest edge, lie the asphodel fields, in the kingdom of Hades, and there my soul is trapped until such time as it repents."

"You mean, it isn't sorry for what you've done?" asked Gentleman Jim.

"No," said Orion, and both Gentleman Jim and Pico looked shocked.

"Why not?" asked Pico. "It seems to me that you were a very bad man."

"I am, or was, the mightiest of hunters," Orion said defensively. "What is the hunter without the chase? And the hunt itself is sacred to Artemis. No," he said, rustling. "My only crime lay in foolishly boasting about it. My soul must repent that boast. But first it must remember that I ever made it."

"You mean—it can't even remember?" asked Pico, looking even more shocked than before.

Orion looked as sad as a constellation can look. "The asphodel fields are a place of forgetting," he told them, "where each soul drinks deep of the waters of the River Lethe. Water that numbs the mind and makes it forget. The souls of the damned descend to Tartarus, place of torment; the souls of the blessed go to the Elysian fields, where all is laughter and delight. But the souls of the rest of us, those who have distinguished themselves neither by great goodness nor great crime, they are lost forever in the asphodel fields, the place of unremembering."

"I'd've thought that killing every animal the earth ever produced might be considered a crime," muttered Gentleman Jim.

"I've told you before—I am the greatest hunter that the world has ever known," Orion said a little snappishly. "It is unfair that I am being made to suffer for what I am. Does the bird suffer for flying? Or the fish for swimming? Or—"

"Yes, yes," said Pico hastily. "But if you know where your soul is, why do you not simply go and get it?"

Once again the stars gave their rustling sigh.

"Each night I traverse the globe," Orion said. "I have seen the Gates of Darkness by the palace of Hades many times. I can see the asphodel fields, but I cannot descend into them. I have no substance, you see. I am fixed to the sky. Not even my faithful hounds can help. Because they too are trapped in the sky and parted forever from their souls."

Pico hopped with excitement on top of Gentleman Jim's skull, which wasn't comfortable. "Well, then," he said. "You must permit us to assist you."

"Assist me?" Orion said. "How?"

"What my tiny friend means," Gentleman Jim said, determined not to let Pico do all the talking, "is that he thinks he can help you to find your soul."

Once again the stars rustled, but this time they sounded as though they were laughing.

"You?" Orion said. "What can you do? I have been searching for thousands of years without success."

"Exactly," said Gentleman Jim, but Pico said pertly, "Then you obviously need our help."

Orion stared at him. "How can you help me?" he said. "It is my doom. And yet—I have paid, many times over, for my crimes. By rights I should be enjoying the delights of the Elysian fields, Isles of the Blessed, where the sun never sets. There I would meet all my old friends, the noblest of heroes from the golden age of man. There I could rest in peace finally with my two beloved dogs. Yes," he said, with infinite sadness. "That is what I should like. But there is no way of repaying my debt to the earth."

Gentleman Jim and Pico had the same thought simultaneously.

"Well," said Gentleman Jim, "there is one way."

Pico almost fell over himself in his hurry to tell the starry giant about the prophecy made by the mistletoe—that only the greatest hunter of all could help to prevent Ragnarok by blowing his horn. He said "Ragnarok" very quietly, but the earth still trembled. Orion listened patiently.

"Ragnarok?" he said, and once more the ground quivered and shook.

Gentleman Jim's stomach lurched. "Stop saying that!" he said.

Orion's face was very grave, and his stars shivered. "I have heard of this. But it is not of my world. So what am I supposed to do?"

"You are supposed to blow your horn," said Pico.

"Ah," said Orion.

"Ah?" said Gentleman Jim. "Is that a problem?"

Orion hung his massive head and sighed, and his sigh was full of tears. "I can no longer blow my horn," he said. "That is part of my punishment. This horn was given to me by Zeus as a reward for being the greatest hunter that ever lived, and the note it sounds is like no other in clarity and purity of pitch. It can be heard throughout the nine worlds. But because I have offended the gods by abusing my gift, it no longer works. Until my soul repents and is allowed into the Elysian fields, I can no longer blow this horn."

"Are you sure?" said Pico.

"Of course I'm sure," said Orion. "Listen," and he raised the great, glistening horn to his lips and took a huge breath, but the sound that came out of it was, *Phtttht.*

"Ah," said Gentleman Jim.

"Do you not think I would blow it if I could?" demanded Orion. "If I could blow my horn, my soul would hear it and awake from its forgetful sleep."

"I see," said Gentleman Jim. "Hmmm," and he was about to say that it was all over then, there was no point trying, but Pico jiggled up and down on top of his head.

"There is only one thing to do," he said. "We'll get your soul back for you."

"What? From the underworld?" said Gentleman Jim.

"Wherever it is. We'll find it!"

If Pico hadn't been on top of his head, Gentleman Jim would have nipped him. But the little dog went on, "That's what dogs do, you know—we retrieve things."

"Only if we can find them, of course," put in Gentleman Jim.

"But we already know where to look," Pico said.

Orion looked at them, and there was the faintest glimmer of hope in his starry eyes. "It is true," he murmured, "that my own dogs cannot help, for they are lost in the underworld as I am. But would you really go down into that dread place, into Hades itself, for my sake?"

"Well—" said Gentleman Jim, but Pico said, "Of course!"

"Of course," said Gentleman Jim. "You don't know anything about it, do you? How to get there, how dangerous it is, how to recognize his soul when we've found it . . ."

"I can tell you all those things," said Orion.

"And how to make it remember," finished Gentleman Jim. "Really, I've heard worse ideas in my time, but I can't remember when."

"Your haggard friend is right," Orion said.

"Who are you calling haggard?" said Gentleman Jim. "And to cap it all off—we don't know how to get back out of Hades when we've got there—"

"But we've got to try," said Pico earnestly. "For Jenny's sake."

All Gentleman Jim's arguments faded in the face of such absolute conviction. But he summoned a final objection. "All right then," he said. "Tell me. How are we supposed to get there?"

"You will walk through the galaxy with me," said Orion, and Pico gave a small gasp of delight.

"Yes!" he said.

"Walk through the—hang on a minute," said Gentleman Jim. "You do know dogs aren't meant to fly, don't you?"

"You will travel with me, in the place of my dogs," said Orion. "Canis Major and Canis Minor."

"WOOF!" said Pico joyously.

"Oh, dear," said Gentleman Jim. "Oh, dearie dear. I knew I shouldn't've got up this morning. I knew it was going to be a bad day."

Gentleman Jim did not want to admit it, but he really wasn't keen on heights. He didn't often have to face them, but he had once been in a lift all the way to the thirty-first floor of the office building where Gordon worked. He hadn't liked it at all and had expressed his feelings by widdling copiously over the feet of all the other people in the lift, so that Gordon had come to the conclusion that it was probably better to leave Gentleman Jim at home. But Pico was speaking again.

"Fear not, my starry friend," he said. "We will travel with you to the ends of the earth, and if your soul can be found, we will find it and return it to you. Consider it done!"

Orion's stars gleamed with emotion. "My friends," he said huskily. "No one has ever volunteered to help before you—not in all the ages of the world. We will travel together on the shining pathways. But first you must leave the earth and join me in the sky."

"Yes, about that," said Gentleman Jim, but Orion merely stretched out his fiery hand.

There it was before them, the edge of the world, rolling away into nothingness. The sky was a great black emptiness, pricked with stars and constellations. One of which was holding out its hand.

"Right," said Gentleman Jim, not moving, but Pico said, "Leap, my friend, leap! Do not hold back. We must join the starry giant on his immortal journey."

"Of course we must," said Gentleman Jim. "What else would we do? Go home and lead a peaceful life? Why would anyone want to do that?" He closed his eyes. When he opened them, the edge of the world was still there and the great, starry hunter still hung suspended before them. No way, he thought.

"Okay," he said. He braced himself. Slowly he lumbered forward, awkwardly and clumsily at first, then faster and faster toward the ridge. And even though he was climbing steeply uphill, he went on gaining speed, his legs powered by some strange force, until he reached the summit. There, no longer able to pause, he closed his eyes and leapt dizzyingly into the sky.

CHAPTER 22

The Greatest Love

Baldur was horribly changed. He was gray and withered, covered in strange patterns of frost and mold and lichen. With a pang of horror, Jenny realized he was becoming part of the tree. She nudged and nuzzled and licked all the parts accessible to her, but his arms and fingers were indistinguishable from the twisted roots. They even tasted like bark. And he seemed aged beyond measure. His withered flesh had taken on the patterns of vegetation, and his graying beard was tangled into the spindly roots twisting out from the main root.

Jenny felt as though her heart was breaking. This was Baldur the Blessed Youth, with a face like the sun, perpetually shining with innocence and joy. Now he was decomposing before her eyes. Worse still, she could sense that far within him, a muffled heart still faintly beat and thin blood trickled slowly through shriveled veins. As she reached his face, his filmy, milky eyes, tree-colored, opened blearily toward her.

"Ley-sa," he breathed in a dry, crackling voice. "What have you done?"

If she had been human, Jenny would have sobbed aloud, but all she could manage was a broken whimper.

"Master," she whimpered, "Master."

It was all she could say for the moment. Her breath came out in short, panting gasps. She thought it might melt the ice on him, but it formed itself into little patches of frost on his flesh, and each time she breathed, he flinched.

"Oh, Master," she said. "I wanted only to save your life."

Baldur spoke slowly and painfully, as if each word cost him a mighty effort.

"You . . . have . . . brought . . . me," he said, "to . . . a . . . living . . . death."

Then Jenny could find no further words. Her head bent forward in sorrow until her nose rested on his chest. But Baldur was speaking again.

"The . . . mistletoe . . . dart," he said.

"I took it," Jenny said, miserably.

"You must . . . pierce me . . . with it."

"No!" said Jenny. "No—I can't."

"Leysa," said Baldur, and his voice was like a trembling caress or the rustling of leaves. "You must set . . . me . . . free."

That was the meaning of her name, Leysa. But she hadn't known until now that it was also her purpose.

"I can't," she whispered.

"Pierce . . . my . . . heart," he said, and his voice died away in a rattling moan, and he closed his eyes.

Now Jenny knew that her heart was broken. This was her beloved master, for whose sake she had leapt into the Void. If he had asked her to die for him, she would, but to kill him—that seemed impossible. It went against every instinct she possessed.

As if he knew that she would fail him, Baldur turned his face away. Somehow, this was worse to Jenny than any reproach. She lifted the dart that she had carried all this time so faithfully and pointed it at his chest. Then, with a moan that came right from her paws, she drove it deep into him.

Baldur shuddered once and writhed in agony. Then he sagged inward, seemingly collapsing in on himself. His face withered and twisted; his hair twined itself into the surrounding root. The mottled fungus spread over his flesh, and his flesh in turn disintegrated into bark. It was like watching a sped-up film of the process of decomposition. Within moments there was nothing left of the master she had loved.

Jenny lifted up her voice and howled—a long bitter howl of desolation and despair. She flattened herself into the bark where he had been, longing only to follow him into the darkness.

CHAPTER 23

Sam Finds a Way

Wearily Sam let himself back in.

"Sam!" his mother exclaimed. "Where have you been? And what's happened here?" she added, gazing in dismay at all the scorch marks. "You haven't been playing with matches, have you?"

"Of course not," said Sam, and he sank miserably onto the nearest chair.

"Sam—you're soaked through," his mother said. "What on earth have you been doing?" Then for the first time, she noticed how miserable he looked. "What is it?" she said, crouching down next to him. "What's the matter?"

"Jenny's gone," said Sam, and he put his head on his arms and wept.

"Gone?" his mother said stupidly. "Gone where?"

But Sam was too distressed to point out that if he knew that, he could go and get her.

"Oh, Sam," his mother said reproachfully. "You didn't let her off the lead, did you?"

"NO!" shouted Sam. "She wasn't in when I got here!"

"All right, Sam, all right," said his mother, getting up. She gazed distractedly out of the window. "This storm's getting worse," she said.

"I know," sobbed Sam. "And Jenny's out in it. Mum, you've got to help me look for her."

"Not in this, Sam," said his mother. "We'll have to wait until the storm's died down."

Sam begged and pleaded, but his mother remained firm.

"She'll probably make her own way back," she said. "Dogs do."

"She won't—I know she won't!" bawled Sam. In the end, to console him, his mother said that they would write out some signs for shop windows and take them to the shops in the morning.

"Now!" said Sam. "I want to take them now!"

So they wrote out five signs:

LOST

One Jack Russell terrier, white with brown markings, answers to the name of Jenny. If found, please return to . . .

And his mother went with him to the shops, though by this time the storm was so bad that they could hardly see.

Then there was nothing to do except stay in, listening to the wind shriek and moan and hailstones battering themselves against the windows. The telly went fuzzy and wouldn't work; Sam couldn't concentrate on his homework, and he didn't want any tea. He went to bed early and lay awake for a long time, worrying about Jenny.

Late in the night he woke, thinking immediately of Jenny, and his heart sank all over again when he realized she wasn't there. He also realized he was very cold. The heat must have gone off. But he wanted to get up, to check downstairs, just in case she had somehow found her way back. He reached out for his dressing gown, and his hand fell on a mass of hairy wool. It was the sweater his aunts had knitted for him.

Normally, of course, Sam wouldn't be caught dead in that sweater. But right now, he didn't care. He tugged it on and trotted downstairs in his slippers, calling Jenny's name softly.

There was no response. The house still felt empty without her. Sam was about to turn around again and climb the stairs dejectedly when he saw a colored light gleaming through the glass of the back door. He opened the back door and gasped.

There, in the darkness and fallen snow of the backyard, was a rainbow. Sam had never seen a rainbow up close before and certainly not in his backyard. All the colors in it gleamed and shone, from deepest indigo to a bright, pure red, illuminating the yard and curving away from him, rather like a bridge.

Sam suddenly felt very sure that the rainbow was, in fact, a bridge, and that it would take him to where he needed to go. A wild hope flared in him that it would take him to Jenny. He glanced back over his shoulder for a moment but decided that he couldn't possibly tell his mother. She would never let him set off alone in the middle of the night, crossing a strange rainbow. He closed the door softly behind him and stepped into the yard. All the rainbow colors glowed softly, invitingly, as he took his first step onto the mysterious bridge.

CHAPTER 24

The Bowels of the Earth

Boris landed first, with an impact that seemed to drive all four paws into his skull. Although the earth was soft, like ashes, he lay where he was for a moment completely winded. His stomach didn't seem to have landed yet, and there was a rushing noise inside his head. He had just about summoned the energy to suck in some air when Checkers landed on him, effectively pumping it out again.

"*Ppphhnngggh,*" said Boris.

"Boris?" said Checkers, then, "Boris! Boris—where are you? *Bor-ris!*"

Boris knew he had to stop Checkers from shouting. But there was no breath left in his body.

"BORIS!" yelled Checkers. "I'm okay. I've landed on something soft!"

"I know," Boris managed to say at last. "Me."

Checkers scrambled off him. "There you are!" he said. "I thought I'd lost you."

"No," said Boris shortly, struggling to his feet.

"'Ere, boss, that was some fall, wasn't it? How far do you think we fell? Miles, I shouldn't wonder. Hundreds and hundreds of miles. How do you suppose we get out again? Where is this place?"

Boris couldn't answer any of these questions. Impulses were reaching his brain but failing to connect. With a sickening lurch he realized his stomach had landed after all. He opened his eyes and wondered why he still couldn't see anything. A single message began the long trek along his optic nerve to his brain, then flailed around hopelessly before finally fizzling out.

"I don't know," he said finally.

"Well, I hope we're not stuck here," said Checkers. "What happens next? Where do we have to go? Do you think this is where the Guardian lives? And if so, how do we find him?"

Boris wasn't good with questions at the best of times. He shook his ears and a shower of soot fell out. Then he spat what felt like soot and ashes out of his mouth.

"I mean, if he's a Guardian," Checkers said, "then he'll be guarding something, won't he? We'll probably bump into him sooner or later. Do you think we'll recognize him when we do? Maybe we should just set off and see what happens. But which way?"

"Checkers," said Boris.

"Yes, boss?"

"Shut up."

"Oh," said Checkers. "Right." And he managed to stay silent for almost a minute while Boris tried to think. Then he said, "Can you hear a rushing noise in your ears?"

If Checkers could hear it too, Boris thought, then there were two possibilities. Either it was the effects of the fall, popping their eardrums until it sounded as though two very small brass bands had become lodged inside their skulls, or else it was . . .

"A river!" cried Checkers, and he bounded off.

Boris sighed the sigh of the unutterably depressed. He had no choice but to run after Checkers. He didn't want to lose him in this place.

There was a dim and fitful light from an unseen source, as though they were traveling through a very dark wood on a windy night, lit by a tiny moon that had developed blood pressure and was emitting a reddish glow. But all around them was the stench of decay, as though no wind had blown in this place for thousands of years. Yet the noise did seem to be the sound of a river, moving slowly and inexorably, and mixed in it were the sounds of voices, yowling and gibbering.

Checkers stopped suddenly, and Boris fell over him.

"I don't think much of this place," he said. "Where are all the ice-cream trucks? And the rabbits?"

Patiently Boris started to explain that there were no ice-cream trucks in the underworld, it was just the Harpies, luring them in, but Checkers crouched suddenly to the floor.

"What's that?" he whispered in a hushed and terrified voice.

"What?" said Boris, unnerved.

"Can't you see them?" Checkers moaned. "Oh, they're horrible—horrible—don't let them get me!"

"What?" said Boris again. "Where?" Fearfully he looked all around. He couldn't see anything. But Checkers went on whining and cringing, and Boris could get no sense out of him.

"There it is again!" moaned Checkers, flattening himself further.

"Checkers," Boris said. "What is it? I can't see anything."

They seemed to be on a kind of road, with tall rocks on either side. Ahead, in the distance, the darkness seemed to be moving, and Boris thought that must be the river. A kind of murky fog swirled around it.

"Oh, stop them!" Checkers whimpered. "They've seen us now. We're lost—lost, I tell you! Doomed."

"Stop *what*?" said Boris, losing patience.

"*Them,*" moaned Checkers. "Look!"

"Checkers," said Boris. "You do know that your eyes are shut, don't you?"

"They can't be," said Checkers.

"They are," said Boris. "And anyway, there's nothing there."

"Can't you see them?" said Checkers. "Monstrous beasts. Fluttering phantoms. Lots of legs and arms. Far too many heads. More than you'd want. It can't be useful, having that many heads. All their tongues lolling out and their eyes dangling. You *must* be able to see that!"

"No," said Boris. He too shut his eyes. Unsurprisingly, he couldn't see anything. Then he saw a small mass of something, glowing and quivering. With a lurch of horror, he realized it was one of Mrs. Finnegan's experimental meals. It seemed to have come to life and was beckoning him. It was making slurping and sucking noises though it had no lips and wriggling suggestively. His eyes shot open again in dismay.

"Told you," said Checkers, whose eyes were still firmly shut.

Boris swallowed nervously. He shut his eyes again. There were more of them now—the turnip and mung bean surprise slithering over the rocks toward him, the squid custard dribbling menacingly near his feet. Boris shuddered all over. They meant to eat him, he thought suddenly. There were hundreds of them, every foul meal he had ever digested returning to take its revenge.

"Don't let them get me!" whimpered Checkers.

Boris forced himself to open his eyes. Instantly the food disappeared. It occurred to him that he and Checkers were seeing different phantoms. With his eyes shut, Checkers was seeing hideous forms and grotesque monsters, while he, Boris, was seeing Mrs. Finnegan's experimental cookery. Boris had a rush of insight, which was such a new experience, he had to sit down.

"Checkers," he said. "Open your eyes."

"Oh, I can't look!" whined Checkers.

"Open them!" Boris said sternly. Wincing and flinching, Checkers opened his eyes. "I can't see anything!" he said in a different tone.

"No," said Boris. "That's because nothing's there."

"But I saw—"

"You saw your own fear," said Boris. "That's what fear does. It makes you look away. When you look straight at it, it goes away."

"I don't understand," said Checkers.

"No," said Boris. "Just keep your eyes open, whatever happens. There's nothing to be afraid of except your own fear."

With a show of determination he did not feel, Boris set off, expecting at any moment to be attacked by a prawn-and-parsnip pie.

Cautiously, still cowering, Checkers followed Boris as he picked his way over stones and clumps of what might have been dead things. The noise of the river grew louder, and the soft earth changed to the mud of the riverbed.

A signpost read *Styx, River of Doom*, only someone had crossed out *Doom* and written *Despair* on it instead, and someone had crossed that out and written *Death.* On the other side of the sign, it read, *Abandon hope, all ye who enter here.* Fortunately, neither dog could read. But as they looked at the river, they got the general idea.

It didn't so much flow as slurp, and again Boris was reminded sharply of Mrs. Finnegan's experimental cookery. It was greenish brown, like her pudding, and from time to time menacing bubbles broke the surface, expelling noxious vapors into the reeking air. It looked as if some enormous giant had blown his nose, discharging a boiling river of snot into the oozing bed.

"Right," said Checkers, looking worriedly over Boris's shoulder. "Er, you first."

Boris looked at him.

"You can swim better than me," said Checkers, though he had the grace to look a little shamefaced since this was a direct lie.

"I don't think we're meant to *swim* it," said Boris, shuddering. "Don't we have to wait for the ferryman?"

"The ferryman?" said Checkers. "You mean the grumpy old coot who's been in a bad mood since before the dawn of time?"

"That's the one," said Boris. "I think we're supposed to give him this"—and he jerked his head to dislodge the flowering branch, which, miraculously, was still tucked inside his collar. It straggled and drooped from his mouth, looking, if not dead, then at least deeply depressed.

"What are we supposed to do with that?" hissed Checkers. "Beat him with it?"

But before Boris could answer, there was a roar from far out on the river.

"You there—whoever you are—take not another step! This place belongs to the shades!"

Checkers shot backwards barking furiously. Boris quivered all over but stood his ground. He could dimly see, through the swirling mists, a black speck getting larger. Soon it was large enough for him to see that it was the figure of an ancient man, standing in a boat that seemed to have been sewn together from the skins of long-dead creatures and plying a pole through the turgid water. He was filthy and ragged, but his eyes burned like coals. The sound of wailing and lament accompanied him as he pressed his way through the foul slime, and, as Black Shuck had warned them, he did seem to be in a shockingly bad mood, though this was hardly surprising, Boris thought, if he had been stuck in this unpleasant working environment for all eternity.

"Who dares to trespass in the Groves of Doom?" he roared as he approached, and both dogs finally got a good look at him. In fact, a much better look than either of them wanted. He was as skinny as famine, and a tattered beard hung down to his bony knees, which protruded through the rags he was wearing. His fingers resembled the yellowing claws of a bird of prey, and deep in their bony sockets, his eyes glowed red. But he had a good, strong voice, like the bellows of a furnace.

"Speak!" he roared. "I am Charon, Ferryman to the Dead!"

Boris had forgotten what he wanted to say. But Checkers, who felt ashamed of his impulse to run, managed to say, in an unnaturally squeaky voice, "Can we have a lift?"

"A lift?" thundered Charon. "This isn't a taxi, you know."

"I can see that," said Checkers. "You haven't got one of those little signs on the top."

Boris found his voice and hushed Checkers as Charon glared down at them both. "If you please, sir," he said, "we have to get to the other side."

"Are either of you dead?" said the ferryman.

"I don't think so," said Boris.

"Then why do you want to cross the river of death? Don't you think I've got enough to do, ferrying all the lost souls, without wasting my time on the living?" And he gnashed the few teeth he had. **"No living soul may enter the abode of death,"** he said.

"But we've got to fight the Guardian," said Checkers, and added, "OW!" as Boris nudged him, hard.

Charon stared at them both, as if all three of them had lost their minds. Then he put back his head and laughed. It wasn't a good laugh. It sounded unpleasantly like the cries of the damned. Besides, they could see the rotting stumps of his teeth.

"Fight the Guardian?" he gurgled, slapping his bony thighs. **"Fight Cerberus? The monstrous keeper of the gates, who puts terror even into the bloodless shades? The brazen-voiced hound of Hades, whose three jaws are rabid with hunger and whose massive back writhes with fifty venomous snakes? Whose howl sends even the gods to destruction?"**

"That's the one," squeaked Checkers, behind Boris.

"We don't have to *fight* him," insisted Boris. "We just have to persuade him to come with us."

Charon laughed again. It didn't suit him, and he obviously didn't do it often. It made him cough, a long, horrible cough. When he had finished, he looked at them with his red eyes watering and said, **"Only once has any mortal successfully tackled the Guardian of the Dead. Hercules, king of heroes and a god among men, had, as his final and greatest labor, to bring the infernal hound to Eurystheus, king of Mycenae. But the monstrous beast so frightened Eurystheus that Hercules had to bring him back."** Charon shook his tattered beard, remembering. **"That was many millennia ago,"** he said, and sighed. **"Those were the days,"** he added.

Boris was feeling distinctly depressed. He began to wish that he hadn't run away from Mr. Finnegan. Even the dog pound was better than this. Checkers, however, was still making a show of bravado.

"So," he said. "Where does he hang out then—this monstrous hound?"

Charon laughed his wheezing, rattling laugh, which ended once again in a terrible cough.

"You want to take something for that," said Checkers.

"Forgive me," said Charon. **"It's the damp. It gets to your chest after the first few thousand years. The watchdog of the underworld lives in his den on the infernal side of the river."** He looked out across the sludgy water and both dogs followed his gaze, but the river was too wide for them to see the other side. **"He greets the souls I ferry across the water. Unfortunately for them, they are already dead, so they cannot die of fright. However, most of them do wish, at that point, that they had never been born. And he makes sure that none of them return from Hades."**

Charon looked at the two dogs quite kindly for a moment. **"I cannot ferry the living,"** he said. **"Return to your homes, small, hairy creatures. Forget this foolishness, and consider yourselves blessed."**

Dumbly, Boris turned to go. But Checkers blocked his way. "We can't go back now, boss," he said. "We've come this far. And what'll happen to the others if we give up? Besides, we don't know the way."

Boris knew this was true. But his heart was filled with dread, and his stomach felt as though he'd swallowed an enormous stone. He wanted nothing so much as to lie in his basket at home in front of a nice, cheerful fire. He wouldn't even mind the baby chewing his ears, he thought.

"Come on, boss," Checkers said sternly. "Chin up."

Boris made a feeble, protesting noise. "But we can't get across the river," he said, "if he won't take us."

"He will take us," Checkers said.

"No, he won't," said Boris.

"No, I won't," said Charon.

Checkers reached forward and nudged the limp branch in Boris's mouth. "Go on," he said. "Give it to him."

Boris stared at him dully until Checkers took the branch from him and proffered it to Charon.

"There you go, gov," said Checkers. "We've got something for you."

Charon looked taken aback. **"For me?"** he said. Then a look of something almost like awe crossed his ancient features. It seemed even less at home there than his laugh. He reached out trembling fingers toward the straggling branch. **"The Golden Bough,"** he said in a hushed voice. **"Its golden foliage illuminates the darkest shades of Tartarus. This is the vine from whose pliant green stems blossoms the breath of gold flowers, like stars to comfort lost souls through their endless night."**

Checkers and Boris looked in surprise at the limp twig. After all their adventures, it had only a few leaves clinging to it and a single flower.

"If you say so," said Checkers doubtfully, but Charon went on looking at the branch as if enchanted, delicately touching the flower. **"You bring me priceless treasure,"** he breathed.

"Really?" said Boris.

"I accept your payment. You may enter the boat."

"D'you hear that, boss?" said Checkers. "We're in!"

"Oh, dear," said Boris.

But Checkers had already leapt excitedly at the boat, which rocked wildly as he landed. Boris sighed and followed him rather less enthusiastically, shuddering as he was forced to wade into the slimy water. Charon, meanwhile, miraculously kept his balance, still gazing entranced at the weedy twig, then without a word he tucked it into the folds of his cloak and grasped the pole. As he pushed it, the boat moved slowly through the grimy foam, which seemed to gasp as they passed through it, so that a terrible stench went up. Grayish weeds clung to the water's edge as if hoping to drown themselves. Only Checkers's spirits seemed undampened.

"We're going to fight the Guardian!" he said. "Hurrah!"

Boris couldn't help feeling that Checkers might have missed the point, but he couldn't think of anything useful and positive to say, so he said nothing.

"Do you think we'll recognize him when we get there?" Checkers asked. Boris had opened his mouth to say that since they were talking about an enormous hound with three heads and serpents hissing along his spine, spotting him probably wouldn't be a problem, when suddenly there was a mind-mangling explosion of noise.

"Ah, the brazen-voiced hound of Hades," said Charon when the noise subsided and both dogs lay stunned in the bottom of the boat. **"He is ravenously hungry,"** he added, failing to cheer them up. **"It is a while since he has eaten. You wouldn't have any honey cakes steeped in soporific herbs, would you?"**

"Er, no," said Checkers, picking himself up. "We must've forgotten them."

"Pity," said Charon. **"He likes them."** For a while no one said anything else. Then, when the horrific noise blasted through the underworld again, he added conversationally, **"Now, where would you like me to drop you off?"**

About a million miles away, please, Boris thought, but his brain felt as though it had been hammered by giant bricks, and his jaw lolled around uselessly, incapable of speech.

"I'll tell you what I'll do," Charon went on when neither dog answered. **"I will not drop you at the mouth of his cavern, where one or more of his heads will instantaneously devour you. I will take you a little farther down the shore, where you may at least have time to plan your attack. Before he eats you."** And he turned the boat around midstream.

"Here you are," he said moments later. **"You'll excuse me if I don't stay and watch. I never could stand the sight of blood. I told Zeus that when he gave me the job, but does he ever listen?"**

"Come on, now. Out you get," he went on as neither dog moved but remained cringing in the boat, and he poked at them with the pole until, very reluctantly, they clambered out. **"I've got souls to ferry. It's been a pleasure meeting you, and I'm sorry our acquaintance has been so short. I hope your deaths are quick and easy—the long, lingering kind never did anyone any good."**

Both dogs watched dismally as Charon plied his boat away from them, rapidly fading from view. Checkers was the first to speak.

"Well, boss," he said in what was for him a whisper. "Looks like this is it."

And looking around the desolate shore, which was even more gloomy than the other side, Boris couldn't help but agree.

"We might as well get on with it," Checkers went on, beginning to walk along the shore. "Now, if he'd only make that horrible noise again, we could work out where he was."

"I don't think that'll be a problem," said Boris, who had just bumped into something unspeakably foul. The two dogs gazed at it in silent awe, wishing they'd left their sense of smell behind them. It was a huge mountain of dog poo, about five times larger than Gentleman Jim.

CHAPTER 25

The Chapter of
Being Foxed by a Wolf

Well, well, well," said Hati as Flo appeared in her line of vision. She slowed herself down to get a better look. She was so near to the moon now that a few bounds would take her to it, and she was confident enough to believe herself invincible. Besides, it wasn't every day that you got a chance to see the hounds of Hel roped together midair by what looked like a pink poodle who was having a *very* bad hair day. Hati licked her own shining fur as she waited. She herself was immaculately groomed.

"Why, Skoll," she said pleasantly. "How good of you to join me. And you've brought all your friends!"

"Stow it, Hati," Skoll growled. "Make yourself useful and get rid of Miss Freak Show here and set us free."

Hati laughed, a delicate, silvery laugh. "Of course," she said.

Flo eyed her warily. She could see, without being told, that Hati was in a different class from Skoll and his band, who were little better than a troop of hired thugs. For one thing, she was very beautiful—silver and gleaming in the moonlight. Her eyes too were a pale silver-gray, cold as moonshine, and her pelt looked polished. She emanated enough evil to make Henry look like a cuddly kitten. Flo licked her chops, which were suddenly very dry. She had come this far, she told herself. She was a very different dog from the creature who had slunk away from the croft, anxious only to preserve her own skin. She was a poodle with a mission.

"But you haven't introduced us," Hati said, and there were mingled cries of, "Get on with it!" and, "Don't talk to her—eat her!" Hati ignored them. "What is your name?" she asked Flo.

Flo tried to disentangle the thread of destiny from her teeth. "My name is Flo," she said. "And I'm here to stop you from devouring the moon!"

"Fascinating," said Hati. "I suppose you've stopped Skoll from devouring the sun? Yes," she said, glancing over to where the sun throbbed with orange light. "I can see you have. Well done," she said admiringly, and Flo felt a ridiculous urge to preen. "When exactly did you learn to fly?"

"I—what?" said Flo, distracted.

"She can't fly," said Garm, behind Flo. "Get that thread off her and she'll plummet to the earth!"

"Splat!" said another wolf.

"Pink poodle jam!" said a third.

"Gentlemen," said Hati reprovingly. "Let the lady speak."

Flo felt hypnotized by the intensity of Hati's gaze. "I didn't *learn* to fly," she said slowly. "It just kind of happened."

"Oh, dear," said Hati, and the wolves said, "Told you!"

"She can't do nothing without that thread!"

"Get it off her, Hati!" and so on.

Flo had enough sense to know when she was being undermined. It occurred to her suddenly that she didn't need the heckling wolves— they would only get in her way. Hati was enough to deal with on her own. The thread tugged gently against her teeth and she gave in to her impulse to bite.

" 'Ere, what's going on!" cried Skoll as the whole bundle of wolves drifted off.

"You can't do that!"

"Untie us!"

Hati watched with interest as they drifted a little way off, then hung around, hovering uselessly, like a malignant parcel in the sky.

"Ah, the female of the species," she said, smiling indulgently at Flo. "More deadly than the male, they say."

Flo said nothing. She still had the ball of thread in her mouth, leading her forward, and she was trying to work out how she would get it around Hati. She could attempt to throw it, of course, but that would mean letting go of the ball. And then she might indeed plummet to the earth.

Hati was prowling up and down now in midair. "Is that really the thread of destiny?" she inquired.

"It is," said Flo. "Perhaps you'd like a closer look?"

Hati gave a low, throaty chuckle. "Those tactics might work on Skoll," she said with a twitch of her tail. "But really, you'll have to come up with something much better for me."

Flo could see that she was right. As well as menace, Hati radiated a dark intelligence. She was formidable as well as beautiful. Flo realized with a pang that she did not have a clue what to do. She hoped the thread had some ideas of its own.

"Come on then," Hati said in her silky voice. "What's the plan?"

Flo hardly liked to say that there wasn't one. Not for the first time that day, she wished she'd stayed at home.

"Well," said Hati, with the briefest yawn. "I'd love to stay here chatting, but there's a moon to devour. And you don't seem to have many ideas, really, do you? I must say, I'm astonished at Skoll," she went on, "allowing himself to be defeated by you. Whoever does your hair, dear? Didn't you try biting them? I'd give them rabies if I were you. Or maybe you already did. That would explain the overall effect."

At last Flo had the glimmering of an idea. "It is true that I am not so beautifully groomed as you," she said humbly. "I don't know how you find the time to take care of such a magnificent pelt. The way you've got it combed over those bald patches is truly remarkable."

Hati stopped prowling. "What bald patches?" she said with a flick of her tail.

"Oh, you can hardly tell," Flo assured her. "It's just here and there that the scabs are showing through."

"Scabs?" said Hati with unutterable scorn. "Bald patches? I do not *have* scabs *or* bald patches. I am Hati the Magnificent, and my pelt is unsurpassed. No one, in all the nations of wolves, can compete with me. My beauty is unrivaled, and age has not dimmed a single hair."

"That's what they've told you, is it?" said Flo kindly. "Well, I suppose when you can't see yourself in a mirror . . ."

"I have no need of mirrors," said Hati, baring her magnificent teeth. "I am immortally, ineffably, *incandescently* beautiful and my pelt is as the Arctic snow or the long grass waving silver in the moonlight—"

"Except for the bald bits, where the scabs show through," said Flo.

For a moment she thought she had pushed Hati too far. Her lips curled right back from her terrible fangs, and the whites of her eyes shone. Flo was horribly aware that a fight to the death with Hati really wouldn't take too long. She watched, fascinated, as vanity vied with rage and finally won.

"*What* bald bits?" Hati said in a low voice but with terrible menace. Flo was ready for this question.

"Well, the one between your shoulder blades, for a start," she said, knowing that Hati couldn't see that particular spot, even though she twisted around, trying. "One on your neck." Hati jerked around the other way. "And then there's really quite a nasty one just at the base of your tail. Terribly scabby, that. Looks as though it might be infected."

Hati writhed around and around, chasing her tail. "I can't see anything," she said.

Quietly Flo crept up toward her, the thread of destiny forming itself into a great loop. Just as Hati turned another complete circle, she flung it toward her like a lasso. It dropped toward Hati's body, falling to her paws, and Flo held her breath. But at the last moment, Hati twisted in a lightning movement like a snake, caught it between her jaws and pulled. Before she understood what was happening, Flo shot forward in midair and the rope wound itself around her own paws. Taken by surprise, she hung, trussed like a chicken and upside down, between the paws of the great wolf. She could feel Hati's icy breath on her face.

"You didn't think I'd fall for that one, did you?" murmured Hati.

Flo wasn't going to give in that easily. She bucked in midair, thrashing wildly, but all her feet were tightly bound. As she reared and thrashed like a kite on a windy day while Hati remained quite still, she felt a dreadfully familiar sinking feeling.

I told you, she said in her mind to Jenny. I told you I wasn't the right dog for this job, and, It's all over now.

Hati lowered her muzzle toward Flo's throat, and Flo twisted again, trying to avoid the savage teeth. However hard she twisted and strained, she seemed only to draw closer to Hati. This is it, she thought, and her mind went blank with fear. She stopped struggling and lay quite limp and submissive with the great wolf towering over her.

"That's better," Hati said. "Now . . ." and Flo shut her eyes tightly, waiting for the terrible grip of Hati's teeth.

"Hmmm," said Hati, obviously enjoying the moment, and she gave Flo's throat a gentle squeeze with her teeth, so that Flo felt all the breath being pressed out of her, then slowly the grip relaxed.

"Well, little dog," she said, and her words dripped venom. "What shall I do with you now?" And she prodded Flo one way, then another.

Stop playing with me, Flo begged her silently. Get it over with.

"The thing is," Hati went on, "we need to get this thread off you and give it to someone who knows what they're doing with it," and she tugged at the cord around Flo's paws, but it only pulled tighter. "Someone who could devour the sun after all," she mused. "Now, who would that be? Oh, I know, yes."

Even with her eyes shut, Flo could feel the great wolf smiling.

"I know what to do," she said, and she lifted her muzzle and howled, a heart-stopping, chilling howl that froze Flo's blood. It was both a war cry and a lament and something else, like a summons. With a sickening pang, Flo realized what she was doing.

Hati was summoning Fenrir.

CHAPTER 26

Shot from the Sky

If I asked you where we were," said Gentleman Jim morosely, "would I regret it?"

No one responded. Orion was striding with determination through the Milky Way, and Pico was traveling beside him in silent awe, his mouth open as though trying to catch the stardust. Above them blazed the millions of stars in the galaxy. Pico had never seen anything so beautiful, so enchanting. For the first time in his life, he had the sense of vast, incomprehensible distances and scale. Out here, suns burst into life and galaxies bloomed. There was no longer any sense of up or down since in all directions the view was the same—millions and millions of stars suspended miraculously in the depths of infinity. Pico the two-pound Chihuahua should perhaps have been daunted by the sheer immensity of space, but he wasn't. He knew that he was little more than a transient particle, winking in and out of existence, but it didn't matter. Just to have taken part, for a moment, in the glory of the universe was enough. He felt part of the mystery and immensity of being. When a shooting star went past, his eyes filled with tears.

Gentleman Jim, on the other hand, merely felt sick. He felt as though his stomach was being used as a soccer ball by a particularly aggressive striker. He only opened his eyes intermittently to make sure that the earth, a blue and shining ball, was still there.

"Just tell me when it's all over," he said. Then he didn't say anything else in case he was suddenly sick and quantities of dog vomit would suddenly be released over unsuspecting people in the world below. Or wander off, out of the earth's gravitational field, and form a little colony of its own, gradually evolving into a civilization.

Gentleman Jim knew that the lack of gravity and air pressure must be getting to him since his thoughts were no longer making any sense. He kept his eyes and his mouth shut and concentrated on keeping the contents of his stomach firmly in place.

Then at last Orion, who for some hours had said nothing apart from, "Look—the Pleiades," or, "There goes Cassiopeia," said suddenly, "This is the place," and lurched forward horribly in midair.

Gentleman Jim said, *"Unnngghh,"* and Pico said, "Where?"

"There," said Orion. "You see below you the Plains of Darkness."

Gentleman Jim peeped quickly with one eye. He could see the earth and its oceans, rolling and lurching horribly far below, and there, in the center of a landmass, there was a great dark spot. He blinked and had a sudden, fleeting sense of inky blackness.

"This is where you must land," said Orion.

"Right," said Gentleman Jim. "Er, how, exactly?"

"I have a plan."

"Oh, good."

"I shall fire you from my bow."

Gentleman Jim managed a short, yelping laugh. "That was a joke, of course."

"No," said Orion. "You will be perfectly safe."

Gentleman Jim boggled. This was obviously some definition of *safe* he didn't understand. "When you said *plan*," he said, "I assumed you didn't mean us plummeting to the earth like stones. This isn't a suicide mission, you know."

"You will travel to the earth on a beam of light," said Orion. "It will disappear as you enter the realm of Hades, where most light cannot penetrate. But you shouldn't fall too far. And anyway, you should land in the soft earth of the asphodel fields."

Gentleman Jim was unconvinced. "When you say *should*—" he began, but Pico said, "How will you know the exact spot?"

"I cannot know the exact spot," replied Orion. "But I do know where the asphodel fields are. We are above them now."

Gentleman Jim looked down, but all he could see was a dark spot on the face of the earth, which was rather like the red spot on Jupiter. It seemed as though the earth, at that point, was covered by an impenetrable gloom.

"Ordinary mortals cannot see the abode of darkness," Orion said. "This is where all light ends."

Gentleman Jim rather wished that he couldn't see it either, but Orion was speaking again.

"I will draw as close as I can to the earth's atmosphere," he said. "Then I must fire my arrows of light and disappear. Dawn is approaching. The rest will be up to you."

"How will we know your soul?" asked Pico as Gentleman Jim struggled to assemble an argument. "Will it look like you?"

"All souls on the asphodel fields look alike," said Orion. "There are countless thousands of them, like points of light above the asphodels. They have forgotten who they are, you see."

"Well, that's helpful," muttered Gentleman Jim, who was really beginning to wish he'd stayed at home. In spite of Maureen. And the vet.

"You must call me by my name," Orion went on. "Each soul responds only to its own true name. As it responds, it will take on the semblance of its former self. Mine will be rather good-looking," he added modestly. "I had a noble face."

"Not the face of a murdering butcher, then?" asked Gentleman Jim, but Pico said, "What must we do with your soul when we have found it?"

"The river that runs through the asphodel fields is the Lethe, the river of forgetting," said Orion, ignoring Gentleman Jim. "The souls there are thirsty and drink continuously. But at its source, near where it joins the River Styx, there is a pool of remembering. You must lead my soul to this water and make it drink. It will not want to because to drink from this pool is to remember past pain and regret and to be subject to the torments of the Furies. That is why the souls drink continuously from the Lethe, so that they will not have to remember. But if you can get my soul to the pool and make it drink, then finally it may repent."

Gentleman Jim wasn't happy. He had almost lost count of the number of things he wasn't happy about. "Furies?" he said. "What's a Fury? You never mentioned them before."

"The Furies are terrible," Orion said with a kind of shudder. "Bat-winged, with snakes for hair and blood dripping from their eyes. They are the avengers of crime. Revenge, Rage and Jealousy—their faces are like dogs' faces, and their home is at the entrance to Tartarus, the deepest pit of Hades. They attack all those who repent with brass-studded scourges."

"Now, just hang on a minute," said Gentleman Jim, but Orion went on as if he hadn't heard.

"When my soul repents, you must not let it slip into despair," he said, "for the Furies can sniff despair at a distance of a thousand miles. It is like meat and drink to them. My soul must pass into the Elysian fields, not sink into the depths of Tartarus."

Gentleman Jim was speechless for almost a minute. There were many things he wanted to say, none of them polite. In the end, all he said was, "So, what will you be doing while we're fending off these bat-winged, dog-faced, snake-headed monsters? And how are we supposed to fend them off, if you don't mind me asking—before they kill us and eat us?"

"They will not harm dogs," Orion said distantly. "They look after dogs. It's a kind of hobby. My soul should fend them off if it does not slip into despair."

Gentleman Jim was not convinced. "There are a few too many *if*s and *should*s for my liking," he said. "I can't see that it'll work. And I'm not happy about this plummeting-through-the-air business. We could land anywhere. Hard."

Orion bowed his silvery head. "It is true." He sighed. "But the alternative is to stay with me here and travel the skies."

Gentleman Jim couldn't think of anything to say to this. He certainly didn't want to spend the rest of his days in space. But Pico said, "Well, there is nothing I should like better than to stay with you and roam the universe for the rest of eternity, or at least for as long as I have left to live. But if anything I can do will bring you peace, then I shall do it—even at the cost of my own life. We are not afraid to die."

"Speak for yourself," said Gentleman Jim, but Orion said, "Dear friend, your heart is great, though your body is so incredibly tiny. All the nations of the world should honor your name. But as for your death, it will not come to that, I hope."

"Good," said Gentleman Jim.

"See, we are approaching," Orion said. And indeed, all the time they had been talking, they had been drawing nearer to the region of darkness. Gentleman Jim made himself look, but it was impossible to see anything through the impenetrable gloom. Orion raised his bow, and a beam of light appeared in the center of it, poised and quivering. Then he released it, and it hurtled forward at breathtaking speed into the heart of the darkness and disappeared.

"I have fired many such arrows," said Orion, while Gentleman Jim was still gasping with horror. "In the hope that one should pierce the awful gloom somewhere near my soul and remind it of me. It does not seem that I have been successful. But if you will dare to ride the arrow, you will land in the asphodel fields."

"And break every bone in our bodies?" said Gentleman Jim. "No thanks."

"Do not worry, my friend," said Pico. "I will go first." And with Orion's help, he ascended to the center of the fiery bow.

"Pico," said Gentleman Jim urgently, "don't do it!"

But he was too late. Orion drew back the quivering bow, and with a cry that might have been, "Tally-hooooo!" the tiny dog hurtled forward through space, disappearing into the inky blackness below.

Gentleman Jim's ears and tail went down. His stomach appeared to be lodged in his throat.

"Well, my friend," Orion said. "Will you let your tiny friend face the realms of darkness alone?"

Many rude thoughts passed through Gentleman Jim's mind. But it was true that he couldn't leave Pico unaided. And he certainly didn't want to be stuck in space. With a sigh that shook him from his ears to his tail, he pointed his nose upward and began to ascend.

A beam of light passed beneath him as he took up a position in the center of Orion's bow. Gentleman Jim felt a tingling sensation pass from his nose to his paws. It was warm and oddly soothing, but Gentleman Jim did not feel comforted. Any moment now, he would plummet through the skies to an unknown destination.

"Ready?" asked Orion.

"No," said Gentleman Jim. He wanted to ask if there was any alternative or at least if Orion could fire his arrows more slowly, but his tongue appeared to be stuck to the roof of his mouth. He felt a sensation of quivering behind him as Orion tensed the bow and he shut his eyes tightly. He remembered something desperately important he had to say . . .

. . . but the next moment all the breath rushed out of his body and there was a terrible yowling noise in his ears. He wished that whatever it was would stop making it, then realized it was him, crying, "Noooooooooooooo!" as he hurtled forward through time and space.

He felt the first impact as he hit the earth's atmosphere. The beam of light disappeared, and he tumbled over and over, enveloped in darkness.

This is it now, he thought sadly as images from his past life flashed through his mind. Images of training Gordon, sniffing the scents of field and forest, capering joyfully with his friends and even of lying on a mound of squealing puppies and feeding from his mum flickered past as though on a fast-forwarded film. There was so much more capering and sniffing and feeding left to do, he reflected mournfully, but now he never would.

I wonder . . . , he thought, but he had no time to find out what he wondered because the next moment the ground, soft and springy with asphodels but not quite soft and springy enough, rushed up and hit him, driving all remaining thoughts out of his mind.

CHAPTER 27

Cerberus Wags His Tail

Boris and Checkers stared at the mountain of dog poo. Neither of them could think of a single thing to say.

"Blimey," Checkers managed at last. He was about to add that he wouldn't like to meet the dog that came from when he realized there was no point. They were about to meet him. In fact, they had to track him down and fight him.

"Boris," he whispered. "What are we going to do?"

Boris's eyes were watering freely. This had to be the stench Black Shuck had talked about—the one that passed all understanding. He stayed where he was, with his tail curled between his legs and his nose pressed to the ground, trying not to breathe. He felt as though he was in a very bad dream, and if he stayed very still and didn't do anything unexpected, he might just be able to wake up.

"Boris," Checkers whispered again. "We have to do something."

Boris didn't want to do anything. Over the years he had perfected the art of doing nothing, and it had always served him well. Sometimes he experienced the urge to do something, but if he waited, it always went away again. Now he didn't have to wait. The urge to do anything at all had completely left.

Very unusually, Checkers was also standing still, but he was quivering all over. "Boris," he said again, "we have to find him—" but he was cut short by the deafening blast that was Cerberus's cry.

All around the plains of hell it rolled, churning the River of Woe, the River of Fire and the River of Wailing. The Gates of Hades vibrated in the blast, and the River Styx boiled and churned in its bed. Gorgons, Harpies and Furies flapped their wings and rose, shrieking, into the air. Boris's heart did a little pirouette and his lungs clapped. His eyes felt as though they were leaking out of his ears.

"I guess we won't have to look too hard," Checkers said as the dreadful noise finally died away.

Boris was dully astonished that Checkers was still able to speak. His own voice rattled feebly in his throat, then died away.

"Best get a move on," Checkers was saying, and he stepped forward with a determined air into the cave.

Boris had no choice but to follow Checkers. If he had known the way out at this point, he might well have taken it, even if it had involved swimming the dreadful Styx. But he didn't know the way, and he didn't fancy wandering around the underworld on his own. Besides, he had to look after Checkers. All that was left of him that was recognizably Boris was the spark of loyalty that meant he could never leave his friend alone. Though he wished, very much, that his friend wasn't such a complete and utter lunatic.

"Come on, Boris!" urged Checkers. "We've got a monster to fight!"

Boris didn't even have the heart to contradict Checkers. Cerberus's howl had driven all thoughts of peaceful negotiation out of his mind. Very reluctantly he took a step forward and then another one into the hollow mouth of the cavern. His legs felt like wool and the ground beneath his feet crunched unpleasantly. He stepped forward again and crunched some more. When he looked down, he couldn't see much in the horrid gloom, but then he realized, with a pang of horror, that he was stepping on bones. Big bones and little bones, scattered all over the floor of the cave. There were skulls too, grinning unpleasantly up at them as if to say, *You'll look like this soon.*

"Can't be far now," said Checkers.

Boris wondered why his friend wasn't more frightened. Or depressed. That was how he felt—terrified and depressed in equal measure. But Checkers was trotting forward as though he didn't know what fear meant. As though he was just going to meet his friends on the croft, on one of those happy days that now seemed so long ago.

"When we get up to him," Checkers was saying, "you'll have to attract his attention."

Boris had no desire at all to attract the attention of the monstrous, three-headed hound. He looked at Checkers in dismay. There was not even a trace of the nervousness Boris had seen in him before, though he was trotting to certain death. His tail was up and his ears pricked and alert. What's got into you? Boris thought.

What had got into Checkers was the lust for battle. He could feel the ancient call of it, surging through his veins. *At last, at last!* it was calling. He felt as though all his life, he had been preparing for one great fight. As though all the generations of fighting dogs that had sired him were cheering him on now, and that every little spark that had driven him to tackle ordinary enemies such as cats and other dogs and the settee was culminating in a fiery urge now to fight whatever the cost. He didn't know that he would win and he didn't even care. The lust for blood, even his own blood, had come upon him.

"Checkers," said Boris.

"What is it, boss?"

"I can't remember why we're doing this—can you?"

"Doing this? Well, of course I can. We have to, don't we? Because if we don't, then . . . And besides, we, well, in any case, we're here now, aren't we, so—"

Suddenly he tripped over something. Somehow he managed to restrain himself from barking fiercely. Boris bumped into him from behind, then they both stood and considered the thing that Checkers had fallen over. It was long, thick and scaly, like an enormous snake, but it culminated in a point, and as the two friends looked at it, unnerved, it twitched. Swiftly they dodged away as it made a great, powerful movement from side to side. It was a tail, though it was like no tail of any beast they had encountered before. It was ridged along its upper surface into scaly spines, and as they scrambled backward to avoid it, it swung itself powerfully against the walls of the cave. The cave walls shook, and the reverberations were felt throughout the underworld.

Cerberus was wagging his tail.

CHAPTER 28

The Chapter of
Facing an Invincible Foe

FEN-RIR!" howled Hati, and the parcel of wolves, bobbing by on the wind, joined in. "Fenrir, Fenrir, Fenrir!" they chanted.

Nothing happened. Flo, who was cowering beneath Hati, remembering the terrible howl she had heard on the croft, managed to look up and around. No one was there.

"FEN-RII-IR!" howled Hati again, and once more the parcel of wolves joined in. But there was no reply.

Trembling and desperate as Flo was, she felt a faint, encouraging spark. She even managed a smile. "Well—" she said, and she was about to make a witty comment to the effect that some people were never around when you needed them when suddenly, the universe coughed.

It coughed and spat out an enormous wolf, right next to Flo.

His eyes were like blowtorches and his teeth, bloody fangs. From his massive jaws dripped an electric drool. Flo tried urgently to pass out.

YOU CALLED? he said in an enormous voice, and it was Hati's turn to smile.

"Fenrir," she said. "This poodle has been playing games with destiny."

HAS SHE? boomed Fenrir, turning his scorching glare on Flo. WHAT HAVE YOU BEEN UP TO? he said.

"M-me?" said Flo weakly, somewhat surprised that she could speak at all. "N-nothing."

"She tricked Skoll," said Hati venomously. "She bound him and his gang with the thread of destiny and prevented him from devouring the sun!"

Tattletale, thought Flo, wondering why her brain wanted to make flippant comments, now of all times.

DID SHE? said Fenrir with a low growl that rumbled around the sky like thunder.

"She *tried* to bind me," Hati continued, adding with a scornful flick of her tail, "as if!"

INDEED? said Fenrir, prowling dangerously close to Flo. DO NOT IMAGINE THAT YOU CAN BIND ME, LITTLE DOG. NOT EVEN THE GODS COULD BIND ME. THEY HAD TO FORGE A SPECIAL CHAIN FROM THE FOOTFALL OF A CAT, THE SPITTLE OF A BIRD, THE BREATH OF A FISH, A WOMAN'S BEARD, THE SINEWS OF A BEAR AND THE ROOTS OF A MOUNTAIN. AND SEE—THAT CHAIN IS BROKEN!

Flo peeped around him and could see that indeed there was the broken end of a chain dangling from his neck.

"Go, Fenrir!" shouted the parcel of wolves, and Hati smiled exultantly.

"The-chain-that-may-not-be-broken *is* broken!" she said. "Now nothing can stop us! Rip out her throat, Fenrir, then we can divide her into pieces and share the spoils. Then you can devour the sun and put right the damage that has been done."

RIGHT, growled Fenrir, and he moved toward Flo.

A terrible trembling traveled along Flo's spine from her tail and rattled her teeth. "I—I—I w-wouldn't d-d-do that if I were you," she managed to say.

NO? said Fenrir, pretending to be surprised. WHY NOT?

Flo couldn't think of a single reason that Fenrir would be likely to accept. *Because I really don't want you to* was hardly likely to work. Fenrir grinned, a horrible, ravening grin. He opened his jaws so wide that Flo could only see the horrifying darkness within. Then he snapped them shut on the thread of destiny around Flo's paws.

I MIGHT NEED THIS, he said, TO LOOP AROUND THE SUN. BEFORE I SWALLOW IT. WHOLE.

Flo clung desperately to the thread. "You can't," she said, playing for time, though she hardly knew why.

CAN'T WHAT?

"Can't swallow the sun. How could you? No dog can."

Hati and Fenrir laughed, but not in a good way.

I AM NO ORDINARY DOG, said Fenrir. I COULD SWAL-LOW THE WHOLE UNIVERSE IF I CHOSE. And he pulled Flo nearer as if he would swallow her too in a single bite.

"Bet you couldn't," she said, pulling away.

DO YOU DARE DOUBT ME? said Fenrir with an ominous growl.

"I'm just saying—that's all," quavered Flo. "You boys are all the same—always got to show off—*I swallowed the sun today. Well, I swallowed a whole universe.* You've always got to boast about something."

Flo never understood how she dared to say all this. It must have been the knowledge of certain death that was prompting her into uncharacteristic boldness.

Fenrir howled. It was a long, appalling howl of destruction and ravening rage. Flo almost dropped the thread. She was rattling like a set of castanets. *This is it now,* she thought. The choice between the jaws of the wolf and a fall through infinite space.

DO YOU DARE TO DOUBT ME? Fenrir howled very loudly.

"Well, show me, then," squeaked Flo.

Hati snorted in contempt. "Do not let her bait you!" she snarled, baring all her horrible fangs. "You are worse than Skoll's rabble! Destroy her now!"

Fenrir paused, his jaws gaping wide. Flo could see that he was torn by the need to demonstrate his prowess and the desire to rip her apart. For a second that stretched on to infinity, Flo could neither speak nor move but only stare at him like a terrified rabbit in the path of a train.

Fenrir opened his massive jaws. And he went on opening them, wider and wider, until Flo could see at last how a single wolf might be able to swallow the sun, the moon, and all the stars. They went wider and wider still, and the sound that came out of them was indescribable. It was like the roaring and howling of many beasts, the screeching of parrots, the yowling of a thousand cats being pushed through a cheese grater. There was thunder and hurricanes and erupting volcanoes in it, and all around Fenrir the skies flashed in torment. Even Hati thrashed around in agony, and the tied-up wolves yowled and gibbered. Flo felt her eyes rolling back in her skull, her brain clawing its way out of her ears. She lost all sense of where and what and who she was, only that somehow she had to stop that horrifying noise.

Then Fenrir snapped the thread from Flo's paws. He swallowed it and went on swallowing, more and more thread disappearing into his throat like the longest snake in the world. He tore at the thread that bound the wolves and swallowed that too, and in their haste to get away from him, the parcel of wolves began to plummet from the sky.

All this Flo saw in a lightning flash before she too plummeted earthward with a terrified wail.

CHAPTER 29

A Chapter of Souls

From a long, long way off, Gentleman Jim heard something calling his name.

Gordon, he thought, and felt a distant impulse to move. It traveled all the way from his spine to his brain before fizzling out.

"Gentleman Jim, open your eyes," the voice said, and something wet nudged him.

Impossible, he thought. *I'm obviously dead.* He ignored the voice, assuming that whatever it was would sooner or later realize he was dead and leave him alone.

But the thing, whatever it was, tugged his ear.

With a momentous effort of will, Gentleman Jim forced one eyelid up. He was staring at a greenish, tangled plant. So ugly and contorted was it that it hardly deserved the name "flower." A sickening grayish green with tangled spikes rather than petals, it emitted the kind of vapor that made you wish you had lost your sense of smell, and an air of corruption, obscenely malign.

"Gentleman Jim," it said.

Gentleman Jim wasn't having it. If there was one thing worse, he thought, than hurtling through impenetrable darkness, it was landing on a bed of grotesque, talking flowers that stank like satanic cabbage.

"Gentleman Jim," persisted the horrid bloom, "you have to wake up! It's me—Pico!"

Gentleman Jim wrenched both eyes open at this. And there was Pico, standing some way beneath the tangled foliage that looked as though someone had remade the TV show *Gardeners' World* into a horror film.

"P—" he said.

"It's all right," Pico told him. "We've landed, and we're safe!"

There was that word again—*safe*. Just didn't seem to mean what he'd always thought it meant. Must look it up in the dictionary, he thought.

"—ico," he said.

"That's right," said Pico. "We've made it. We've landed in the asphodel fields!"

Gentleman Jim's senses were finally relaying messages to his brain, but he really wished they weren't. He was surrounded by appalling flowers that seemed to be releasing a sticky fluid onto his pelt, and the stench was nauseating. With a huge effort he lifted his head. It wobbled dangerously on his shoulders for a moment, causing the world around him to lurch and rock unpleasantly, then it steadied itself, and he drew in his breath.

All around him, as far as his eyes could see (which wasn't too far, given the unnatural gloom), the ground was carpeted by the tortured and sickening flowers that emitted a greenish glow. Hovering above them, rising and falling gently, were thousands of points of light, in all the colors Gentleman Jim could name, and several that he couldn't. They hung poised above the asphodels, then delicately descended, as though *feeding* from them, and rose again, fluttering, this time with a greenish energy.

"Wow," said Gentleman Jim, and what he meant was, These must be all the souls of all the men, women and children that ever lived, apart from the heroes, of course, and those people who managed to be exceptionally bad. They look so beautiful, hovering above those nasty flowers, in all those different, iridescent colors—I never imagined there could be so many—but what are they doing landing on those hideous blooms? They seem to be taking something from them, but when they rise again, they look different somehow, as though contaminated by those unnatural plants—yes—there goes another one, lowering itself to a monstrous bud, and now as it rises, it has lost something of its beauty and uniqueness.

"Let me see," said Pico, jumping up and down impatiently. So Gentleman Jim, holding his breath, lowered his nose so that the tiny dog could clamber up it, and when Pico was settled on his neck, he began the difficult job of getting up. His spine seemed to have buckled, his knees were locked into position and his hips had given up. But finally, on the fourth or fifth attempt, he managed it, and both dogs gazed in amazement at the scene around them. It had an eerie, enchanting beauty. The points of light rose and fell, rose and fell as though in an hypnotic dance. Forgetful of time and urgency, Gentleman Jim and Pico stood and stared.

"Well," whispered Gentleman Jim finally, and Pico murmured, "Yes," and then both were silent again, for it seemed a violation to speak aloud.

"Well," said Gentleman Jim again, and Pico said, "Yes?" more loudly this time, but neither of them said anything else. The truth was that they both felt unnerved. Then, after a pause that seemed to go on forever, Gentleman Jim said, "We'd better get going, I suppose."

"Yes," said Pico, and cautiously, as though the asphodels might try to trip him up or bite, Gentleman Jim stepped forward through the tangled plants. The points of light moved away from them as they approached, then closed behind them quite silently. Despite all the movement, the overall impression was one of stillness.

"Do you suppose they can see us?" whispered Pico.

"I don't know," said Gentleman Jim in the same hushed tone.

"How do we know which one's Orion?" he said after another silence.

"We have to call out his name, remember?" said Pico.

"Oh yes," said Gentleman Jim. "Well, go on, then."

Pico said nothing. He was resisting the urge to snap as a bluish light drifted toward him like a beautiful insect. "Are these really souls?" he said.

"That's what the man said," replied Gentleman Jim, then he jumped as one brushed his flank and he felt a small current of electricity. He too was resisting the urge to snap. Mustn't swallow the souls, he told himself.

"Orion?" said Pico hesitantly to a greenish point of light. He felt rather foolish addressing it, but it just drifted past. "Orion?" he said again, to a yellow light this time.

"This is hopeless," said Gentleman Jim as Pico called Orion's name a third time. "Have you seen how many there are?"

The asphodel fields seemed to stretch on forever, with the myriad points of light hovering above them.

"Well, it's what we have to do," responded Pico. "Orion?" he said again to a red glow.

"It's ridiculous," said Gentleman Jim. "Do we have to ask every single one?"

"That's what he said," replied Pico, though he too was feeling rather discouraged. The points of light seemed to be multiplying if anything and swirled around like multicolored snowflakes.

"Did he say we'd be stuck here for the rest of eternity?" said Gentleman Jim. "Oh, and did he say how we get out again? No? Thought not."

Pico felt suddenly cross. Largely because it was true that Orion hadn't told them how they would get out. "We would get on better if we both called out his name," he said sternly.

Gentleman Jim muttered something to the effect that if anyone had told him that morning that he would be spending the rest of his day in the underworld, talking to points of light, he would have bitten them. Then he lifted his voice suddenly and bellowed, "OR-I-ON!" scattering the points of light to left and right.

"Good grief!" said Pico, who had almost fallen off Gentleman Jim's neck.

"Well, we weren't getting very far your way," said Gentleman Jim, and he bellowed again, "OR-I-ON!"

The points of light quivered all around them, then slowly settled again.

"Go on then, you try," said Gentleman Jim.

Pico, as you know, had a very loud voice. Louder even than Gentleman Jim's. He didn't like using it in this strange, quiet place—it seemed like sacrilege. But he could see the sense in what Gentleman Jim said. So he summoned all his strength, and took a great breath, and he too bellowed the name of the mighty hunter, only it came out like this:

"WOOF!"

"OR-I-ON!" bawled Gentleman Jim.

"WOOF!" bellowed Pico, and together they stepped through the underworld, making enough noise to wake the dead.

And finally, when they were almost hoarse, another voice spoke.

"WHO IS IT THAT WAKES ME FROM MY PEACEFUL DREAM?" it said.

Gentleman Jim spun around so fast that Pico almost fell from his neck. There before them a light of the palest blue-green was expanding rapidly and taking on contours.

Gentleman Jim and Pico could see that the form of a man was taking shape. He was sitting on a grassy verge, with his feet buried in asphodels and his chin propped up on his hand as though he was deep in thought. He was almost, but not quite, transparent, which made him difficult to see, apart from his eyes, which still glowed with the pale blue-green light.

"Orion!" said Gentleman Jim, for indeed the transparent, faintly glowing figure was recognizably the same as the giant star man in the sky.

"I know that name," the figure said, more quietly this time. "But I do not know where from."

Gentleman Jim was speechless for a moment, but Pico said, "It is your name. Do you not remember it?"

"My name?" the figure said, looking at them both in a puzzled kind of way and speaking as though in a dream. "Who are you, who claim to know my name?"

"My name is Pico," said Pico, "and this is my friend, Gentleman Jim. We have been sent to return you to your rightful place."

The shining eyes glimmered at Pico for a moment. "I am here," he said unnecessarily. "I have always been here. This is where I am."

"But you haven't always been here," said Pico earnestly. "Do you not remember that you were a mighty hunter, in the days when the earth was young, and all the stars more brilliant than they are today, and the morning breeze fragrant with all the scents of nature? You were the greatest hunter the world has ever known, but Gaia the angry goddess sent a scorpion to kill you—remember?"

Orion glimmered some more. His eyes gazed into the distance, as though looking for something very far away and long ago. The two dogs waited eagerly.

"No," he said at last, and their ears went down. "I remember nothing."

Gentleman Jim had felt quite hopeful when they had first met Orion, but now his hope began to fade. He could sense a massive apathy and inertia in the figure before him.

"You made a boast, remember," he said sternly, "that you could kill any animal on the face of the earth. That was why Gaia sent the scorpion."

Orion looked at him with a concerned expression, and for a moment Gentleman Jim thought he had struck home, but all Orion said was, "What was your name again?"

"Hopeless," said Gentleman Jim to Pico, then, more loudly, "It is time for you to leave the asphodel fields."

Orion's soul looked at him as though from a vast distance. "Hopeless," he said wonderingly. "What kind of a name is that?"

"No, *I'm* not hopeless," began Gentleman Jim crossly, but Pico said, "If you please, sir, we have been sent by your great counterpart in the sky to release you from the asphodel fields."

Even sitting down, Orion was an impressive size. Not as big as the constellation, of course, but still, much bigger than your average man. A spark of interest gleamed in his eyes for a moment, then faded, as though he was sinking back into his dream.

"Why?" he said in his faraway voice, and Gentleman Jim snorted with impatience. "It's no use trying to explain," he said to Pico. "We have to get him out of here whether he wants to or not. You have to come with us," he said to Orion.

Orion glimmered at him again, then he looked at Pico. "Why does Hopeless keep saying that?" he said.

"You have to leave this place and go to the Elysian fields," said Gentleman Jim, feeling as though he was losing track. "To repay your debt to animal kind."

Orion stared at him. "What debt?" he said.

Pico tugged at Gentleman Jim's ear. "This isn't working," he said. "He can't remember anything. We have to get him to drink from that pool to make him remember."

"Who are you?" said Orion. "And who am I?"

"Your name is Orion, mightiest of hunters," said Pico. "You have been too long in the place of forgetting. It is time for you to remember."

The shadowy figure crinkled his transparent brow. "What for?" he said.

"So that you can return to your former glory," said the little dog, looking up at him earnestly. "So that you can undo the curse of the gods and help to save mankind. Don't you want to remember?"

Orion looked at him blankly. "Remember what?"

"Whatever it is you have forgotten."

"I don't *think* so," said Orion dubiously. "Why should I, when I can forget?"

There didn't seem to be an answer to that one, but Gentleman Jim tried again. "Look, Orion—" he said.

"What is that name?" said Orion.

"Don't start that again," said Gentleman Jim. "Why don't you come with us for a little walk? A change of scenery, eh? Do you good."

"Why?" said Orion. "My place is here—where I can drink from the sacred river and feed from the wondrous nectar of these flowers. It is peaceful here," he said, looking around for the first time. "Why should I want to leave? And anyway, who are you?"

Gentleman Jim groaned, but Pico changed tack. "Are you often thirsty?" he asked.

"All the time," replied Orion promptly. "That is why I stay here, by the river."

He gestured behind him, and the two dogs saw that there was indeed a river, so wide and slow-moving that it looked like a dark, glittering lake.

"The River Lethe," murmured Pico, captivated by the noiseless flow, which was rather hypnotic.

But Gentleman Jim said, "We know of a place where you can drink, and the water is much, much nicer than here. Don't we, Pico?"

"Wondrously nice," said Pico as Gentleman Jim nudged him. "It surpasses the water of this river as the light of the sun surpasses the moon's."

For the first time, Orion looked interested. "Nicer than here?" he said, as if he didn't believe them.

"Much," said Pico firmly. "That's why no one wants you to drink from it. That's why they've all left you here."

Orion looked at them doubtfully. "Who has left me?" he said.

"Everyone," said Gentleman Jim. "Did you never wonder why you were alone?"

"No," said Orion, considerably surprised. "Should I not be?"

"Definitely not," said Gentleman Jim. "They've all gone off to the party and left you here on your own. Typical, I call it."

Now Orion just looked confused. "But who—" he began.

"Never you mind," said Gentleman Jim reassuringly. "Don't worry your head about it. Some people get the best water; others have to make do. I can see you're not a person who minds other folks doing better than him, and that's good. We can't always be first, that's what I say. Someone has to make do with second best. . . ."

Orion rose to his considerable height. "I have no interest in *second best*," he said, with a sudden energy, and both dogs could see that in life, he would have been fearless and arrogant. "Show me this water," he said.

Pico and Gentleman Jim exchanged glances. The plan, such as it was, was working. Their only problem was that they didn't actually know where the pool was. *At the source of the River Lethe,* the starry Orion had said, *near where it joins the River Styx.* Well, of course, they didn't know where that was, but they did know how to follow the river upstream, where hopefully it would join the other river and form a pool. So they set off along the riverbank, where the asphodels nodded and sighed out their reeking breath across the water, and Orion strode with them, seeming almost energized. And behind Orion streamed thousands of points of light, but what they were, the two dogs didn't know, and they didn't ask, so intent were they on fulfilling their task.

Fortunately, in the underworld, neither time nor distance operates as we know it. The thickly carpeted ground flew beneath Gentleman Jim's paws, the points of light streamed past and before long the River Lethe was narrowing in its bed, and they could hear the noise of another river, flowing much faster and more noisily.

"We're getting there," Pico said in excitement from between Gentleman Jim's shoulders. "Now all we have to do is find the pool and get him to drink."

"When you say *all*," said Gentleman Jim, but he was interrupted by a crashing, rumbling, tumbling noise. One river was pouring into the other by means of a great waterfall, and the waterfall ended in a kind of pool.

"This must be it," said Pico, staring down over the edge between Gentleman Jim's ears.

"He can't go down there," said Gentleman Jim, scandalized. "He'll kill himself. Er, oh," he ended, having realized his mistake.

"Is this the place?" said Orion.

Both dogs looked over the edge. The water looked black and bitter, foaming with a greenish foam. It did not look in any way inviting. But it was the only pool.

"Er," said Gentleman Jim, but Pico said, "This is the place, yes."

"With the better water?" asked Orion.

"Definitely," Pico said.

Orion looked at the churning sludge. "What does Hopeless say?" he asked.

Gentleman Jim glared at him. "Drink," he said.

Orion looked as doubtful as he possibly could. Then he said, "I know that you would not try to deceive me, for you are honorable dogs," and both Gentleman Jim and Pico had the grace to look a little ashamed. "Will you not drink with me?" Orion said.

Pico began to say that they would love to but it would be much harder for them to get down to the pool, but Gentleman Jim interrupted him. "This water is not for dogs," he said firmly.

"I see," Orion said. "Then I have no way of knowing that what you say is true."

Gentleman Jim and Pico looked at each other in despair. This wasn't going to be as easy as they had thought. Then Orion made a movement as though he would leave, but Gentleman Jim stood in front of him.

"Look," he said. "What harm can it do? You're already dead. What have you got to lose?"

"I don't know," said Orion. "Why don't you tell me?"

"If I can get behind him," said Gentleman Jim in an aside to Pico, "maybe I can push."

But Pico was gazing up at Orion. "You are right, of course," he said. "If you are afraid, we had better return."

Orion lifted his transparent chin. "I am not afraid," he said.

"We can offer no guarantees, no assurances," Pico said. "As far as we *believe*, that is the water that will make you remember everything about yourself and why you are here. But we do not *know* because we have not drunk it. If you prefer to forget, that is your right. We do not know what will happen if you drink."

Gentleman Jim held his breath. Pico had told the exact truth. That was a novel approach, he thought. He eyed Orion warily. *You can bring a soul to water, but you can't make it drink,* he thought.

Orion seemed to be assessing them both from a vast distance.

"You are right," he said at last. "It is good that you have given up your foolish attempts to deceive me. And you are right when you say I have nothing to lose. I will try the water," he said, and before their eyes he returned to his former shape of a glowing light and disappeared over the edge of the ravine.

Gentleman Jim and Pico rushed to the edge. They saw Orion's light glimmering over the surface of the water, hovering like a large, pale insect. Then suddenly it dipped downward and, just as suddenly, disappeared.

"Now what?" whispered Gentleman Jim, but Pico could find nothing to say. It was as if the water had swallowed Orion's soul.

"Where's he gone?" said Gentleman Jim, and both dogs gazed in consternation over the edge.

The water below them began to churn more rapidly than before. It was almost as though it was boiling. The surface of it bulged for a moment, then sank down again.

"Orion?" called Pico. "Or-i-on!"

The water bulged again, and bubbles broke the surface.

"GO AWAY!" said a voice drenched in misery. In agitation, Gentleman Jim ran along the edge of the ravine one way and Pico the other. The surface of the water bulged into the shape of an enormous man, but rapidly the shape disappeared.

Gentleman Jim licked his lips. "Orion?" he began.

"DON'T LOOK AT ME!" cried the anguished soul, and he disappeared beneath the surface of the water again.

Gentleman Jim and Pico looked at each other in dismay. "Orion, you have to come out," said Pico, but Orion only howled again.

"I CAN NEVER COME OUT!" he cried. "I DESERVE ONLY TO DROWN!"

"Now, look here," said Gentleman Jim. "There's no use wallowing around! You have to come out and face up to what you did—"

He was cut off by a terrible howl. "I CAN NEVER FACE UP TO THIS!" cried Orion. "IT IS MONSTROUS, HORRIBLE! I DESERVE ONLY TO DIE!"

And as this howl faded, it was taken up by another, far more terrible and unearthly. A vengeful, hate-ridden shriek, as if all the bad thoughts in the world had been condensed into a single cry, punctuated only by the rapid beating of wings.

Gentleman Jim and Pico stared at each other, remembering suddenly, with horrible clarity, what the starry Orion had said.

The Furies were coming.

CHAPTER 30

The Monster's Tail

Course, it might mean," Checkers pointed out, "that he's in a good mood."

Boris said nothing. He was too busy trying to dodge the shower of stones and skulls dislodged from the walls and roof of the cave. The tail had settled down and was thumping erratically on the floor of the cave. Every time it thumped, the cave quivered, and Boris was drawing unpleasant conclusions about the size of the beast attached to it.

"If we could get right up to him," Checkers said, "we could have a sniff at his bum."

Boris's look said it all.

Dogs can tell a great deal by sniffing the bums of other dogs. They can tell what mood they're in, hostile or friendly, how well they fight, what they've eaten recently and so on. Normally, sniffing the rear end of another dog was a good first step to establishing a relationship, but when it came to the hound of Hades, Boris was unsurprisingly reluctant. He thought that there must be a better plan somehow, if only he could think of it.

The tail was lifting itself now and thumping downward, once, twice, then, on the third time, it remained lifted.

The two friends waited. Nothing happened. The dreadful thumping was replaced by a terrible silence.

"Right," said Checkers. "I'm going in."

And before Boris could shout, "Wait!" or, "Don't do it, Checkers!" or, "What! Are you nuts?" Checkers was running under the tail.

"Checkers, don't!" Boris called at last, in a strangled bark. "It's a trick!"

But Checkers went on bounding forward, following the length of the enormous tail.

Boris groaned aloud. He didn't even bother about being quiet. Cerberus knew they were there, he was quite sure about that, and Checkers was bounding forward to certain death. Which meant that he, Boris, had to bound after him.

With a hopelessness born of utter despair, Boris plodded after Checkers. He tried to stay to one side of the mammoth append-age, which was twitching evilly above him, but every time he tried to dodge it, it shifted position slightly, just as if it were tracking his every move. As in fact it was, Boris realized, and he would have had a sinking feeling, except that there was nowhere further for his spirits to sink.

Above him, the tail was growing in size and thickness, and Boris knew they must be reaching its horrid end.

"It's here!" Checkers shouted excitedly. "I can see it now! It's a big one—I can smell it from here! I'll just see if I can get my nose tucked right in—"

"Checkers, no!" panted Boris, but he was too late. Checkers had clambered onto a rocky ledge and thrust his nose upward, right under the root of the tail.

At that precise moment, two things happened. Checkers stag-gered backward, reeling from the smell, and the tail coiled itself inward with lightning speed. Boris barely had time to flatten himself against the sides of the cave before it swept past him, wrapping it-self around and around Checkers. And as soon as it had got him, it began thrashing around, thumping him against the walls, ceiling and floor. Boris stared aghast as Checkers was butted into the wall barely a foot away and the cave shook with the force of the blow.

"Gnnngggh!" said Checkers, landing again next to Boris.

"Ppphhhnnngg!" he said as the great tail drove him powerfully into a nearby rock, and, *"Ggglllrrrkkk!"* as he pounded the wall again.

"Checkers!" cried Boris in distress, clambering uselessly after his friend. He realized that Checkers was trying to tell him something, but he was greatly hampered by being squeezed to death. Checkers struggled valiantly in the coils of the tail, and Boris ran from side to side after him, trying to keep up.

At last, Checkers got his muzzle free. He shouted something at Boris, but Boris couldn't hear and was finding it hard to concentrate, what with the cave falling in all around him and the imminence of death.

"What?" he cried uselessly. "What did you say?"

The great tail stopped thumping briefly as Boris scrambled over fallen rocks to get to his friend. Checkers was a sorry sight. His ear was bleeding and both eyes were swelling up.

"I think I've got him cornered," he managed to say as Boris reached him. "Now all we've got to do is—"

But the tail lifted again before he could finish the sentence, swinging him high into the air before battering him into the ground.

Boris growled and gnashed at the tail, trying to bite it, but it was too fast for him. All his life things had been too fast for Boris, and now his lack of speed was going to prove fatal to his best friend.

"Boris," Checkers said as he hit the ground again and lay still for a moment. "Boris, I think I'm done for."

"Don't say that!" panted Boris.

"It's true," moaned Checkers. "I can't fight this one. You'll have to fight him for me."

"Me?" gasped Boris as the great tail swung Checkers up again. "I'm no fighter, Checkers. I've never fought another dog in the whole of my life."

"Well—now's—your—chance!" panted Checkers, and with each word the monstrous tail pounded him into the rocks.

Boris wanted very much to protest. He wanted to say that he had never felt the urge to fight; he just wasn't that kind of dog. And if he was going to start a fight for the first time ever, it wouldn't be with the hound of Hades, whose mounds of poo were five times larger than Gentleman Jim. He wanted to say that he wished he'd stayed in bed that morning, or let Mr. Finnegan take him to the dog pound, but everything he wanted to say caught suddenly in the back of his throat. A surge of rage the like of which he had never experienced before boiled up in him. It was rage at all the injustice he had ever experienced, rage at his owners and their fiendish infant, but most of all, it was rage at the diabolical hound that was pounding his best friend into a pulp. Suddenly he knew himself to be what Jenny had said he was, the guardian and protector of Checkers. Rage coursed through his veins and into his muscles and pumped upward into his throat so that he released a savage howl.

"SPAWN OF THE PIT!" he howled, taking Checkers completely by surprise, and tensing all his muscles, he sprang at the tail as it descended once more, driving all his teeth into it as far as they would go.

CHAPTER 31

The Darkest Hour

Jenny had lain for a long time, prostrate in an agony of mourning.

She didn't know how long she had lain in the place where the body of her master had been because time had lost all meaning. She simply slumped, crumpled and abject as though all hope had gone, with her eyes firmly closed.

Behind her, on the darkest shore, the corpses were gathering. She knew they were waiting for her, but she didn't even care.

A black bridge appeared silently, lengthening itself over the stretch of water that separated Jenny from the shore of corpses. She didn't even need to look, she knew that it was there and that she was expected to cross it. Once she had crossed it, the bridge would disappear again, leaving her on the shore of no return.

I don't care, she thought. *I have nothing to live for now.*

But even as she thought this, a different thought nagged at her.

What about your friends? it said. *What about Sam?*

Sam. The small boy who had given her his heart.

If Ragnarok broke out in Sam's world, he would be in terrible danger. Her friends were probably already in terrible danger, all because of Jenny. She couldn't just abandon them to fight alone.

Slowly, and as if it was unutterably heavy, Jenny raised her head. She kept her eyes closed, afraid of what she might see if she opened them. Despair and fear battled with loyalty in her mind. Baldur, she thought, then, Sam.

She had no idea how to return to Sam's world or what she could do, if she got there, against all the forces of Ragnarok. It would be better, and far easier, to enter the darkness.

Yet against her will, a picture of Sam's face swam into her mind. Every day, when he saw her, his face lit up. Every afternoon, when he returned from school, he looked as if seeing Jenny had made his day.

Sam, she thought, and it was as though she was calling him. *Sam!*

He was her golden boy now, and holding the bright image of him in her heart as protection against the dark bridge and the gathering corpses, she finally opened her eyes. And there in front of her was the rainbow.

CHAPTER 32

The Chapter of
Not Being Destroyed by Furies

The bat-winged, dog-faced monsters were approaching, and the air whirred with the beating of their wings.

"Orion!" shouted Gentleman Jim and Pico together. "You have to come out now!"

"NO!" said the muffled voice. "LEAVE ME ALONE! I DESERVE TO DIE!"

"But we don't!" Gentleman Jim pointed out. "You can't leave us to the Furies! Come out and fight like a man!"

"LET THE FURIES COME!" said Orion, now clearly visible in the murky water. "LET THEM DO THEIR WORST! NOTHING CAN BE WORSE THAN THIS!"

"For goodness' sakes!" muttered Gentleman Jim, pacing up and down anxiously. "We've got to get him out of there. Pico?"

Pico was slithering down the sides of the rocky drop toward Orion.

"Pico!" cried Gentleman Jim. "Pico—come back!"

"Orion!" called Pico. "I am coming to you!"

"Oh, great," groaned Gentleman Jim. There was another hateful shriek, and he ventured a look upward, then immediately wished he hadn't. The Furies were circling above him; he could see their masklike faces twisted by rage. Blood and venom dripped from their eyes, and in their talons they held long whips. Gentleman Jim felt his throat tighten, so that his voice came out in a husky squeak. "If you felt like coming out and saving my life," he managed to call to Orion, "now might be a good time."

Meanwhile, Pico landed in the water next to Orion with a loud *plop*. He surfaced, kicking furiously, and waited to be assailed by feelings of remorse and despair.

Nothing happened.

He paddled around to where Orion could see him.

Nothing happened some more.

"What are you doing here?" moaned Orion.

"I have come to get you out," said Pico.

"I cannot come out," said Orion. "I have been bad. Very, very bad."

"All the more reason to come out," said Pico, "and face your doom."

Orion shifted in the water, turning his back on Pico. "No," he said, sulkily. "Go away and leave me alone."

Pico paddled again until he was facing Orion once more. "I bet you haven't been that bad," he said.

"I have," said Orion.

"Bet you haven't," said Pico.

"Yes, I have," said Orion. "What would you know about it?"

"All right, then," said Pico. "What have you done?"

"Look around you," Orion said. "Can you not see them all?"

Pico craned his neck. But he could see nothing apart from the cliff walls and Gentleman Jim's anxious face peering over, with the thousands of points of light that had followed them clustering behind. "I see nothing," he said. "What do you see?"

"All the animals! The soul of every animal I ever killed! Hundreds and thousands of them! They have returned to haunt me now."

Pico began to understand. *That's* what the points of light were. He looked up and swallowed. They did seem to be clustering over the edge, looking down. And Orion had remembered everything and was seeing his whole life in a different, crueler light. He had thought he had only to repent of his boast, but now he was seeing himself as the animals saw him. No wonder he was horrified, Pico thought.

"But you were a hunter," he began, but Orion only moaned and turned his face into the water.

"Stop them looking at me," he groaned.

Far above them, Gentleman Jim cleared his throat. "Ahem," he said. "I don't suppose you could get a move on, could you? The Furies are getting closer, and it's not a pretty sight. In fact, I don't know when I've ever seen anything quite so hideous. Like a cross between your worst nightmare and a horrible accident. I've thrown up better-looking things—"

"How kind," said the nearest Fury, descending right next to him.

"Now, you listen to me," said Pico to Orion. "You may have done terrible things, but you were a hunter, and it was in your nature to kill. Does the lion go around apologizing? Or the shark?"

"Yes, but they're only animals," said Orion, and Pico stared at him sternly.

"I think you'll find," he said, "that attitude is what got you into this mess in the first place."

"They're not nearly as bad when you get close up to them," called Gentleman Jim as the second and third Furies descended. "Quite nice-looking, really, in a certain light . . ."

"I'd quit while I was ahead if I were you," said the nearest Fury, in a voice that felt like fingernails on the blackboard of his soul. *"And don't look so worried. We don't torture dogs."*

"Are you sure?" said Gentleman Jim.

"Quite sure," hissed the second Fury, with the voice of a thousand snakes. *"Only humans suffer guilt and remorse. Animals aren't nearly so much fun."*

"That's why your friend down there isn't having any problem with the Water of Memory and Regret," commented the third, whose voice was like the slime on the riverbed. *"Only humans have the kind of conscience that enables us to torture them."*

"And we will torture this one," said the first Fury, flapping her wings a little in glee. *"We will have fun with him for all eternity!"*

Oh, dear, thought Gentleman Jim. Oh, dear, oh, dear.

✳ ✳ ✳

". . . So, if you don't get me out," Pico was saying, "I shall stay here with you. And I will surely drown. And then you'll have another death on your conscience."

Orion looked at him wearily. "Why would you want to die for me?" he said.

"I don't," said Pico. "I'd much rather you got me out."

"*Or-i-on,*" sang all the Furies, in hideously off-key voices. *"Come to us!"*

"We'll deal with them when we get to them," said Pico firmly. "Now—get me out."

With a sigh that seemed to come from the depths of the water, Orion extended a hand toward Pico, cupped him and lifted him free of the water.

"I shall save you, little dog," he said. "I shall leave the water and face my doom."

"That's the spirit," said Pico encouragingly as Orion started to climb, still muttering about how worthless he was and how he deserved only death.

Above them the Furies fluttered their wings, rising and falling in an ecstasy of anticipation.

"Stand back," said Gentleman Jim. "Stand back and give him some room."

It was hard work, climbing with only one hand, but at last Orion emerged, dripping, over the edge of the cliff and still carrying Pico. The Furies gave a heartstopping shriek.

"At last!" they cried with one awful voice. *"At last—you are ours! Come and take your punishment. You belong to us!"*

And they rose, flapping about his head and brandishing their whips.

"Oh no, he doesn't," said Pico as Orion merely stood shivering, with his head bowed. "Anyone attacking Orion has to get past me first. I stand with him!"

"Pico—" began Gentleman Jim as the Furies howled with laughter, but the little dog would not be silenced.

"If you want to hurt him, you must get past me," he repeated. Gentleman Jim groaned aloud.

"No, Pico," said Orion. "Save yourself. I have deserved my fate." And he tried to put Pico down, but the small Chihuahua hung on.

"No one can be abandoned to fate while they have one true friend," Pico said, realizing as he said it that it was true. "I am your friend, and so is Gentleman Jim. We stand together!"

Leave me out of it, thought Gentleman Jim.

"Stand with us!" Pico cried to him. "Together we will face the worst they have to offer!"

"*Typical!*" snorted the nearest Fury. "*Man has enslaved you, disposed of you, bred you into mutant runts—*"

"WOOF!" said Pico.

"*Yet now you would stand by him, even to the horrid end. And believe me, my friends, your end will be horrid!*"

"Gentleman Jim!" called Pico, ignoring her. "Stand with us!"

The Furies cackled like fiendish hens. "*Your lumbering friend has more sense,*" said one.

Now it was true that Gentleman Jim had been backing away. He couldn't see that he should have to die as part of the deal, and secretly he thought that Orion probably had deserved everything that was coming to him. He rather resented Pico's assumption that they would all stand together in the face of the Furies' cruel revenge, yet he wasn't about to stand by and be cackled at. Besides, he knew that he couldn't leave Pico. And somewhere in the depths of his memory, he heard a bugle blowing—the immortal sound that every hunting dog recognizes—the call to fight.

Knowing that he would regret it, he plodded over to stand at Orion's side. "I stand with them," he said, and for the first time, Orion looked up.

"My friends," he said, in a broken, humble voice. "I do not deserve you."

No, you don't, thought Gentleman Jim.

"Well, sisters," shrieked one of the Furies.

"It is rather unorthodox," said another.

"But if these foolish beasts are offering themselves up to an eternity of torment—"

"Then who are we to stop them?"

And with a terrible, anguished shriek they descended, their talons outstretched and their eyes dripping gore.

Galvanized, Orion raised his bow and began firing arrows at them in all directions as they batted around his head. This caused them to shriek some more and to double the ferocity of their attack. Gentleman Jim leapt upward, snarling and snapping, and was caught across the back with a whip. The pain burned fiercely, maddening him, so that he rolled over howling, then, in the next moment, Pico was swept to the ground by another whiplash. Orion stood alone, firing his arrows toward one Fury while another descended on him from behind. . . .

But at that exact moment, Boris sank his teeth into Cerberus's tail and the great dog bellowed from all three throats as he had never bellowed before.

CHAPTER 33

In Which Flo Meets a Norn

Flo plummeted downward, at a speed that drove all the breath out of her body. Just before her eyes disappeared entirely into the back of her head, Flo glimpsed something advancing toward her rapidly. It looked like a small, horned woman, with wings and a breastplate.

No, Flo thought, before all her thoughts fizzled out.

But the small, horned woman was in fact there, and she continued to hurtle toward Flo. "Gotcha!" she said, grasping Flo by the collar.

"*Ooommmph!*" said Flo, and, "*Glkk!*"

Then the pressure on her neck released, and she seemed to be floating lightly at the side of the small horned lady, whose braided hair streamed behind her in the wind. In fact, they were still traveling at a considerable speed, but compared to the speed of plummeting to certain death, it felt gentle and slow. Flo felt sure that she had seen the small horned lady who was holding on to her somewhere before, but only when she said, "Well done, Flo. You've stopped them from swallowing the sun and moon and put Ragnarok on hold for now—I knew you had it in you," did Flo recognize her and gasp in disbelief.

"Aunty Dot?" she ventured, hardly believing her eyes.

"That's one of my names," said the short, stout lady briskly.

Flo felt too dazed to speak. "But—Fenrir—" she managed to say, "and the sun . . ."

"Well, it is ninety-three million miles away," said Aunty Dot. "It'll take him a while to get there. Just about enough time for us to descend into Hades."

"Wh-what?" said Flo. "Where?"

"Don't worry about it," said Aunty Dot. "You'll be quite safe with me. We've just got to give the others a bit of a helping hand, that's all. Now, where were we?"

Flo hadn't a clue.

"Ah, yes," continued Aunty Dot. "What I was going to say was— I am one of the three Norns, Spinners of Destiny. Or at least I am in one world. In the world we're about to enter, I'm one of the three Fates. Same job, really, bit more thread. Whereas in your world, I'm simply one of Sam's aunties. See?"

"No," said Flo.

"You look confused," Aunty Dot said kindly, and even in her dazed state, Flo thought this was a bit of an understatement. "It *is* terribly confusing when the worlds collide," Aunty Dot went on. "But do you mind if I explain it as we go? There really isn't much time."

Flo nodded, then shook her head. She wished that her thoughts would assemble themselves into some kind of sense. It was a long time since anything had made sense.

"Now we're descending into a different world," Aunty Dot said, and Flo didn't even try to understand.

"I expect you're wondering what's going on," said Aunty Dot.

Flo blinked. She had given up wondering altogether.

"We're about to descend into the underworld. There's nothing to worry about, really. I just need to reunite you with your friends. All those wolves you just met will be falling to your earth, and chaos will ensue. I've got to get everyone back up there and ready to fight."

"F-fight?" said Flo. She was about to explain that fighting was not something she did when Aunty Dot cried, "There we are!"

Flo looked down.

Below them, the earth seemed to be seething into a mass of darkness.

"There's Hades now," said Aunty Dot cheerily. Then she said suddenly, "Hark!"

Flo harked. There was the eerie sound of a cock crowing.

"The second cock of Ragnarok," said Aunty Dot in hushed tones. "That's not good. That means that Hel and her minions can still burst out of the abyss. And she won't be happy now that her wolves have failed to swallow the sun and moon. We'd better get a move on. We need Orion to blow his horn."

And before Flo could ask any questions, she was hurtling forward once more at a mind-numbing speed.

"If you'll excuse me," yelled Aunty Dot above the noise of rushing air. "I'll have to change."

"Change?" echoed Flo, and before her eyes Aunty Dot started to elongate. She burst out of her armor, which changed into flowing white robes, and tendrils of gray hair flew around her head like snakes.

"You don't mind, do you, dear?" she said in an ancient, creaking voice. "Different world, you see." Flo felt that she wouldn't know how to mind anything anymore. She *thought* she recognized this new apparition as one of the three hags she had seen in the mirror, but she no longer trusted anything that her brain was telling her. They hit a wall of noise, as though the universe had just fired a shot, and Flo felt simultaneously that she had turned inside out, then immediately they began plunging into the heart of darkness.

CHAPTER 34

The Rage of Cerberus

The mighty hound, Cerberus, burst out of his cavern and charged through the underworld, howling.

The underworld rumbled and shook. The ground around Gentleman Jim and Pico began to slide from under them, and rocks cascaded down. The Furies shrieked, but the noise was lost against the greater cacophony of sound. They folded their bat wings around their ears, causing them to plummet, maddened, to the ground. A great gale of noise blasted past Gentleman Jim. His ears and chops rippled backward with the force of it, his brain batted around his skull like a demented moth. His last clear thought was that he might as well pass out since it seemed pointless to even try to do anything else.

The monstrous hound thundered toward the River of Forgetting, all three heads howling at once. He pounded his mighty tail as he ran, and Checkers flew out of it yelping, but Boris hung on like grim death. It was almost as though he'd forgotten how to let go.

"Cerberus!" moaned the Furies, covering both ears and eyes, and Pico, Orion and Gentleman Jim stared in horror as the hideous beast lumbered into view. His three heads gnashed their horrible teeth, and each fang was larger than Gentleman Jim and a good deal more pointed. His six eyes glowed like furnaces and rolled in agony. Poisonous foam flew from his jaws, and all along his scaly neck, diabolical serpents hissed like countless pressurized valves releasing steam.

Yep, definitely a good time to pass out, Gentleman Jim thought.

But the horrendous hound was careering directly toward them, maddened with pain. Orion's bow shook crazily in his hands; it was anyone's guess who he might hit with his arrow. Cerberus lashed his tail with supreme violence, and Boris finally flew off. He hit a jagged rock and lay stunned and sickened by the foul venom in the monster's tail. Cerberus didn't pause but went on lunging toward Orion, who was the only creature he could dimly see and who, therefore, he was determined to punish for the pain in his tail. Checkers, crushed and feeble but undaunted, hobbled after him as well as he could, determined to find Boris and rescue him. But it was Pico who ran to meet the demonic hound.

"DIE!" shrieked the three heads of Cerberus. **"YOU WILL ALL DIE!"**

"WOOF!" said Pico, taking the diabolical dog completely by surprise. His three heads thrashed around.

"I SAID, YOU WILL DIE!" they howled.

"WOOF!" said Pico again.

Cerberus's three heads looked down, then down again. He couldn't even see Pico. **"WHO ARE YOU THAT SAYS 'WOOF'?"** he bellowed, so Pico said it again.

Cerberus lowered his mighty neck. His six eyes struggled to focus. He hadn't mentioned it to anyone, but lately he suspected he had been getting a little nearsighted. Or at least, three of his eyes were nearsighted. The others seemed, if anything, to be getting farsighted. He supposed it was only to be expected since all his eyes were thousands of years old, but it was a bit of a nightmare, really. He couldn't see anything properly. And he really didn't want to start wearing glasses. Besides, where would he get them?

Gradually, as he lowered his enormous neck, he became aware of six specks standing in a group on the ground. They jiggled about a bit, some standing closer than others, but as he lowered his heads still further, they slowly resolved themselves into one tiny dog.

"WOOF!" it said.

Cerberus's three heads banged into one another in disbelief. He hadn't even known a dog could *be* that small. He opened his horrid mouths, blasting Pico with the incomprehensible stench of his rotting breath . . .

. . . and laughed!

Or at least, two of his heads laughed, howling and shrieking in mirth, as though they'd just been told a really funny joke. The third head gnashed its rotten teeth in rage that something as tiny as Pico dared to defy him.

"OUT OF MY WAY!" it bellowed.

"WOOF!" said Pico yet again, and Gentleman Jim, who had quite failed to pass out, trembled like Jell-O in an earthquake for what seemed like the inevitable demise of his little friend, while behind Cerberus, Checkers limped up and down, barking and snapping.

"RIGHT, THEN," said Cerberus. **"I'VE HAD ENOUGH OF THIS,"** and he raised an enormous paw, with talons like a dragon's talons, and looked set to bring it down on Pico, crushing the little dog out of existence . . .

. . . when suddenly Flo and Aunty Dot, in her new guise as one of the Fates, crashed down through one of the openings to the underworld, straight into their midst.

CHAPTER 35

Over the Rainbow

Even in her stupor of grief and fear, Jenny blinked. The rainbow hadn't been there before. As she stared at it, it began to tremble, as though something or someone huge was striding over it.

Jenny felt too maddened by grief to be afraid, yet against her will her hackles rose, the hair on her back bristled and her lips drew back in a snarl. If this rainbow was the bridge she had heard of, called Bifrost, then Jenny knew there was reason to be afraid. Because it linked the different worlds and was the means by which all the monsters and demons, trolls and giants would invade Sam's world in Ragnarok.

Whatever was coming, however, there was only one of it. Single footsteps rattled and pounded the shining bridge, and as they reached its apex, a long shadow fell across the surface. Jenny crouched, ready to spring. She had suffered enough and was more than willing to make someone else pay.

The shadow lengthened as the footsteps approached.

Jenny rolled her eyes upward, ready to view her enemy before she attacked. She had never met a giant before and didn't know quite what to expect, but she was taken by surprise to see a small boy in a large, misshapen and ridiculously yellow sweater.

"Jenny!" cried Sam.

CHAPTER 36

Reunited

Berry!" cried Aunty Dot, and Cerberus stopped bellowing mid-thrash.

"Aunty Atropos!" cried the enormous hound, and the next few moments were literally pandemonium as the great beast lumbered toward Aunty Dot, lowering its hideous heads, and she flung her arms around his vast, scaly necks.

Everyone stared in amazement. There seemed to be so much to take in.

"Aunty who?" said Pico, glancing over to where the tall, ragged woman with milk-blind eyes and hair like snakes was embracing the monstrous, three-headed hound of Hades. Everyone looked questioningly at Flo.

"Don't ask," Flo said.

Gentleman Jim was the first to move. He stumbled over to Pico, who seemed to be rooted to the spot, and scooped him up out of harm's way.

"I don't know whether you're a hero or a complete lunatic!" he growled to him as he set him down again. Pico shook himself.

"Flo?" said Checkers, limping up excitedly. "Pico? Gentleman Jim—where's Boris?"

"Here I am," said Boris, lumbering slowly toward the group. "What's going on?"

"Blowed if I know, mate," said Checkers, and he bounced Boris playfully, to say thank you for saving his life, and when Boris got up again, he sat on him and chewed his ears.

"Don't look at me," said Flo as everyone did.

"Who's this?" Checkers added, looking at Orion, and, "Blimey, who are they?" nodding toward the Furies, who were flapping about again in consternation.

"Sister," moaned the Furies together. *"Sister, this is not your place."*

"Sister?" said Gentleman Jim to Flo, who just shook her head hopelessly. "She *says* she's Aunty Dot," she said as Gentleman Jim gaped at her. "At least, she was before. Then she . . . changed."

"Sister," the Furies droned again with one voice, but the strange gray being claiming to be Aunty Dot ignored them. She and Cerberus were too busy nuzzling each other to take notice of anyone or anything else. Aunty Dot scratched the spines on his scaly neck, and Cerberus made little gratified, whimpering noises and slobbered all over her. It was kind of grotesque.

"Best guard dog I ever had," said Aunty Dot, turning around at last and wiping her milky eyes. "Until Zeus took him off me and said he had to guard the underworld instead."

"Yes, I know, I know," she said as the Furies began flapping and moaning again. "But I am here for a good reason. Where's Orion? It is time for him to repent so that his soul can go to the Elysian fields and he can blow his horn."

Orion glimmered faintly in shock. Then he stepped forward.

"Orion, King of Hunters," said Aunty Dot in a loud, resonant voice that all the dogs recognized at once. "Persecutor of the animal kingdom. What have you to say for yourself?"

Orion hung his head and mumbled something.

"Eh?" said Aunty Dot, sounding, just for a moment, uncannily like Aunty Lilith. "What was that?"

Orion hung his head even further and mumbled again.

"Can't hear you," boomed the strange being known as Aunty Dot. "Speak up, man!"

A spasm of irritation crossed Orion's handsome, transparent face. "I said I'm sorry!" he snapped.

"Sorry for what?" said Aunty Dot sternly. "You once claimed to be sorry only for boasting about your misdeeds."

If possible, Orion turned even paler than he already was. But he looked straight into Aunty Dot's milky eyes.

"I am sorry for all the damage I have done," he said clearly. "I am sorry for my arrogance in thinking that the animal world was put there only for me to destroy. I am sorry for abusing my skills as a hunter and for killing without rhyme or reason. I am sorry for setting myself above nature and for misusing my considerable talents."

He finished with just a touch of the old arrogance. Aunty Dot held up one skinny, clawlike hand. "You are sorry," she said, "for taking all these lives?"

And suddenly the underworld was full of animals. A shady multitude of stags and wild boar, cattle, sheep, horses, wolves, warthogs, tigers, lizards, fish, even insects filled the gloomy plains surrounding them and gazed at Orion with glowing eyes. A murmuring roar swelled, then subsided. Checkers, Flo, Boris, Gentleman Jim and Pico huddled together in dismay, and Orion groaned aloud in anguish.

"Orion, Master of Hunters," said Aunty Dot in ringing, yet sorrowful tones. "You boasted that you could kill any animal that the world produced, and you made good your boast. Look around you. See the results of your arrogance, and your thirst for blood."

"No—no!" moaned Orion, but Aunty Dot was inexorable.

"Because of you, all these animals that might have lived happily on earth, enjoying the sun and the moon and the fruits of forest, field and sea, have been condemned forever to the gloomy caverns of Tartarus, where no light shines. You placed yourself above all the living creatures of the earth, and that is where your light shines now. The light from your stars irradiates the earth, and all mankind looks up to you. Because of you, all of mankind has continued to lay waste the animal kingdom. What have you got to say for yourself?"

Orion's great shoulders heaved. "What can I say?" he cried. "It is true. I deserve only to die!"

"You cannot die, immortal one," said Aunty Dot as the Furies hissed. "You can only change. And you can only do that if these animals forgive you."

Now Orion hung his head again. "I do not deserve forgiveness," he said through clenched teeth.

"I'm inclined to agree with you," said Aunty Dot. "But it is not up to you. Only the animals have the power to forgive. It is up to them."

Aunty Dot finished speaking, and there was complete silence in the underworld. The ghostly multitude of animals remained motionless. Orion closed his great, shining eyes, and two shining tears fell from them.

But before they could fall to his feet, Pico dashed toward him. "I forgive you," he said as Orion looked down at him in wonder. "You are my friend."

And as if this action broke some kind of spell, the swelling murmur began again, rising to a roar. Slowly the sea of animals moved toward Orion. Vast and numberless, animals old and new, with any number of legs and eyes, some with tails, some without and some of them completely unidentifiable, they wreathed around him like smoke, pushing and jostling, and he reached out to them and lifted up his head and wept.

Then, from the heart of the vast multitude, two dogs pushed their way to Orion. One was much larger than the other, but they both gleamed like starlight. They pushed their muzzles into his hands, and his face shone suddenly with astonished joy. Then as he sank to his knees, they licked his face.

"Sirius!" he cried. "Procyon! Oh, my two faithful companions! My beloved dogs!" and he buried his face in their pelts.

Aunty Dot sat back on a rock and watched them with a faint

smile on her lips and her milky eyes full of tears. "I love a happy ending," she murmured, and Cerberus laid all three heads in her lap.

Only the Furies didn't seem too happy. *"You have interfered with our prey,"* the nearest one screeched, rising and batting about Aunty Dot's head. *"Orion was ours!"*

"Oh, get over it," said Aunty Dot. "Because of what has happened here, the whole of the human race can change, and we can get on with building a better world. Which reminds me . . ."

And she rose to her feet and gave a piercing whistle.

Flo, Checkers, Boris, Gentleman Jim and Pico all felt the summons immediately and tore themselves away from the ghostly beasts surrounding Orion. They each came to stand by Aunty Dot, feeling that they had experienced something wonderful and overwhelming. Around Orion the crowd of animals grew still, and Orion looked up at last, with the tears still streaming down his face. Aunty Dot smiled at him. She seemed somehow to know where he was and what was happening, in spite of her milky eyes.

"Berry?" she said, and the great hound of Hades gazed up at her adoringly. "It's up to you. Will you let Orion's soul pass on now that he has repented to its place of rest?"

"Whatever you say," the great beast purred. It was impossible to imagine the hound of Hades purring, yet that is what he did. Aunty Dot stood up.

"These beasts will accompany you to your new home in the Elysian fields," she said, and Orion gasped. "There, with your soul at rest in the land of endless delight, the stars in your constellation will emit more benign rays of peace and harmony upon the earth, and man will never again be at war with the animal world. When you reach the Elysian fields, you must blow your horn finally, one last time, then the new era can begin. Go now and be at peace."

Just for a moment, Orion blazed with joy, as brightly as any constellation, illuminating the whole of the underworld. The Furies flapped off squawking, then perched behind a ridge of rock and covered their faces with their wings.

"I can never thank you enough!" he cried. "Pico, little dog, great heart—I will never forget you!"

"WOOF!" said Pico, looking quite emotional. But Orion turned and, buoyed along by all the animals, made his way to where the road left the asphodel fields and divided, one way going down into Tartarus and the other way, broad and shining, to Elysium.

"Now," said Aunty Dot. "We're all together at last."

The five dogs looked at one another.

"Not quite all," Pico said, and he looked up at the great, grayish being that was Aunty Dot.

"Aunty Dot," he said earnestly. "Do you know what has happened to Jenny?"

Aunty Dot looked down at him kindly. "I cannot know that," she said. "I can only hope that she has fulfilled her part of the quest. If she has, she will have returned to your world, which is where we must go now. There is work to do."

"What? *More* work?" said Gentleman Jim.

"Yes, indeed," said Aunty Dot. "Have you forgotten Ragnarok?"

And at that dread word, all the caverns of the underworld quivered.

"All those wolves have fallen to earth. It'll be a terrible shock for everyone when they land. And the forces of Hel may still burst from the abyss. When the third cock crows, the gods will go to war, the seas will boil and the heavens will be rent asunder. Fenrir may already have swallowed the sun and moon. And Berry here is the only one who can fight him. Berry, my angel, will you take us out of here?" She patted the neck of the monstrous hound, and he wagged his terrible tail.

"You know I will," he said adoringly.

"That's my boy," said Aunty Dot approvingly. "Climb up, everyone!"

"What? On that?" said Gentleman Jim, appalled.

"Certainly," said Aunty Dot. "Berry here will take us wherever we want to go. You do want to get out of here, don't you?"

Gentleman Jim did of course want to get out, but he couldn't help looking dubious. However Aunty Dot patted Cerberus's back encouragingly and said things like, "Come on," and, "Up you get," and, "You do want to see Jenny again, don't you?" and one by one the dogs all clambered onto the great hound's back, Checkers taking good care not to be near the tail, which had done him such damage before. Besides, the experience of sniffing the rear end of the hound of Hades was not one he was likely to forget.

Once they were all on his back, Cerberus bounded away with ever-lengthening strides, straight through the rivers Lethe and Styx, so that water splashed up around them on all sides, and Charon stared after them, too astonished even to shake his fist.

"I don't know," he muttered. **"What's the point? What is the point of being the ferryman when people just come and go as they please? Come on in, all of you—"** He waved at the souls clustering anxiously on the banks of the river. **"Don't mind me—just come on in!"**

CHAPTER 37

The End of the Rainbow

Now, rainbows, as you probably know, are bridges between the worlds. Which is why, whenever you see a rainbow, you can never really tell where it ends. It ends in another world. The rumor that there is a pot of gold at the end of a rainbow was started by trolls in order to lure beings from all the different dimensions into their own, where they would promptly mug them—thus creating their own pot of gold. Jenny had heard the rumors about rainbows and was sensibly wary. However, when she saw Sam, she was so astonished and delighted that she ran to him at once, temporarily forgetting her sorrows and wagging her tail so hard that it could hardly be seen.

"Sam!" she cried. "What are you doing here?"

Sam fell to his knees and scooped her up, squeezing her so tightly that it was hard to breathe. "I thought I'd never see you again," he whispered, and she licked his face.

"How did you get here?" she managed to ask when he had stopped squeezing.

"Dunno," said Sam, looking rather dazed. "I think I must be dreaming. It must be a dream," he went on, "or I wouldn't be wearing this." And he plucked in disgust at the baggy, shapeless sweater that fell to the floor.

"Hey, you can talk!" he added. "Cool!" And he ruffled the fur behind her ears, and she jumped and wriggled and licked his hands enthusiastically. In her pain at losing Baldur, she had forgotten that she could love again.

"But what happened?" she asked.

"Well, I woke up," Sam said, wrinkling his brow. "And went

downstairs looking for you. Then I saw this light out of the back door. So I opened it, and there was this rainbow! And somehow, I knew it'd take me to you. So I followed it, of course."

Jenny was so pleased to see Sam that she forgot to give him a cautionary lecture about the dangers of following strange rainbows. Besides, it did look as if this rainbow was the only way out of Niflheim, and she no longer had any desire to return, not even to try to find her beloved master on the Shore of Corpses.

"Where are we, anyway?" said Sam, looking around.

"Niflheim," said Jenny.

"Where?"

Jenny sighed. There was so much that Sam didn't know. "Niflheim," she said. "The far northern region of darkness and cold, where the bitter winter of despair breathes icy fogs of desolation."

"Oh, right," said Sam, "I thought it was a bit nippy. I never thought I'd say this, but I'm glad I've got this sweater."

Together they gazed at the black bridge, on the other side of which the corpses had gathered silently. "Er, what's on the other side of that? Are we going to explore?"

"No," said Jenny, shuddering slightly. "That is Nastrond, shore of corpses. And on the other side of that is Helheim, where Hel herself, Queen of the Monsters of the Abyss, greatest of the giantesses, awaits the final battle so that she can burst forth in destruction onto the earth."

Sam shook his head. "Just say that again, will you?"

As briefly as she could, Jenny told her tale. About coming from another world, where Baldur had been her master, and running away with the mistletoe twig, and Fenrir coming to find it because with it he could rule, Lord of Ragnarok, over the nine worlds.

"Nine worlds?" said Sam.

"Yes," said Jenny. "There are nine worlds, connected by a single tree. This tree," she said, indicating the great root.

Sam stared at the tree. He opened his mouth, then shut it again. Then he opened it once more. "So, what's in the other worlds then?"

"I do not know them all," said Jenny. "Your world is one and the world I came from another. Boris and Checkers, Gentleman Jim and Pico have gone to a different world to fight the Guardian of the Darkest Way and return with the greatest hunter of all time."

"Why?" asked Sam.

Jenny did her best to explain. But even as she spoke, she was remembering her friends and the terrible danger they were in. "There is no time," she said urgently. "Ragnarok is coming! We have to return to your world now, Sam, before Hel breaks loose."

"But I was just getting used to it here," said Sam, peering over her shoulder to where the thick mists of Niflheim ominously swirled. "Aren't we going to explore?"

"No," said Jenny, shuddering slightly. "If we explore, we will meet Hel. And trust me, we do not want to do that."

"Are we going back, then?" said Sam, trying not to sound disappointed.

"Yes," said Jenny, trotting toward the rainbow bridge. "We must return to fight in the final battle at the end of the world!"

"Cool!" said Sam, hurrying to catch up with her. "This is a great dream, this. I hope I don't wake up! Mine are usually dead boring!"

But even as he spoke, there was a rumbling, grinding noise and the ground beneath them lurched, flinging them both to one side. Great jagged lines appeared in the stony earth and the rainbow bridge itself began to split.

"What's happening?" cried Sam, trying and failing to pick himself up as the ground shook beneath him. Jenny scrambled toward the rainbow bridge, but she slid backward in a shower of small stones. The bridge was disintegrating before her eyes.

"Jenny!" cried Sam. "What is it? What's going on?"

Jenny rolled over as the earth shook again and another split appeared. She gazed in despair at the disintegrating bridge, and then, through all the noise, both Jenny and Sam heard plainly the sound of a cock crowing.

"Ragnarok!" she said.

CHAPTER 38

Ragnarok!

Meanwhile, back in the city, strange things were happening. The cold had intensified overnight and snow fell until all the traffic was brought to a halt. Children were sledding in the middle of the roads; some enterprising people were skiing to work. Cars slewed into one another and piled up. Somewhere outside of time, a cockerel crowed loudly enough to wake the dead. Then wild yowling noises seared through the wind as the wolves fell.

Irma Nail, who lived next door to Gordon, was setting off as usual for her morning paper. She was not easily distracted from her routine, even by the Apocalypse. She stepped out of her house in her purple rain boots, muttering about the freakish weather, and glanced up at the sky just as a wolf fell out of it.

"Outrageous!" she snorted as it lay stunned at her feet. "I've heard of raining cats and dogs, but this is ridiculous!" and she stepped over the stricken beast, putting her umbrella up in case more wolves should tumble, uninvited, from the sky.

Myrtle Sowerbutts was worried about Flo. She opened her front door and stood on her doorstep in the fresh air for the first time in years. She lifted her arms in a gesture of helplessness and surprise at the huge flakes of snow falling all around, just in time for an enormous wolf to fall into them.

"GRRRRR!" said Skoll, and Myrtle shrieked like a steam engine and dropped him, running back indoors. And on her way to Gordon's house, Maureen was suddenly flattened by a falling wolf.

All over the city chaos reigned as more wolves fell from the sky, hitting the roofs of cars and rolling off. The streets exploded with people running for their lives and screaming, pursued by howling wolves. Then, as the different worlds collided, primordial light spewed into the sky and matter exploded.

Garbage men raced past Mr. and Mrs. Finnegan's house, pursued by an army of garbage cans. Seconds later, a lamppost uprooted itself and marched purposefully along the street. The walls of the dog pound bulged and collapsed, and all the dogs ran out barking and yowling and fighting the wolves. A lonely policeman fled back to his station gabbling about wolves and the walking lampposts and was made to sit down while his sergeant brewed him a cup of tea.

Then things got seriously weird. Sea creatures that looked as though they belonged in the bottom of the ocean where no one could see them stormed out of the sky. Sam's mum opened her curtains and screamed as one of them slapped up against the window.

Then, with a noise that tore the sky apart, the earth itself started to split. Smoke and flame belched out of it.

And at exactly that moment, Aunty Dot, Flo, Boris, Checkers and Pico burst through the walls of the underworld on the back of Cerberus. The lollipop lady at the corner of the main road opened her mouth wide enough to swallow her own lollipop as they thundered past, followed by other monstrous creatures from the same world, Harpies and Furies and Gorgons, centaurs and nymphs.

A reporter from the *Daily News* who had run onto the street to catch the story quietly passed out.

"Everyone dismount!" cried Aunty Dot, who was now looking like Aunty Dot again. The dogs didn't need telling twice. They leapt from Cerberus's back in relief, only to be surrounded by snarling wolves.

Cerberus ran at the hellhounds, who scattered, yelping.

"Never mind them!" yelled Aunty Dot. "It's Fenrir you want! You've got to stop him from swallowing the sun and the moon!"

Cerberus raised his massive heads. And in that same moment, darkness descended on the face of the earth.

"Oh no!" cried Aunty Dot. "He's done it! He's swallowed the sun! Get him, Cerberus!"

Cerberus crouched down low. Then, with a terrific bound, he leapt into the sky.

"Go, Cerberus!" yelled Aunty Dot, and the great hound flew, soaring gracefully into the utter blackness of night.

Up and up soared the monstrous beast, guided by hunting instincts he'd forgotten he had. Without the sun, the night air grew bitterly cold, but still he hurtled upward, through all the layers of the earth's atmosphere and out into the unimaginable regions of space.

Fenrir was having a hard time trying to digest the sun. It was giving him terrible heartburn. Flames licked his bowels, and his entire body felt as though it might combust. He was just wondering whether he'd have room for the moon as well when the giant, three headed hound of Hades landed right on his back.

"*Whhoooommmmmppphhh!*" said Fenrir, and coughed up the sun. Flames shot from his nostrils, and both dogs tumbled backward, dazzled by the glare.

Fenrir bucked and thrashed in agony, but Cerberus gripped him with all three jaws, and the next moment, both hounds were plummeting downward, and the earth gaped to receive them into the abyss.

Buildings crashed and tumbled as the earth split; dogs, wolves and people fell over one another and were buried in rubble. Trees burst into flame, and all were caught in the fierce glare of the newly released sun.

Gentleman Jim was flattened by a flying pig. *I knew I shouldn't have got up today*, he thought. Flo was encircled by ravening wolves. Her choice seemed clear, to run away or faint, when a train, running entirely clear of its tracks, ran into them all and carried them off. Checkers, mad with excitement, ran around and around barking until a huge garbage truck collapsed sideways, spilling its contents all over him, and Boris, who couldn't quite work out what was going on, was running to save him when the street upended itself, and he shot past at dramatic speed. Only Pico was safe. He scuttled around underneath a fallen plant pot that for some reason he couldn't shake free.

"WOOF!" he said, and "WOOF!" again.

The earth gaped further, and more wolves spewed forth from the abyss. Hel herself, greatest and most terrible of the giantesses with an entirely blue face and scorching eyes, began to rise out of it while a vast serpent, venom dripping from its jaws, wound itself around and around the ring road that encircled the city.

"Berry!" screamed Aunty Dot as Cerberus and Fenrir, looking like one four-headed, eight-legged monster, plunged past her toward the abyss. She clung to a lamppost, but the lamppost was charging away from the city as fast as it could go. Letting go of it, she rolled over and over in the rubble, narrowly avoiding a swimming pool that flew over her head.

Fenrir howled as he hurtled toward his mistress, and Cerberus released his grip and howled with him. Hel howled back. All the remaining buildings of the earth were flattened by the mind-blasting noise.

Then, in the midst of the fury and chaos, Aunty Dot suddenly knew what she had to do. "ORION!" she shrieked, then, in the kind of voice that only a stressed-out Norn can produce, she bellowed, "O-RI-ON!!"

High in the heavens, far above the chaos and storms of the city, Orion was rising. He felt peaceful and happy for the first time in centuries. Was not his soul on its way to the Elysian fields? He rose blissfully accompanied by his beloved hounds, Canis Major (Sirius) and Canis Minor (Procyon), and together they radiated a pure and tranquil light. Now that his soul was at peace, he was receptive to the beauty of the blue planet, which seemed to him exquisitely serene.

Then suddenly the peace was shattered by a universe-splitting yell.

"O-RI-ON!!!" howled Aunty Dot.

Rudely interrupted, Orion glanced down with his supernatural eyes and took in the terrible scene below. All at once he remembered that he had forgotten to do something vital.

"Oh no," he said. "If I don't do something, the heavens will be rent asunder and the stars will fall into the abyss!"

"WOOF!" said Canis Major and Canis Minor.

"But what was it I had to do?" he mused. "Oh, dear, oh, dear!"

He was starting to panic. Canis Minor nipped him. "The horn!" snapped Canis Major. "Use the horn!"

"B-but I don't know if I *can*!" Orion protested.

Canis Major rolled his starry eyes. "Try!" he said.

Orion's fingers fumbled at his belt. He raised the glistening horn and blew, and a note of astonishing sweetness and clarity, unbearably pure, flew out of it, halting the stars in their courses.

On earth, Hel raised her gory arms just as Cerberus and Fenrir flew into them, and all three collapsed backward in a sheet of flame that burst from the abyss. Black smoke belched forth, wrapping the city in a vast and terrible silence.

CHAPTER 39

The End, and a Beginning

Meanwhile, back in Niflheim, Sam and Jenny were crouched together under an overhanging boulder as the world around them collapsed. The earth quaked and split apart, giant rocks cascaded all around them and they were deafened by the rumbling, crashing, grinding noises. It was like being in a very small bedroom, with the world's loudest rock group playing all around your bed. Sam huddled beneath the boulder, hoping very much that it wouldn't come crashing down on top of them and clutching Jenny, who was quivering all over.

"Never mind, Jenny," he whispered during a momentary pause. "As long as we've got each other, we'll be all right."

Jenny briefly licked his hand. But she didn't feel Sam's confidence. She was aware, as he couldn't be, of what the terrible noises meant. She knew that only Ragnarok could shake the foundations of Niflheim, and if Ragnarok was happening, then she had certainly failed. In despair, she thought of her friends, who had gone into the unknown so bravely to help her in her impossible task and who would now face certain doom. She had lost Baldur, her beloved master, and now she had sent her friends to their deaths. And she thought of Fenrir and of what the nine worlds would be like under his total rule. It was hard not to feel that it was somehow all her fault, and she couldn't stop shuddering in Sam's arms.

Then, as suddenly as it had all started, it finished. The thundering noises were replaced by a deafening silence.

Sam and Jenny didn't move.

There was more silence.

Timidly Jenny peeped out from the crook of Sam's arm.

They were almost entirely surrounded by rubble. There was just a little space between the overhanging boulder and the avalanche of stones.

Sam looked at Jenny, and Jenny looked at Sam.

"What do you think?" Sam whispered. He was afraid to speak too loudly in case he set off another cascade, but nothing happened. "We'll have to get out of here somehow," he murmured, and he stood up and set Jenny down on the rubble.

They started to climb. It wasn't easy because the stones kept shifting and sliding beneath them. Every time Sam got a grip, stones above him would loosen and come tumbling down, bouncing off his shoulders and head. Jenny kept clambering up, then sliding down again, but eventually she caught hold of the bottom of Sam's sweater with her teeth, and he hauled her upward and began to squeeze his way through the gap at the top of the rocky pile . . .

. . . and they emerged, bruised, battered and shell-shocked, into a world completely unlike the one they had left.

There was no swirling mist, no black bridge, no shore of corpses. There was no sign of the root of the great tree. Instead there was a kind of rocky path, climbing steeply upward into darkness. Great stones and rocks jutted out from the path, almost like a makeshift ladder, but it was too dark to see where it led to.

Sam looked at Jenny, and Jenny looked at Sam.

"Well, we can't stay here, that's for certain," Sam said in a low voice, and he tucked Jenny under one arm and began the steep ascent.

"I wish I could see where I was going," he said as he hauled himself upward with one arm. He had stopped whispering, but he was already out of breath, and his voice came out in gasps. "A—bit—of—light'd—be—handy."

And no sooner had he said this than a light began to shine. It was a dull yellow light, not golden, but a dirty mustard color. It seemed to be coming from Sam's sweater, soiled and muddy though it was.

"Weird," breathed Sam. Then he saved all his breath for climbing as the strange, muddy yellow light all around them grew stronger and more golden with each step.

Slowly Aunty Dot picked herself up. She brushed the dust and rubble from her tunic and, seeing that the small horned helmet had rolled away from her, picked it up and replaced it, battered though it was, on her head. Then she found her spectacles, miraculously undamaged, in the pocket of her tunic. She used the hem of her tunic to wipe them clean, put them on (the frame was slightly bent), looked around and saw . . .

. . . the devastation of a city.

Buildings had crashed and tumbled to the ground, cars and other vehicles lay piled in heaps of wreckage, shops and houses had spilled onto the street, their contents scattered over the roads. Smoke and dust billowed everywhere. Worst of all, there were no signs of life. The ruined city was empty and desolate.

Painfully, because her knees hurt, Aunty Dot began limping through the rubble and chaos that had been the city. She hardly knew where she was going or what to do. But as she passed one ruined building, she caught sight of a wheel and a handlebar poking out of the wreckage. Her bike!

Moments later, she was tugging it out of the wreckage. It was more battered and bent than ever, but it was still recognizably her bike, the basket hanging drunkenly off the frame. It wobbled dangerously as she pushed it, and the seat was at a crooked angle, yet she clambered onto it and was soon pedaling lopsidedly through the ruined streets.

Through the devastation of Ragnarok careered Aunty Dot on her rickety bike, calling "Sam! Jenny! Pico! Flo!" but nobody replied.

"Boris!" called Aunty Dot. "Checkers! Oh, someone answer, please!"

But no one did, and soon she came to the great gaping hole left by Hel in the middle of the main street.

She stood over it for a moment, looking almost as desolate as the city itself. Then she leaned right over the hole, as far as she could without falling in, and called something in an old, strange language.

And a light began to shine from the darkness.

It grew and intensified in brightness until it was as though the sun was shining underground. And someone was climbing out of the hole, and that someone was—

"Sam!" cried Aunty Dot.

"Hello, Aunty Dot!" said Sam. "What have you got on your head?"

"Oh, Sam!" breathed Aunty Dot. "Sam!"

It was all she could manage to say because she felt quite tearful and overcome. And because she was dazzled by the light that now seemed to be shining not only from Sam's sweater, but from his whole body—streaming from his face and hair and hands.

"The Shining One returns!" whispered Aunty Dot.

"Eh?" said Sam. "Give us a hand, will you?"

Speechlessly, Aunty Dot extended her hand. And the beautiful youth rose from the abyss, his face shining like the sun, his small dog still tucked under one arm. The light from his face bathed the ruined city in pink and gold, so that even the dust and smoke seemed illuminated and slowly began to clear.

"Blimey," said Sam. "What's happened here?"

CHAPTER 40

A Tangled Thread

Well," said Aunty Dot. She looked at Sam and started to speak, then changed her mind. "This'll take some explaining," she said, shaking her head. "I might need some help with this," and she took a small horn from her belt and blew on it, a short, noisy blast.

"What's that?" Sam started to say, but just then the air in front of him parted like a curtain and out stepped Aunty Joan.

Except that she was dressed like an elf. All in green, with pointed ears. "Hello, Sam," she said.

Sam blinked at her.

"Where's Urd?" said Aunty Dot.

"I'd blow again, a bit louder if I were you," said Aunty Joan. "You know she's deaf."

Aunty Dot blew her horn again, louder and longer this time, and even before she'd finished, everyone could hear Aunty Lilith's voice.

"Yes, all right," it said irritably. "I'm coming, I'm coming. Keep your hair on." And the air parted again, and Aunty Lilith climbed out backward, carrying an enormous horn. "Hello, Sam!" she said cheerfully. "Fancy seeing you here. And Jenny too!"

Sam was speechless.

"He wants to know what's going on," said Aunty Dot, and the three aunts exchanged significant glances.

"Don't we all," said Aunty Lilith. "Go on then. Tell him."

Aunty Dot raised her arms, then let them fall again. "We are the three Norns," she said. Sam looked at her blankly. "On earth, you know us as your aunties—Lilith, Joan and Dot. But in another world we are the Norns, Urd, Verdandi and Skuld. And in yet another we are the three Fates. Don't worry too much about it," she said as Sam looked stunned. "All you really need to know is that we preside over the past, present and future. Over the lives of men and gods and the fate of the earth."

"Wow," said Sam, and Aunty Joan smiled her worried smile.

"Well, yes," she said. "But it does have its downside." She sighed. "Let me start at the beginning."

"I should start at the beginning, if I were you," said Aunty Lilith.

Aunty Joan sat down cross-legged on a patch of grass, and once they were all sitting with her, she began.

"In the beginning there was only Ginnungagap, the Void. Ymir was the first being to come out of this Void, and he fathered a race of giants, as well as Odin's own father, Bor. So great and terrible did Ymir become that Odin was forced to slay him, and from his body he created the universe. In order to support the universe, he created an ash tree, Yggdrasil. It supports, links and shelters all the nine worlds. And he asked us, the three Norns, to look after it, with sacred mud and water from the holy well."

"But—" Sam interrupted, and Aunty Joan smiled at him kindly. "Yes?" she said.

"But I thought you said that there was only the Void," Sam said, wrinkling his forehead. "Where did this Ymir bloke come from? Come to think of it—where did *you* come from? And what is a Norn anyway? None of this makes sense."

Aunty Joan sighed and smiled at the same time. "Yes," she said. "Mythology is like that. You can't ask it questions. It just doesn't work that way." She petted Jenny, who was feeling for the first time that things did make sense. She had always known there was something unusual about the aunts.

"Suffice it to say," Aunty Joan went on, "that we Norns were also born from the Void and are almost as old. You see, as soon as anything begins to *be*, it has to have a past, a present and a future. And that's where we come in. We preside over the fates of men and gods. We were the natural choice to look after the world tree. Without us, it would wither and die. And all the nine worlds would be destroyed. Do you see?"

"No," said Sam. "But go on anyway. It's kind of cool. Just the three of you and all that power!"

Aunty Joan looked faintly gratified. "You'll find us in most mythologies," she said. "In theory, the gods rule. In practice, there's always a group of three women somewhere who actually pull all the strings."

"And cut 'em and spin 'em," put in Aunty Lilith, who was using the enormous horn as an ear trumpet so that she could hear.

"Yes, well, that's the point," said Aunty Joan. "In return for us looking after Yggdrasil, Odin accepted that the fate of gods and men rested with us. We were left in charge of the threads of destiny."

"Women's work, he said." Aunty Dot sighed, and Aunty Lilith snorted. "Typical man," she said.

"Actually, none of us *likes* spinning," said Aunty Joan. "I always wanted to try woodwork."

"A bit of pottery'd be nice," said Aunty Lilith wistfully.

"We just got a bit bored," said Aunty Dot. "Two million years of spinning and weaving was definitely enough."

"So you took to climbing the tree," said Aunty Lilith.

"That's right." Aunty Dot nodded, and Aunty Joan said, "As soon as she learned that each branch ended in a different world, there's been no stopping her. She was always the adventurous one. And once or twice she talked us into going with her. Which is how we first came into your world."

"But—" said Sam, but Aunty Joan lifted a hand to stop him.

"When we went exploring with Aunty Dot," she said, "yours was the first world we came to where we didn't have much to do. You may think that your world has troubles of its own, and indeed it has, but it's a holiday camp compared to the others. Look at the Nordic world—all bloodbaths and Valkyries. Look at the Greek myths! But in your world there was much more freedom—everyone getting on with his or her own thing. No one knew about us or expected us to weave their destinies—we came and went as we pleased. If we dropped a few stitches, no one bothered, they just carried on without us. It was such a relief, I can't tell you. They'd forgotten about us, you see. That's the thing about your world, Sam, it's a place where people forget. Different gods and religions come and go. Some of them set up home there and no one even notices.

We loved it. We bought a nice little house there and planned our retirement. We even fostered a little girl—your mother, Sam. And we took up knitting, just as a change from all the spinning and weaving—"

"I signed up for that pottery course," put in Aunty Lilith. "And the line dancing."

"—And Aunty Dot took to looking after dogs, which was her real passion. Then one day, we sent Aunty Dot to the shop for more wool for our knitting, and she forgot all about it. We sent her out again, and she bought the wool, but she must have dropped it on the way home because *she gave us the wrong wool by mistake.*"

Aunty Joan gazed meaningfully at Sam, but he didn't catch on.

"Unfortunately," Aunty Dot said, "it was the wool we used for your sweater, Sam."

Sam stared at her as the penny finally dropped. "You mean?" he said.

"Yes," said Aunty Dot, nodding slowly. "Your sweater is knitted with the thread of destiny. So the fates of three different worlds have become horribly tangled. Just the three of them, thankfully—if we'd kept on knitting, who knows what might have happened to the other six. Anyway, that's when Jenny managed to catch the dart that should have slain Baldur."

"Horribly tangled's right," said Sam, looking down at the monstrous yellow mess. "You might not be very good at spinning and weaving, but—you're *terrible* at knitting!"

"Well, we're still learning the art," said Aunty Joan defensively. But Sam was looking at his sweater with new respect.

"Do you mean to say," he said, "that this sweater's knitted out of . . . fate?"

"We do," said the aunts.

"Cool!" said Sam. "What happens if I pull this bit here?"

"No—don't do that!" chorused the aunts in alarm. "You might cause a war or an earthquake!"

"Cool!" said Sam again, but he stopped pulling the thread.

"Actually, we do have to unravel the thread," said Aunty Joan. "But very carefully—one stitch at a time. We don't want to send all the worlds into shock."

"What worlds?" said Sam, still confused about this.

"There are nine of them altogether, Sam," said Aunty Dot. "You hear about them in mythology. The world of ancient Greece, the Old Norse world, Egypt and Babylon, the Aztec and Inuit worlds—"

"That odd little world that none of us understands," put in Aunty Lilith.

"Well, there are several of those," said Aunty Dot. "Then there's your world, of course. And the underworld, which seems to be a kind of mishmash of all the worst aspects of the other worlds. But every aeon or so, all the worlds are supposed to renew themselves. Which is where Baldur comes in."

"Who?" said Sam.

Between them, the aunts explained that Baldur was the son of Odin and Ragnarok was the doom of the gods, the last battle at the end of the world, where the forces of chaos and destruction were unleashed.

"But so long as Baldur dies," said Aunty Dot, "the world can renew itself and the golden age begin."

"But Baldur didn't die," said Jenny. She lay with her head between her paws, feeling all the old pain at the mention of her master's name.

"No," said Aunty Dot. "And that was our fault too. We were in your world, Sam, knitting your sweater with what we thought was ordinary wool while the game of the gods was taking place. Loki shaped the mistletoe into a dart and gave it to Baldur's blind brother, Hod, to throw. It should have killed him, but instead Jenny here jumped up and caught it and ran off with it."

"I must've dropped a stitch," said Aunty Lilith.

"So while Ragnarok was set in motion—" said Aunty Joan.

"And the end of the world was nigh," boomed Aunty Lilith.

". . . there was no chance of it all renewing itself," said Aunty Dot. "And then Jenny here leapt into the Void and emerged in your world, still carrying the mistletoe dart, and Fenrir of course followed her because he'd worked out that if he had the mistletoe dart, then the world would never renew itself and Ragnarok would never end. Worse than that, the forces of chaos would spread throughout the nine worlds and Fenrir, as hound of Ragnarok, would have total rule and never be chained again. Do you see?"

"Er, no," said Sam, sounding rather dazed.

Aunty Dot patted his hand. "No," she said. "It is rather a lot to take in. Even we didn't work it all out until the Fimbulwinter began. And it doesn't matter now. Because Jenny here got the dart to Baldur just in time, and he died as he was supposed to and now, well, here you are!"

"But what have I got to do with it?" asked Sam, looking more confused than ever.

"And what about Boris and Checkers, and Gentleman Jim and Pico, and Flo?" asked Jenny. The aunts exchanged significant glances once more.

"Ah," said Aunty Joan.

"Well . . . ," said Aunty Lilith.

"Yes," said Aunty Dot. "They're part of the bigger picture, you see. There was only one dog in all the worlds who could defeat Fenrir, and that was my darling Berry. Boris and Checkers went to fetch him, and they did their job the best way they could. And meanwhile, Gentleman Jim and Pico went to fetch Orion's soul back from the underworld."

"Yes, but why?" asked Jenny.

"Well, Orion shines above all the worlds and has had a very bad influence on each of them," said Aunty Joan. "He made a boast, remember, that he could hunt and kill any animal on the face of the earth. Because of his influence, mankind has believed it can lay waste the animal kingdom and create a world in which humans rule and there is no place for other beasts. Things have got terribly out of balance. We don't want that to happen again, when the new golden age begins. So we thought it would be much better if Orion repented, for the killing as well as the boasting, and then he could blow his horn, sounding a whole new note for the new era."

"We're tired of this endless cycle of birth and destruction and death," said Aunty Dot. "We don't want it all just to happen again over and over. The human race has to learn. And it needs to learn from the animals. And where better to start than with dogs?"

Aunty Joan nodded. "Dogs have a special relationship with man. Civilization as you know it would not exist without dogs guarding and hunting and fighting man's battles. So in this new world," she said, "we want a different star to guide it. Sirius, in fact. The Dog Star."

"And once that's happened," said Aunty Lilith, "we can go into retirement!"

"I can go back to dog walking," said Aunty Dot.

"I can try woodwork," said Aunty Joan.

"And I can take up line dancing again," said Aunty Lilith. "And pottery!"

Sam stared at his aunts and shook his head. "I still don't get it," he said. "Where do I come into all this?"

"Well, we weren't sure at first," said Aunty Dot. "But when I saw you emerging from the abyss—suddenly I knew!"

"Knew what?" asked Sam.

"The world needed a new Shining Boy! And so Jenny brought you from the underworld, to replace the world we knew!"

Jenny barked in astonishment.

"No way!" said Sam. "How?"

"Because of the Sweater of Fate," said Aunty Dot, and the aunts all beamed at one another.

"I said it'd all turn out all right in the end," said Aunty Lilith, who had said nothing of the sort. But Sam was shaking his head.

"Just hold on a minute," he said. "I'm not Baldur—I'm Sam. I'm not the son of Odin or anything mythological like that. I'm just me—and I live with my mum!"

"That's all right, Sam," said Aunty Dot kindly. "Don't try too hard to understand. In this new world, all we need is a new balance between humans and the rest of the animal race. And we need dogs to lead the way. Which will all happen," she said, "once you've created the world anew."

"Oh, right," said Sam, who had obviously decided that his aunts were all barking mad. "So long as that's all I've got to do. But in case you've not noticed—I'm just a boy. I don't create worlds, I just live in them."

"Look around you, Sam," said Aunty Joan gently.

Sam looked. Then he rubbed his eyes and looked again.

The desolate wastes of the city had disappeared. And all around him the world had already begun to renew itself. Blackened trees burst once more into bloom, grass spread along the pavements, smoke cleared and the birds began to sing. They were on a wide, grassy plain, which was green with life. Trees hung close to the ground, weighted down with blossom, the air was thick with singing birds and the light was golden, with a hint of pink. A fresh wind blew and small clouds chased one another across the sky. Everywhere seemed fresh and clean, as if newly rinsed. It was hard to believe in Ragnarok and the forces of chaos.

"How did that happen?" said Sam. The aunts just smiled at him.

"It all seems new," he said, looking around at the brilliant green of the grass.

"That's because it's the morning of the world," said Aunty Joan, "time for everything to begin again."

"All you have to do," said Aunty Lilith, plucking the great horn from her ear, "is to blow this horn."

"What? And then?"

"Then the world will rebuild itself along the lines you choose," said Aunty Dot. "It all depends on what you wish for. It all depends on you, Sam."

Sam took the great horn from Aunty Lilith. It was all too much to take in. At the same time, deep inside him, he felt as though he had known it all along. He gave up trying to understand it fully and allowed the deeper part of him to take over.

"So all I have to do . . . " he said, turning the great horn over in his hands.

"Is to make a wish, Sam, for the world to be as you would like it to be. Then blow the horn," said Aunty Dot.

"But be careful what you wish for," said Aunty Joan.

"Because it will come true," said Aunty Lilith.

Sam thought hard. He thought of every exciting computer game he had ever played and how he'd wished, sometimes, that his life could be more like that. Then he thought about all the fantasy films he'd watched and the books he'd read that had dragons and knights and giants in them. Then he thought about his home and his mum. He wiped the mouthpiece of the horn carefully with his sleeve because it had just been in Aunty Lilith's ear and took a deep breath.

"I wish," he said, and the aunts all craned forward.

"Yes?" said Aunty Joan and Aunty Dot, and Aunty Lilith said, "What's he saying?"

"I wish," said Sam, "that everything could be like it was before. Only better. For humans AND animals."

And he raised the horn to his lips and blew.

CHAPTER 41

Another Beginning

Gentleman Jim woke from a terrible dream in which he had been hit by a flying pig. He seemed to be alone on the croft.

"That's funny," he said to himself. "Must've been something I ate." And he got up without any of the old problems in his back legs and trotted off toward home.

Maureen was waiting for him by the garden gate. He hung back for a moment when he saw her, but she ran toward him with her arms outstretched.

"Oh, Gentleman Jim!" she cried. "There you are! We've been so worried about you!" And she flung her arms around him, and knelt down in the muddy grass, and buried her face in his neck.

Gentleman Jim stood stiffly, bemused by all this attention. But when she lifted her face and called for Gordon, he set off at a loping run toward his old master and leapt into his arms just as Gordon appeared.

Gordon collapsed backward, hugging Gentleman Jim, who licked his face all over.

"Oh, Gentleman Jim—where have you been!" Gordon exclaimed. "I've missed you so much!"

"I'm going to cook you a whole pan full of your favorite pet mince!" Maureen said, beaming. And she did! Gentleman Jim stood in the kitchen while she boiled it up, thinking that something, some-where, was *not quite right*, but he couldn't remember what. And soon the delicious smell of tripe and offal and the remains of long-dead animals filled his nostrils, driving all other thoughts away. He lifted his nose and gave vent to his feelings in a long, baying howl. Gordon and Maureen laughed in delight.

"That's my boy!" said Gordon, ruffling Gentleman Jim's ears in exactly the way he liked. "We've missed that noise!"

Then, after he'd eaten it all up, every scrap, Maureen said, "You look tired, Gentleman Jim. What you need is a nice lie down on your bed." And she led him upstairs to the old bed with the comfortable old mattress that had bumps and hollows in it that were exactly the shape of Gentleman Jim.

Then, after a nice long sleep, Gordon and Maureen took him out for his evening constitutional. Maureen insisted on him wearing the coat she had made for him since it was still a little chilly in the evenings and she didn't want him catching cold.

Gordon laughed at her. "I swear you think more of that dog than me," he said.

"Nonsense," said Maureen, but she gave Gentleman Jim a little squeeze that suggested that Gordon really might be right, and they all set off together toward the croft.

And as they walked, Gentleman Jim realized that all this was really true and not a dream. He lived with two people who thought the world of him, who cared for him more than they cared for anyone or anything else. He had come home at last.

Boris slid all the way to the bottom of his street and lay there, stunned, for a moment. He closed his eyes while the whole world seemed to shake itself like a wet dog. When he opened them again, he was facing his front door.

Boris experienced the familiar feeling of not understanding what was going on.

Door, he thought slowly. He had a feeling of wariness about it that he didn't understand, but after a moment he went right up to it and barked.

Mr. and Mrs. Finnegan hurried to greet him. "Boris!" they cried together, and they made an enormous fuss over him as he plodded past them to the kitchen.

His food bowl was empty, but Mrs. Finnegan said that she'd soon put that right—she'd cook something for him straightaway. Boris's ears went down at this, for reasons he couldn't understand, but he waited patiently in the living room while Mr. Finnegan hugged him and played tug-of-war with him and his favorite toy. And then, minutes later, Mrs. Finnegan called that food was ready, and Boris went into the kitchen with a sinking feeling in his stomach, but determined to be brave . . .

. . . and there, in his bowl, was the biggest, juiciest steak he had ever seen!

Despite his hunger, Boris sniffed at it several times before nibbling it cautiously, sure that there was something about Mrs. Finnegan, and food, that he had to be wary about. But he really couldn't think of why, and soon he was overwhelmed by the glorious, meaty smell, and he wolfed the steak down in a single bite.

Mrs. Finnegan fondled him lovingly.

"I've put the baby in the back room for now," she said. "I thought you might like to watch some telly with us."

And so Boris sat between Mr. and Mrs. Finnegan in the front room, and they all watched the comedy programs together, and Boris even got the jokes. And for the first time in many months he really felt at home.

Checkers clambered slowly out of the pile of refuse. The garbage truck seemed to have gone and with it his memories of the Apocalypse. But he felt a bit bruised and stiff and, well, *sober* for the first time in his life. His coat seemed heavier than usual, matted with dust and mud and rubble. He shook his ears and a mouse flew out. Then he limped slowly and painfully toward his house. He had the feeling that he might be in trouble, but he really couldn't remember why. Something told him he was always in trouble.

The door was partly open when he reached his house. Freda was on the settee, eating an apple and reading a magazine. She hardly looked up as Checkers passed but reached out and patted him gently. "Good boy," she said, and Checkers managed a muffled "woof."

He went upstairs to where John was working on the computer. Checkers had a bad memory about the computer, but he couldn't remember what, and it seemed to be working fine now. John reached out and scratched Checkers behind the ears.

"Hello, Checkers, old son," he said. Then he looked at the muck on his fingers. "My goodness," he said, "where've you been? Do you need a bath?"

Checkers tensed immediately, ready to do battle, but John, noticing this, said, "It's all right, old boy. You don't have to have a bath if you don't want one."

I don't? thought Checkers, considerably surprised. Something told him he was always having baths whether he wanted them or not.

"You're not looking quite yourself," John said, lifting Checkers's face and searching for his eyes among all the hair. "Why don't you come and sit down with me and Freda?"

So Checkers followed John into the living room and sat down on the settee, and John and Freda petted him in spite of all the dirt and didn't try to make him sit on a plastic sheet, and Checkers felt so relieved by all this that he promptly ate a cushion. Then he looked anxiously at his owners, but they only laughed and shook their heads.

"What's a bit of soft furnishing between friends?" John said. "Quality of life, that's what matters," he added, slinging an arm around Checkers's muddy coat. And Freda brought a box of biscuits from the kitchen, and they all sat together and ate the lot, dropping crumbs everywhere and feeling comfortable, safe and warm.

Flo stared around in confusion. Where had all the wolves gone? Everything had returned to normal, and she seemed to be on the croft. Had she imagined everything? As she turned around slowly, feeling mystified, it occurred to her that she could no longer remember whatever it was she might have been imagining. There were flashing images in her mind, but they were fading, and they didn't make sense. Something funny was going on, but she really didn't know what.

Then someone called her name.

"Flo?" the voice called. "Flo!"

And when she turned around slowly once more, Flo could see Myrtle Sowerbutts approaching her from the other side of the croft.

Myrtle? thought Flo. Because one thing she seemed to remember was that Myrtle never left the house. Yet here she was, walking in a slightly unsteady way toward Flo.

"Oh, you darling dog!" cried Myrtle. "Come to Mumsy right now!"

And she threw her arms around Flo and clipped the lead onto her collar. "Where have you been, my darling poodle-doodle?" she cooed. "And whatever's happened to your bee-yootiful coat?"

And when Flo didn't reply, she said, "Never mind, darling. We'll get home and give you a nice hot bath!"

And Flo, who didn't mind baths at all, felt that this, in fact, was exactly what she needed. But Myrtle kept talking to her as they walked.

"We're going to go for lots of walkie-poos together from now on," she said. "I'm getting the hang of all this outdoor business. Though all this fresh air's a bit hard on the lungs at first."

Then she said, "I've decided that hair dye isn't good for you, Flo. So I'm going to let you return to your own natural, gorgeous color. But we can still look the same—I shall only wear white from now on! I'm going to look just like you!"

Flo let Myrtle talk on. She was hardly listening. She felt a mind-numbing tiredness creeping over her, yet as they approached the house and Myrtle let them in, all the old anxiety returned. She had a vivid, flashing memory of something terrible and ginger and frightening, with horrid teeth and claws.

"You'll never guess what's happened to Henry," Myrtle said, walking ahead of Flo into the kitchen. "I sold him, while you were out, to a TV company that makes horror films for pets! They were looking for something orange and mean, and Henry fit the bill perfectly. They promised to take frightfully good care of him and they paid me quite a lot. So there you are. It's just the two of us from now on."

Flo felt a wave of astonished delight. Tremulous with gratitude and fatigue, she made her way over to her bed. She was back in her own home, and she needn't worry about the dreadful beast that used to stalk it. She wondered briefly whether she had in fact died and gone to heaven. Tired but very, very happy, she sank down on her bed in front of the fire while Myrtle ran her a bath.

Finally Pico got the plant pot off him. He struggled out and looked around. Everything had changed. Or rather, nothing had changed. Everything was as it was before . . . before . . .

. . . well, *something* had happened, but he really couldn't remember what.

And now he seemed to be on the croft, but none of his friends were there.

Pico felt quite exhausted from doing something, though again he wasn't sure what. Home seemed a long way away, over dark and dangerous terrain. Nonetheless, there was nothing for it, so he set off bravely in what he hoped was the right direction, pushing his way through clumps of grass like jungles and molehills that were exactly like mountains. He might have lost heart, but fortunately, he hadn't gone very far when he heard Aunty Dot calling for him.

"Pi-co!" she called.

Pico sprang to attention immediately. He opened his mouth and gave his biggest-ever bark. "WOOF!" he barked, and, "WOOFF!" again. And Aunty Dot came pedaling toward him on her bike. She scooped him up, and petted him briefly, and put him into her basket.

And that was it. Pico went back to exactly the same life he'd had before. A life in which he was loved but not overly petted and sometimes forgotten about. A life in which he often got stuck in wastepaper baskets or handbags and in which he peered out at the world from the windowsill or from Aunty Dot's bicycle basket or Aunty Lilith's sleeve.

Yet inside Pico, everything had changed.

He had no direct memory of helping to save the world, yet he felt that within him were distant horizons and marvelous deeds. Stars blazed inside him, and a whole universe was in his heart. In his dreams he wandered along the Milky Way, with comets shooting past and galaxies bursting into existence, and he felt a vast contentment about his own small life.

As for Sam, once he had finished blowing the great horn, he had handed it back to Aunty Lilith, who had thrown it as far as she could until the air had closed around it silently. Then he had tucked Jenny under one arm and set off home with his aunts.

"Mu-um," he called when he got there. "We're back! Jenny's home!"

And indeed Jenny felt that she was.

Life quickly went back to normal, and after Sam's first day back at school, Aunty Dot called to take her for a walk.

They went to the croft, and it was just as she remembered it. She lifted her nose and sniffed, searching the air for the scents of her friends.

Boris was out with Mr. and Mrs. Finnegan, who were pushing baby Sean in his stroller. They were joined by Gordon and Maureen, who were spending quality time with Gentleman Jim. Boris and Gentleman Jim stood together talking while their humans chased a ball around the field. And they were soon joined by Flo, who was walking Myrtle. Myrtle seemed so keen on the outdoor life these days that it was hard to keep her in. Flo joined Gentleman Jim and Boris, and moments later Checkers arrived with Freda and John, who had taken a break from doing his reports. There were more important things than money and work to think about, he said. There was Checkers!

And finally Pico came, trotting along in front of Aunty Lilith since there was no longer any nonsense about him not being allowed to walk on the streets. The five dogs greeted one another rapturously, like the great friends they were. None of them remembered exactly the great events that they had taken part in, yet they all felt somehow, in spite of their near-perfect happiness, as though something was missing from their lives.

Pico saw her first. He trotted over slowly, sure that he remembered her scent. Then gradually he picked up speed until he was running as fast as a two-pound Chihuahua can while Jenny waited for him with her head on one side.

"Jenny!" cried Pico, and he knew all of a sudden what the great gap in his heart had been. Then for a few moments everything was a blur as Pico bounced up and down toward Jenny, and Jenny wagged her tail so hard it could hardly be seen.

Finally, Pico raised his nose to hers.

"Little friend," she said to him. "Your body is small but your heart is great. You have seen distant horizons and done marvelous deeds. In the new world, you can show other dogs that they too can dream of greatness."

And though he had forgotten the old world and his big adventure, as she looked into Pico's eyes, Jenny could see the glimmerings of memory, like a star.

Then Gentleman Jim came over to sniff her. "Well, hello," he said slowly, and he thumped his great tail once, twice, against the trunk of a tree. "Jenny, isn't it?"

The small white dog raised her nose up to Gentleman Jim.

"Dear friend," she said. "Born hunter, your instincts are keen and you have used them well. The new world owes you more than you know, and now you can show other dogs how to use their instincts for the benefit of all."

"Hrrrrummpphh!" said Gentleman Jim, suddenly feeling within him the blood of his ancestors, fierce and swift. Then he stooped and licked Jenny on the nose, and she realized that while so much had faded from his memory, no dog ever truly forgets.

"My turn! My turn!" said Checkers, bounding up, but Boris stood patiently behind, and she turned to him first.

"Dear Boris, natural guardian and protector, you defended the whole world from danger, and now the new world needs you to go on protecting and guarding its young."

"I did, didn't I?" said Boris as a spark of memory dimly returned.

"Me! me!" said Checkers, bounding around in a circle.

"Checkers, natural warrior," the little dog said, "you have accomplished great things by using your gift of courage. In the new world there may still be battles to be fought, and both people and dogs will need to be brave. And you can show them courage."

"That's me!" said Checkers, dashing around again. "The bravest dog that ever lived!"

"WOOF!" said Pico.

But Flo was waiting, overwhelmed by the memories that were flooding back, because out of all the dogs, her memory was the most keen.

"Dearest Flo," Jenny said. "Your wisdom and your perception helped to overcome the enemy. In the new world the young will need your guidance, which you can freely give. Because you have been set free."

"Yes," said Flo. "But it was all thanks to you. You set us free."

The little dog lowered her head modestly. "That was my name—Leysa, meaning to set free," she said. "But you have set yourselves free," and for a moment they stood together, with their noses touching, and each of them felt complete. Then they bounded around the croft for a while, just like ordinary dogs, before returning home with their human, to a new life in a city in which each dog played a vitally important role.

Boris and Flo looked after the city's young, both animal and human, Boris guiding and protecting them as they learned to explore, Flo teaching the puppies her many proverbs so that they could guide their humans.

"Be careful!" she would say. "Still waters run deep!"

"There's many a slip 'twixt cup and lip," and, "Cowardice is just one of the forms of wisdom."

Gentleman Jim helped to rear a new generation of people and dogs who were used to hunting and tracking, and wherever they went, Checkers went with them in case of danger.

But when any animal or human was feeling down at heart or out of sorts, they went to Pico, who would sit with them until they too could see the vastness of the universe and their place in it, which was both immensely significant and immeasurably small.

And so that city changed. It was full of green spaces, where people walked their dogs, and dogs walked their people. There were hardly any cars. Traffic kept to certain roads, while others were made into free dogways. The streets were clean because the dogs foraged in them and kept them clean. There were shops and restaurants where dogs feasted on steak while people sat at tables to one side and ate their salads. The hunting dogs hunted, the herding dogs herded and the guard dogs guarded, and between them they brought perfect order to the city and its people. No dog was homeless; they all looked cared for and loved because it was unheard of for a dog to be lost and alone in this, the City of Dogs.

The biggest change was in the people. No one hurried; everyone looked relaxed. People stood around with their dogs, talking, and no one was lonely or shut up in their houses—they were all brought together by the community of dogs.

The three aunts felt entirely at home in this new city. Aunty Joan took up woodwork as she had always wanted, and Aunty Lilith went line dancing and lost a lot of weight. There was less dog walking for Aunty Dot to do since everyone walked their own dogs, but she would walk along with them and greet every dog by name. And from time to time she would visit her darling Berry in the underworld, where he had settled in nicely in the Elysian fields, far away from Fenrir and the other hounds of hell. The underworld itself was changing, he told her, now that mankind was on the right track, and there were hardly any great sinners left to guard.

Far above this new city shone Orion. It was always possible to see his outline dimly on winter nights, but two of the stars in his constellation were of particular brilliance—Sirius, or Canis Major, and Procyon, or Canis Minor. The great hunter was content to be guided by his dogs because even in his own eyes, he just wasn't that important anymore.

As the years passed, though none of the humans remembered the momentous events that had created their city anew, all the dogs did remember, and they honored the names of Jenny, Flo, Pico, Boris, Checkers and Gentleman Jim. They had brought change, not only to the city, but to the whole world because soon all the cities of the world followed the example of the City of Dogs and restored dogs to their rightful place as the honored guardians, guides and protectors of mankind.

Each time a dog was walked on the croft, he or she took a long time to sniff and widdle, widdle and sniff, because the full legend had to be passed on to other dogs for generations to come.

As for Jenny, she had done her bit for mankind, and she settled into a new, peaceful life in which she remained devoted to Sam. And

Sam was devoted to her. He couldn't wait to get home from school, to play with Jenny till bedtime, when she went to sleep on his bed and both of them dreamed wonderful dreams all night, about a boy with a face like the sun and a small white dog gleaming like a star through the early morning mist.